EXORDIUM

FRANKIE JAMES

CONTENTS

WARNING

This book contains sexual situations and other adult themes. Recommended for age 18+. Trigger warnings include (but not limited to): Dubious consent, Non-Consent (rape), Profanity, Sexual situations, Violance, Death, Blood Play. If you have any specific questions please email me at frankie james153027@gmail.com.

PROLOGUE

ADELAIDE- NINETEEN YEARS AGO

I fell to my knees at the intense pain in my chest and screamed. What the hell was happening? I'd been standing between Jesse and John, making sure the last of the Aurathions had made it to the portal, when suddenly, my chest felt like it had opened, and my heart was being ripped out.

John fell to his knees beside me, "Adelaide, what's wrong?"

Jesse was standing in front of us both, on guard in the form of a Fellat, his teeth bared in a bloodthirsty snarl. I tried to answer, but I couldn't draw in enough air to speak.

"Baby, please! I don't know what to do." John clutched me to his chest in desperation.

Leaning my head back, I looked into his beautiful eyes, raising a trembling hand I cupped his cheek and whispered, "I think we lost Rue and Sly. I can't feel them anymore." I planted my face on his chest and sobbed hysterically.

At my words, Jesse transformed back into his human form and crouched beside us. Both their faces wore identical expressions of agony in response to my words. I could feel the silent communication between the two brothers, but I was too devastated to try to decipher it.

John pulled me to my feet, "Come my love, we must get out of here. We've helped as many Aurathions get through the portal as we could. We have to go."

Jesse's head was on a swivel, making sure we were still safe from the enemy. I knew my inability to stand on my own was freaking him out. I knew this but right now the pain and grief were so intense I couldn't do anything about it.

The civil war in Aurathia had been bloody and hard fought, but despite the powerful abilities my Faction brought to the table, we had been defeated. My men and I had fought side by side until we knew the only choice left to us was getting as many Aurathions as we could through the portal to Earth.

Our world was a mix of technology and tradition. We were born as Passives and couldn't access our abilities until we met and bonded with the people destined to be a part of our Faction. It was a beautiful thing when it was meant to be. When it was forced, it wasn't quite as beautiful.

A Faction was centered around a Nexus. Without a Nexus, a Faction couldn't be formed. A Nexus had the ability to bond Passives through a ritual that had been performed for hundreds of years. Once the Faction had been formed, our abilities were revealed and we lived happily ever after.

At least that's how it should've been.

Unfortunately, some Aurathions never found their Nexus and had to remain Passives for the rest of their lives, never getting to access any abilities. There didn't seem to be as many Nexus in the years past, so the number of Passives living without abilities was multiplying.

The war was fought for just this reason. Upper-class families that didn't want the stigma of having Passives in their line. Families that were greedy for more power and didn't care how they got it. Abilities that became perverted when gained synthetically and not naturally.

"We can't leave them! What if I'm wrong? We have to find them!" Just then, my precious Mira appeared beside me. She was the Fellat I'd bonded with, confirming my Nexus status. A proud, fierce animal that had picked me the first year I was at Emberhold Academy.

The Fellat were found deep in the forests around Aurathia. They were drawn to a Nexus and bonded on instinct. Not every Nexus was lucky enough to bond a Fellat. They were notoriously picky and couldn't be forced. Some chose to stay in the wild, never revealing themselves.

"Nexus be strong. I will find your men and bring them to you. I can feel them faintly through my bond with you." She nuzzled the top of my head.

I was lucky enough that the ability to speak to animals had formed after I bonded with John. The ability had been passed to him from his four-time great grandmother. In turn, everyone in our Faction had gotten this ability. That was rare because most Factions didn't share abilities throughout. The Nexus was usually the only one with that privilege.

John and Jesse urged me toward the portal, but I resisted. Mira bent her head, nudging me to go with them, *"Go Nexus, I will find your men if they are still alive and bring them to you."* She sniffed my stomach, *"You have to protect the future of our world."*

"What do you mean?" I cried as John and Jesse brought me closer to the portal.

"Take her!" She commanded my Faction. *"I will come to you as soon as I'm able."*

Mira turned and blended back into the shadows. As we passed through the portal, I prayed to every ancestor I had that Mira, and my precious Rue and Sly would be returned to me. Something in my gut told me that wouldn't be the case.

CHAPTER 1
REVERIE

"I've checked your oil and put new windshield wipers on your jeep. Did you pack essentials?" Grumpy frowned, not in the best mood since I was leaving. I smiled with affection.

"I think I'm good. You've gone through a checklist with me twice daily since Monday."

John Rasmus Hawthorne was one of the best fathers a girl could ask for. He was a man of few words, but patient and kind, at least with Mom and me. With everyone else, not so much, he could be quite the ass. Pop had taught me to call him Grumpy since I was a baby. He told me it had pissed him off at first, but then it became our thing.

"That's his love language, and you know this," Pop winked.

There were many differences between my fathers. Pop was funny and loud and loved playing practical jokes on the family. No one would ever accuse him of being patient. He would start one project but quickly grow bored and start another. It drove Grumpy insane.

They were twins, and Pop loved to tell me stories of how they switched places in school to mess with people. Mom got extremely aggravated with the amount of female attention they garnered everywhere we went. Apparently, women found matching bookends with over six feet of muscle attractive. Who knew?

Jesse Randall Hawthorne was mischievous, whereas Grumpy was serious, outgoing to Grumpy's introverted personality, always ready to stir up trouble. They were the best fathers a girl could ask for. Their one similarity, other than their faces, was that my mother and I always came first. Our safety and happiness were the most important things to both of them.

"I'm only driving two hours to the portal," I rolled my eyes in exasperation. Grumpy pulled me in, giving me a bear hug.

"You know the drive doesn't worry us, Tater Tot. Although Sly's talent for creating portals would be awesome to have right now."

Pop sighed, "Sly and Rue would have been so proud of you. We've done our best to fill the huge hole their deaths left. I just wish they could see how amazing our little girl is."

Making a visible effort to shake off the sadness, Pop pulled me away from Grumpy giving me his own version of a bear hug. "It's the first time you've been on your own, and the academy can be brutal. It sucks we won't be there."

"I know! But y'all have taught me to kick ass, so I'm not worried," I squeezed Pop and smirked. "Nathan is so protective I'd be surprised if I even got a paper cut."

"Watch the language, little girl." Grumpy narrowed his eyes. The corners of his mouth turned up, and for him, that was like a full grin. A large raccoon we called Rubbish, climbed up his leg to sit on his shoulder.

Pop laughed, "We know you can kick ass, but there're a lot of secrets that must be kept. We can't help but worry that one of you might slip up, and by one of you, I mean Nathan. If the Council finds out, we'll have a huge issue. We've done our best to prepare you, but you're still our little girl." Pop kissed the top of my head.

"I don't think I'll be able to take a deep breath until you complete your initiation." Grumpy sighed, reaching into his pocket and handing Rubbish a carrot.

"You don't give yourselves enough credit. I can take care of myself. Look at Nathan. He sucked when you first started training him, and now he's badass." I chuckled, shoulder bumping Pop.

"I wouldn't call him a badass," Grumpy grumbled, making me laugh. He still wasn't completely sold on Nathan. "Just remember we've kept you apart from other Aurathions for a reason. We love our people, but the Council has become too powerful since the war, and we don't like the decisions they've made lately. Being a Nexus is rare, and finding your faction is difficult enough without their interference."

"Knowing I'm a Nexus this early in the game gives me an advantage over the other Passives," I reminded both of my fathers.

"That may be true, but it didn't come without a cost," Mom said walking out of the house shooing Copper, our mongoose, out of the way. "I think we've prepared our baby girl better than most, and with Nathan in the mix, she's even more protected. You two need to stop stressing."

Adelaide Ophelia Hawthorne, at just 5'3", was a force to be reckoned with. She was one of the most powerful Nexus that ever lived. The fact that she survived the deaths of two of her Faction was proof of that. Her white hair and light amber eyes also made her stunningly beautiful.

Unfortunately, I only reached 5'2" but was lucky enough to have Mom's amber eye color, her small, upturned nose, and full lips. I didn't get her beautiful hair, but inherited Grumpy and Pop's raven color. The dimples in my cheeks came from Rue, and my pale, unable-to-tan skin came from Sly.

I don't think my mom had ever fully recovered from losing her men and her beloved Fellat, who was defending them. My fathers tried to keep them alive by telling stories of how they formed their Faction. I never got tired of hearing the way they met and how each of my fathers fell in love with my mom. We had albums filled with pictures of them together, but Mom kept them in a special cabinet in her room. Sometimes, we would pile up on her bed and she would pull them out and tell me about the stories behind each one. As I got older, I noticed how upset she would be after seeing them, so I stopped asking to look at the pictures.

When my parents were students, the academy was still located in Aurathia. Unfortunately, the original academy had been destroyed during the war. A replica was created in a pocket dimension so Passives could be tested and find their Faction.

Our home was in a small town north of Houston, TX. We lived in a two-story farmhouse that sat on 30 acres. Complete privacy and the freedom to train and use our abilities were important to my parents.

They didn't want to settle too close to the Aurathion communities. After the deaths of Sly and Rue, my mom was in no shape to make any decisions so Grumpy and Pops moved us to a more secluded place to avoid the machinations of the Council. They all needed to recover from their loss and raise their child away from the nightmare that dealing with the Council had become. They only had contact during certain holidays and Council gatherings they couldn't get out of. Nexus were so rare that the Council tried to insist that Mom replace her dead men with new Faction members. There was zero chance of that happening, and as powerful as she was, they couldn't force the issue. I stepped onto the porch to hug Mom.

"I know what to expect. The other Aurathions can't always be trusted, and as soon as my Nexus status is revealed, I'll most likely be inundated with Passives wanting to be Faction." I recited what she had been telling me on repeat the last few weeks word for word.

She smiled, "Just remember what I told you about the way you'll feel when you meet a Passive meant to be yours. Never try to force a connection because even if they become part of your Faction, in the end your Faction will fail."

I nodded my head, "Yes ma'am. The way I felt when I met Nathan will be easy to recognize. Anything less would be unacceptable." I winked at her. "You know I won't put up with any bullshit."

"Hey! Watch that mouth, little girl!" Mom laughed. "Your fathers really need to clean up their language around you."

"I don't think they're the ones with the problem," I grinned.

"That's bullshit, and you know it!" Mom somehow managed to say without smiling.

"Adelaide, I should put you over my knee," Grumpy frowned. Once again, the corners of his mouth were turned up slightly, so no one took him seriously, least of all Mom.

"I don't have a fear of that happening. Mom would zap you to the Cimarron Forest." I joked, laughing at the face Mom was making behind his back.

"Unless she liked it," Pop winked at me.

I started gagging, "OK! That's enough! As soon as the

disgustingness starts, that's my cue to get the hell out of Dodge!"

"You know the disgustingness never ends around here!" Pop laughed. No truer words had ever been spoken. My fathers loved Mom and didn't shy away from showing it. I pretended it grossed me out, but secretly I loved the way they felt about each other.

"We're going to miss you, Tater Tot." Pop sighed tragically, "Who's going to help me prank the old man?" He tipped his head Grumpy's way like I didn't know who he was talking about.

Grumpy smacked him on the back of the head, dislodging Rubbish, who chattered at them in anger then headed to the barn. "I'm only older than you by a few minutes, brother."

I laughed at their antics.

"I'll miss you too, Pop. It might make you feel better knowing I packed two small daggers and my Smith & Wesson boot knife."

Pop smiled, "That helps because I know how deadly you are with them." He frowned, and an intense look came over his face. That expression was so unusual, I gave him my full attention. "Reverie, remember everything you've learned. The initiation will be vicious, and no holds barred. Use every skill we've taught you and don't give away your Nexus status until you and Nathan can perform the ritual. Without it, we wouldn't be able to explain how he became your Faction."

Grumpy nodded his head, agreeing with his brother, "Remember, always be at the ready. The academy can take you at any time, day or night. And please don't let that lunatic you've bonded reveal his abilities!"

"I promise he won't. He may be crazy, but you can't argue that he's protective of me." Unfortunately, I couldn't hide my parentage, so the Aurathions would be watching me closely.

Mom had worked to teach me that confidence in yourself was the key to success. I took that advice to heart, and even when I felt unsure, I tried never to show it. "Fake it till you make it" was my motto.

I was a good student, and I always tried to embody what I thought a Nexus should be. It wasn't hard because I had the best role model. I tried to be kind, but some people confused that with being a pushover, and I was far from that. I couldn't wait to put everything my parents had taught me to the test, and Emberhold Academy was the place to do it.

"I promise I won't forget a single lesson, and I plan on showing them I'm not to be fu-"

"Reverie! I'll wash your mouth out with soap!" Grumpy growled, and I died laughing.

"Fudged with. Fudged was all I was going to say!"

"Riiight!" Mom winked and laughed. "Keep that attitude, and remember that if you need us, we'll come running!"

I kissed and hugged each of my sweet parents and climbed into My Precious, a 1995 baby blue Jeep Wrangler. Grumpy had bought it the summer before. He and I restored it to absolute perfection. Other than my parents and Nathan, it was the love of my life. I'd caught him giving it the evil eye several times-the psycho!

The intense training sessions, late-night reading, and relentless practices led to this moment. With the wind in my hair and Creedence singing *Bad Moon Rising* in the background, my mind drifted to the last few months of preparation.

~�&~

"**R**everie, pick up the pace!" Grumpy yelled as I exited the woods on my second lap around the property. "Conditioning is your friend. It could mean the difference between life and death!"

I groaned but dug deep to increase my speed. I wanted to make my parents proud and wasn't afraid to put in the work.

"Look at her go!" Nathan yelled proudly.

"Less looking and more running, baby man!" Grumpy growled out. "You still have a lot of work to put in before you're good enough for my little girl's Faction."

"You know I'm a machine, Daddy Grump!" Nathen blew Grumpy a kiss.

"Do not call me Daddy! Twenty more laps for you, asshead!" Grumpy growled. He nodded his head in Nathan's direction after making eye contact with the solid black jaguar Samson, lazing on the ground beside him.

"After you get warmed up, I get your candy ass. It's Krav Maga time, baby!" Pop yelled in a gleeful voice.

"If I call you Daddy, will it get me out of it?" Nathan joked, trying to catch his breath.

"Not even if you called me Daddy and meant it!" Pop laughed, "Get your ass in gear."

"If you kill me, my Nexi will be pissed!" Nathan yelled, laughing as he started running again.

"Don't call her Nexi!" Grumpy shouted. "You'll slip up, and everyone will know what she is to you!"

Nathan started running backwards and shot finger guns in Grumpy's direction, giving him a cocky smile. The smile dropped from his face and he shouted in alarm when he saw Samson coming up behind him.

Grumpy sighed, closed his eyes and rubbed the bridge of his nose, muttering to himself, "Don't kill him. Don't kill the boy." but started laughing his ass off when he opened his eyes and saw

Samson holding a piece of Nathan's shorts in his mouth. Nathan was running in terror into the woods with the ass of his shorts torn out and his crack shining in the sun.

Hearing their banter made me happy. At times, I didn't think they would ever get to this point. The laughter Nathan had brought into our lives was worth all the pain we had both endured. I thought Mom even smiled more when he was around.

Since bonding with him, I felt more powerful physically. That really shouldn't happen until my Faction was complete. I wasn't surprised. Nothing about mine and Nathan's relationship was ordinary.

Aurathions were stronger and faster than humans and lived much longer. The exception to this was if we remained Passive, never finding our Nexus. My parents were powerful, so I'd always been just a little stronger and faster than Aurathions of the same age, even before bonding with Nathan.

I was excited to be Nexus. Following in Mom's footsteps was a dream of mine. She was my hero, and rightfully so. The Nexus brought out the latent abilities in their Faction when they bonded. The abilities could range from controlling the weather to invisibility and a variety of things in between. The powers Mom brought out in her Faction were nothing short of amazing!

Grumpy could control and communicate with any animal on land or sea. As long as I can remember, there had been animals everywhere. Thank God we lived relatively secluded because most of the animals were not native to Texas.

Pop, being his twin, had the flip side of his power. Pop could shift into any animal he'd seen in person, on television, and in print. To say he could tell a hell of a bedtime story was putting it mildly. How many kids get to pet the actual characters in their book as the story is read? Reverie for the win!

Even though I was raised with the expectation of being Nexus, it wasn't a known fact until I bonded with Nathan. After becoming

Faction, Nathan gained the ability to teleport, and I had increased strength and speed. When I gained more Faction, I would gain more abilities. As Nexus I shouldn't have access until my Faction was complete.

I had learned everything my parents could teach me, and their knowledge was vast. I had trained in various fighting styles. Krav Maga was the one I enjoyed the most. It combined aikido, boxing, judo, karate, and wrestling. Also, the Aurathion culture had several fighting methods passed down through the generations that I was proficient in. I wish I could say it would improve my odds, but the truth is, most children raised in the Aurathion culture were more than familiar with those fighting styles.

I didn't envy Nathan having to play catch up and train with Pop. His joking nature didn't translate to the training mat. Holding back wasn't something he did. My psycho was going to be bitching about the bruises he was likely to collect on his "perfect ass." I was asked to refer to it as such at his request, but the boy wasn't lying. His ass was nice to look at.

Nathan took it all because even though he liked to rile up my fathers, being able to protect me was his priority. Nathan's power was unstable, but he worked tirelessly to perfect it. I was so thankful he would be waiting at Emberhold. Hopefully, we could meet under the guise of friendship until we could perform the ritual and begin building our Faction in earnest. We had a rocky start, but I couldn't imagine my life without him. I doubt he cared how I felt. He was a stage five clinger from kindergarten to our senior year in high school. No way would he allow me to contemplate life without him. I should have known our bonding would be extraordinarily different.

My thoughts stopped when I pulled up to the trail leading to the portal. It was concealed from all pure-blooded humans. Aurathion illusionists had cast a mirage of a large hillside surrounded by a thick forest. I continued to drive until I saw the massive stone pillars with bright swirls of color rotating lazily in a circle.

This was it.

It was time to see if I had what it took to become the Nexus of an Aurathion Faction.

I had a huge grin on my face as I drove through the portal. I couldn't wait to see Nathan. I had missed his crazy ass. Together we were going to form the strongest Faction Emberhold had ever seen.

CHAPTER 2
REVERIE

The trip through the portal was uneventful. Aurathions that created portals and pocket dimensions were amazingly talented. Emberhold Academy existed in a pocket dimension created so Aurathions could meet and form Factions, learn, and strengthen their abilities without humans discovering their existence. The original academy was one of the first buildings destroyed at the start of the war because it was essential in forming Factions built around a true Nexus.

I stepped out of my Jeep, inhaling the crisp, enchanted air. The beautiful trees that towered above the entrance to the academy had a mix of gold and orange leaves. The main building was a massive gothic structure composed of a black rock native to our world. The rock was almost reflective, so it glowed when light hit the building. Quaint lampposts, benches, and tables lit the brick pathways leading to the dorms scattered throughout the campus. The dorms and training buildings were smaller structures, identical to the main academy building. Houses scattered throughout the forest surrounding the academy were built for fully formed Factions that needed to complete their training.

A small town was also located close to the academy. Most of the businesses were ran by Passives who hadn't given up on finding their Factions. The town consisted of a few cafes, coffee bars, and small boutiques. Java and Jam was a favorite of my family's. My parents often ate at the original, which was destroyed at the same time as the academy.

The gate in front of Emberhold was held up by massive posts made of the same rock as the academy. The gate itself was constructed of material like earth's platinum. Directly in the center of the gate was the Aurathion symbol. It was a triquetra surrounded by a ring of flames, with a smaller triquetra in the middle representing the Nexus.

I had no idea how extensive the forests were but assumed they were significant. There were animals of all kinds, some native to Aurathia. If this was an accurate representation of Aurathia, I could understand why my parents missed it so much. I looked around the half-full parking lot and realized most students probably used the smaller portals. A vehicle wasn't needed to navigate around campus and the small nearby town, but leaving My Precious wasn't an option for me.

My parents had taught me to always expect the unexpected. Sometimes, a quick getaway was the difference between life and death. After the destruction of our world, my parents didn't leave anything to chance. Nathan could teleport anywhere he had seen or been before, but this talent had yet to appear for me and wouldn't until my Faction was complete. Suddenly, I heard a knock coming from inside my jeep. I jumped around and saw Nathan waving at me, sitting in my backseat.

"What the hell?" I jerked open the door and fell inside. "What are you doing here?" I whisper yelled.

"Welcoming my little Nexi to Emberhold, of course," Nathan grinned. He had a boy next door look and he used it to his advantage. Light brown hair with a slight curl, big green eyes, a dimple in one cheek, and perfectly straight white teeth. At 6'1", he was the perfect package- if you were into psychopaths.

Apparently, I was.

"Nathan, you know we need to be careful. You could have welcomed me somewhere a little more discreet!" I growled. Grumpy had warned us repeatedly how desperate Passives were to be part of a Faction. I didn't need that kind of pressure my first few months at Emberhold. Not to mention Nathan becoming Faction without the ritual. The Council would put us in a lab somewhere and probably anally probe us both.

"Now, you sound like a mini-Daddy Grump", Nathan pouted. "I couldn't wait any longer to see you." He wound a piece of my hair around his finger. "I just flashed in with no one the wiser. You know my power is unparalleled."

His arrogance was "unparalleled".

"You shouldn't be using your power at all." I frowned. "And don't call me daddy." The last came out in a screech as Nathan jerked me under him.

"You're wasting a lot of breath arguing with me when your mouth could be put to much better use." Nathan batted his eyes at me. "I've missed those plump lips, and this smell!!" He groaned out while leaning down to take a large inhale of my neck. "Chocolate chip cookies and honeysuckle." He made a smacking noise, "I could eat you up."

I giggled, melting under him. Resisting my psycho was not something I was proficient in.

~☙~

The first day of kindergarten is always hard, but I thought it was harder on my parents.

"It'll be OK, Pop. I'll be home soon," I giggled. Pop held me so tight I could hardly breathe.

"Put Tater Tot down and stop being dramatic!" Grumpy rolled his eyes. "She'll be home in a few short hours, get ahold of yourself, man!"

Mom started laughing and took me from Pop. It was a struggle because he wasn't letting go. Grumpy hit him in the back of the head and Mom was able to pull me to freedom.

"You're going to love school." Mom smiled. "These children are precious, and I know you'll make great friends."

I knew she was right because I wore my most favoritest new dress. It was in the palest pink with darker vertical pink stripes. My hair was in two pigtails with dark pink bows and my sandals glittered bright pink in the sun.

"Damn Adelaide, do you think you could have snuck some more pink accessories somewhere on Reverie's tiny body?" Grumpy eyed all the pink like it was going to bleed over on to his clothes.

"Watch yourself, John!" Mom stuck her tongue out at him. "A girl can never have enough pink."

"That's right, Dad!" I said, sticking my tongue out too.

I looked over Mom's shoulder and saw a little boy with the prettiest green eyes staring at me.

"Give her back, Adelaide. Right now!" Pop demanded. "I haven't gotten enough hugs to last me through the day!" He grabbed my legs as they played pretend tug of war with me.

Suddenly, Pop let out a high-pitched yelp and dropped to his knees. When I looked down, the pretty little boy stood in front of Pop, his fist drawn back to hit him again.

"Oh, my Lord!" A pretty lady with the same green eyes as the boy yelled. "Nathan, what have you done?"

"Looks like a good punch to the gonads," Grumpy said quietly while snickering into his hand.

"What's gonads?" I wrinkled my nose in confusion.

"Never mind that, little girl," Mom struggled to keep a straight face.

Nathen glanced at his mom with a fierce look on his little face. "Saving the princess!"

"I'm so sorry! I have no idea what's gotten into him!" Nathan's mom apologized.

"He was pulling her apart and 'sides that she's my princess!" Nathan scowled.

"No, I'm not! I'm my own woman," I said, looking at my mom for approval. Mom nodded at me and smiled while kneeling on the ground to look at the little boy.

"We're her parents, and I promise we'd never hurt her."

"I don't know how to apologize enough. My name is Sarah, and this little terror is Nathan. Tell the nice man you're sorry." Sarah frowned at her son.

"But I'm not sorry! He was keeping my princess captive, so I punched him where Gramps said it hurts the most!" Nathan continued to eye Pop with suspicion.

"Gramps sounds like a wise man," Mom laughed. "Why don't you walk in with Reverie and ensure she gets to her desk safe and sound?"

"OK, Mrs. Princesses' Mom." Nathen grinned. "Come with me. I'll keep you safe."

As the pretty little boy grabbed my hand to lead me into class, I wondered why my hand felt all tingly and my tummy dipped like when I was on a roller coaster.

⌒☖⌒

Nathan lightly ran his fingers over my forehead, licked my neck, then bit it gently. "I've missed you so terribly, horribly, my Nexi," he whispered. "I can't stand to be away from you for so long or I go crazy."

"Too late, lunatic. You're already there." I smiled, "But I missed you too."

"These next few weeks are going to be absolute hell," Nathen groaned. "I'll be glad when I can claim you in front of everyone. Oh! Look what I did to commemorate the first time we met!" He sat up in excitement and started pulling down his pants.

"What the hell, Nathan?! Tell me you didn't get your penis pierced!"

"What? Is that something you would like, my Nexi?" He froze in contemplation.

"Well, I can't say for sure since, you know, you're the only guy I've ever been with," I smirked.

"True enough, but I'd like to reserve the right to revisit this topic." The psycho grinned. "Look at my new tattoo!" He pulled his pants down to show the bright pink princess crown tattooed right above his dick with "NEXI" in bold black letters right in the middle.

"Why do I find your gesture strangely sweet?" I mused.

"Because it is sweet. But also extremely sexy." He waggled his eyebrows, adjusted his pants, and pulled me on his lap.

"How are you settling in?" I leaned my head on his shoulder and stroked his chest.

"It's going good. You know how lovable I am, it's the usual. Girls want me, and guys want to be me." I rolled my eyes and pinched him. "Hey now! There's no need for violence. You know I only see your sweet face." Nathan grabbed my hand and kissed the top of my head.

"Seriously, is everything going well? Do you remember everything we told you?" I snuggled closer, breathing him in.

"Yes, my Nexi. Everything has gone smoothly. No questions asked after your dad enrolled me and explained to the dean about accidentally stumbling upon our family." He nuzzled his nose in my hair and kissed the top of my head.

"So, was the story about the blood test my mom conducted in her office believed?" I asked.

"Yes. We explained that I had visited her office for a physical and after she got the test results, she researched my family background and found my Aurathion ancestry."

"Fantastic!" I kissed his chest.

"Give me one more kiss, and I'll return to my room... Pucker up, buttercup." I leaned my head back and gave him a kiss and then, being the psycho he was, Nathan leaned forward and bit me hard in the juncture between my neck and shoulder, drawing blood. It should have hurt but instead sent a jolt of heat through me.

"That's new."

He grinned, showing slightly extended incisors coated in my blood. "The taste of your sweet blood on my lips is euphoric." He groaned in ecstasy looking a little confused. "It seemed like the thing to do, so I just rolled with it. I like seeing my mark on you, especially since I can't claim you publicly yet. Until we meet again, Nexi mine." He saluted me, then teleported out.

It was just like Nathan to go with whatever he was feeling without question. It looked like we were dealing with another ability. I would need to contact my parents about this new development. I suspected some of the possessiveness stemmed from him knowing that we would be growing our Faction soon. I grew up in this culture, so multiple mates were the norm for me. Nathan had not, and even though my fathers had assured him on multiple occasions it would feel natural and no jealousy would be involved, he was having a hard time with the idea.

I got back out of Precious and headed to the hall for check-in and room assignments. Hopefully, I got a roommate that was nice and not some snotty assface. I had met plenty of those at the few Aurathion gatherings my family had attended. Entitled Passives who believed they were better than average Aurathions just because they had powerful parents.

As I walked under the giant arched door and into the building, I admired the marble floors and the massive chandelier fifty feet above my head. A beautifully curving staircase was in front of me, with a railing made of the same black stone as the academy. It had a gothic elegance that I appreciated. Signs were directing new students where to go, so I headed toward the register office. Pushing the door open, I saw a blonde lady behind an elaborate counter talking to a massive guy.

"You're in dorm A, and your room number is 402." The blonde lady batted her eyes and sent him a flirty smile. I could see why the lady looked so twitter-pated. The guy had muscles upon muscles with dark hair that reached the top of his shoulders. If the view from the front was as lovely as the back, any woman would be the same.

"Thanks," Mr. Muscles turned after grabbing his packet and walked right into me.

"Whoa, sorry!" I exclaimed, realizing I had drifted too close. I was a little distracted when I realized goosebumps had broken out all over my body at our brief contact. When I didn't get a reaction, I looked up and froze. Wowza, he was

H-O-T! All Aurathions were attractive, that was a fact. But this guy was at the next level: dark brown hair, deep brown eyes, full lips, all on an outrageous body. Also, damn, he was huge. Granted, compared to me, most people were tall, but the top of my head barely reached his nipples. He had to be 6'7". I realized we were staring at each other without speaking.

"Hi, I'm Reverie. And you are...?" He stared a few moments more, then slowly backed out of the office, never breaking eye contact. When the door closed, I turned to find the woman behind the desk staring at me.

"Well, that was rude." She didn't respond and I noticed her gaze was trained on my face in confusion, "Do I have something on my face? Is it a booger? Oh shit, I'm so embarrassed!" I started wiping my nose frantically.

The blonde woman blinked, "No, but the pink princess crown sticker on your forehead is a strange fashion statement."

I blinked my eyes slowly, exited the office and entered a small restroom I had spotted on my way in. Looking in the mirror, I saw the sticker on my forehead. Peeling it off, I screamed so loudly that it would make Jamie Lee Curtis proud.

"NATHAN!"

After pulling up my big girl panties and returning to get my packet and dorm assignment, I headed to dorm B to check out my room. I was on the fourth floor in room 410, the last dorm. I stuck my thumb to the scanner, and the door clicked open. I walked in and was amazed at how big it was. I didn't know what I expected, but it wasn't this. My dorm had a central living room with heather grey walls, an oversized brown sofa, a glass coffee table, and a small kitchenette on the left side. As I walked further in, I saw a small hallway with two bedrooms off to each side, with what I assumed was a bathroom at the end. The rooms had a small scanner beside each door that had initials on a plaque above it. The room to the right had my initials R.H. in bold letters. I saw C.M. on the door to the left. I sincerely hoped my roommate was a good match. I put my thumb to the scanner, and my door clicked open.

The smell of home put me at ease immediately. The fabric softener my mom used and a vanilla candle on the night-stand made me release tension I didn't even realize I'd been holding. My parents and Nathan must have decorated my room as a surprise for me. They truly were the best. The large double bed was covered in a fluffy pink comforter that went well with the same grey walls from the living room. Pink and grey pillows were scattered at the top of the bed, and a grey throw blanket was draped at the end. Two small side tables occupied the space on either side of the bed with a pink lamp on each, a desk, and a large closet finished out the room.

I threw down my backpack with a few essentials: my blades, a laptop, a few snacks from Buc-ee's (the best gas station in the world), and a photo of me with my parents that we had taken at the state fair. I looked around the room and realized this was my home for the foreseeable future. The next phase of my life was starting now. Falling back on my bed I thought, bring it on!

CHAPTER 3
REVERIE

I woke to a light tapping at the door. It took me a minute to remember where I was.

"Hey roomie. I've got donuts out here from Java and Jam. Wakey, wakey. We've got some bonding to do." A cheerful, feminine voice yelled.

"I'll be right out!" I yelled back. Well, that sounded promising. Maybe I lucked out in the roommate department. The donuts at Java and Jam were to die for. I'd tried them when my mom decided to get donuts to surprise Grumpy on his birthday. Getting out of my comfy bed, I threw my long hair up in a messy bun, grabbed my pink fluffy robe and headed into the living room.

"Hey Hawthorne Hottie! I've been so excited to meet you!" The cutest redhead ever squealed as she bounced on the sofa.

"Hello to you too." I grinned. "Even though I sincerely appreciate the hottie title, my name is Reverie."

"Duh! Everyone knows who you are. Your mom is Adelaide!" The redhead screeched.

"Yes. Yes, she is." I laughed. She was too precious. "Can you tell me your name? I can't keep calling you 'the redhead' in my head." I ran that sentence back through my head. I guess it made sense because she answered.

"Oh crap! My name is Chloe Moon. I should have begun with that. I tend to get excited when meeting the daughter of my hero!" She screeched once again.

"The important part of that was daughter. My mom is awesome, but I'm just Reverie. No big deal."

"No just, about it! You are now the roommate of Chloe Moon. We're destined to be best friends. We'll be right up there with the Dynamic Duo, the Wonder Twins, and Brennan and Dale. Do you play the drums? Never mind, that's not important. Are you ready for initiation?!" She patted the couch for me to sit down beside her.

This girl did not just reference the *Stepbrothers* movie! I think I just met my soulmate. Goodbye, my sweet psycho, you've been replaced. Side note: do not say that out loud in front of Nathan. Chloe would disappear.

"I'm as ready as possible, considering we don't know when or what." I sat down and was swallowed immediately by the soft cushions.

"My brothers have been training me like crazy! They're in their third year, so they went through initiation a couple of years ago. Since the academy itself decides on the initiation, no one knows what it'll be. The size of their class went from two hundred and fifty to one hundred ninety-four." Chloe grimaced.

"My parents put me through insane scenarios. Some were things they went through and others were just things they heard from other years. No one knows what Emberhold will design. I questioned them about why we're put through such harsh and deadly trials, especially when our numbers aren't great," I frowned. "They told me it was necessary to weed out the weak or mediocre."

"That seems like a shitty thing to say but, it's basically what my parents told me when I asked them the same question," Chloe said.

"I thought so too. But when I said that to Grumpy, he got a haunted look in his eyes and replied, 'You can't imagine the horror war brings. You only want the strongest guarding your back, and even then sometimes, it's not enough.'" I gave Chloe a solemn look.

"Well, damn! That just gave me cold chills. And think, if we survive initiation, we get to start training with our Faction if we're lucky enough to find one. That's when the S.H.T.F.!" Chloe shivered.

"What the hell is S.H.T.F.?" I asked.

"Shit hits the fan, of course!" Chloe laughed, "Girl, you're going to have to get with the program!" We both started cackling. "Who's this Grumpy character?" Chloe asked still laughing.

I wiped the tears from my eyes, "It's what I call one of my fathers, and believe me he fits the name." I smiled, missing my parents already. "We better dig into these donuts before they get cold, and more importantly, the coffee. I can tell I'll need to be caffeinated to deal with you."

"You have no idea," Chloe grinned mischievously.

"So, do your brothers have a Faction?" I bit into my donut. "Yum! That is amazing!!!" I groaned out loud as the flavors hit my tongue.

"Right? Stick with me, kid and I'll keep you hooked up!" Chloe winked at me. "No, they don't have a Faction yet. Last year, against my advice, they let the queen bitch of their year talk them into doing the ritual. I knew they didn't mesh and so did they, but the boys were so tired of waiting they went for it."

"Do they expect to be Faction or Nexus?" I took a sip of my coffee.

"Everyone always wants to be Nexus, but they're identical twins and would prefer to be Faction so they can stay together. Of course, little miss my-shit-doesn't-stink, Kristine thinks she's Nexus." Chloe sneered.

"Well, she did make it through initiation. There must be a little badass inside her." I leaned back and took a long sip of my coffee.

"Maybe a little, but she probably passed by stepping on the bodies of her dead classmates," Chloe scowled.

"I'm sensing you don't like this girl." I smirked.

"I really don't. Kristine got on my bad side when she acted like she wanted to be friends. I'm used to girls trying to hang out with me because of my brothers, but she laid it on thick. Then, I overheard her talking to one of her followers saying how annoying it was to hang out with Zeke and Zane's little sister just to have the twins in her Faction. Truly, I'm mad at myself for falling for her crap!"

"Well I'm here now, and I think you're amazing." I grinned at her. "And I haven't even met your brothers."

"Maybe you'll be Nexus and the boys will be in your Faction. Then we can be family." Chloe grinned. "That would almost make Adelaide my mom!"

"Slow your roll, I haven't even met them yet!" I laughed. Damn, this girl was something else!

We finished breakfast and then went our separate ways. This was the last day before classes started and we both had things to prepare. After I showered, I threw on some shorts and an old Creed concert tee of my mom's. Then, I went into my room to get things organized for class and memorize my schedule. I sat cross-legged on my bed, opened my packet, and started reading when Nathan suddenly popped onto the bed beside me. I jumped sideways and almost spilled my coffee.

"What the hell, Nathan?" I hissed. "You scared me to death."

Nathan knelt before me, wrapped his hands in my hair, and tilted my face up to his. When I looked into his eyes, I knew playtime was over, and psycho Nathan was in charge.

"How long has it been since I've touched you?" Nathan whispered in his deep, hypnotic voice.

"Too long." I whispered back. I needed him like the air I breathed.

"Right answer." Nathan growled. "Take your clothes off and lay back." I loved how his eyes darkened with desire, and I couldn't help but shiver under his intense gaze.

"Now, Reverie!" Nathan demanded.

I jumped at his sharp tone, but immediately slipped my shorts down my legs and started to pull my shirt over my head. Nathan stopped me before I took it completely off, trapping my arms above me.

"Do you have any idea how beautiful you are? Every time I look at you, I can't believe I'm yours." He leaned in and lightly kissed my mouth, then slowly moved down my body, giving little nips and licks as he went.

Being Nexus to your Faction was a fantastic thing. If you genuinely belonged together, the connection was beyond imagining. I couldn't understand wanting power so much that you would relinquish a connection like I had with Nathan. I could feel his desire for me, and Nathan could feel my desire for him. It made every touch that much more intense, almost unbearable. When he got to the juncture of my thighs, he leaned closer and inhaled my scent.

"Cookies and honeysuckle." He muttered as he gave a long lick with the flat of his tongue along my wet slit. Using his fingers to spread my pussy, he began sucking lightly on my clit. I let out a long moan and untangled my hands from my shirt. I grabbed his hair and arched up into his face, pushing my clit further into his mouth.

"Please, Nathan!" I whimpered, not knowing what I was asking for, just completely drowning in pleasure.

"I know what you need, my Nexi." He kissed the inside of my thigh. "I'll always take care of you. But I think you know I had your hands restrained for a reason." He flipped me over suddenly. "Get on your knees."

Being apart even these few days was ridiculously hard. I had missed him so much. His scent surrounded me, and I knew neither of us would last long. I got to my hands and knees and shivered with anticipation. I could feel Nathan's desire for me warm in my body. He knelt behind me, took his cock in his hand and slowly began rubbing the head in a circular motion around my swollen clit. I felt his warm palm glide down my back, then rub my ass gently. The harsh slap would've surprised me if I didn't know this man so well. We both let out a long moan and I couldn't help but arch closer, urging him to slide his perfect cock inside. Feeling both of our pleasure as Nathan pushed into my core was unreal. I could feel his hard flesh entering me, but also feel how tight I was squeezing him.

"You're so perfect and I need to feel you dripping with my cum right now, so be a good girl for me, yeah?" He growled.

"Yes, please, my psycho! Please!" I hissed through gritted teeth. He straightened back up, but reached between my legs with one hand and rubbed slow circles on my clit. He eased his cock in and out of me at the same speed, and his grip on my hip tightened. He leaned down kissing a path down my neck then suddenly bit down hard, the sensation was too much for us. I clenched around him in ecstasy and he followed right behind in an orgasm that seemed to go on forever. We fell together, with Nathan the big spoon behind me. I shivered as he licked the blood from my neck and sighed in satisfaction.

Still nestled in my warmth, he put his mouth close to my ear and whispered, "I love you, sweet princess. You are the very breath in my lungs, and I'd kill to keep you."

"I love you too, Nathan." I fell into a deep sleep, wrapped safely in my psycho's arms.

$$\sim \triangle \sim$$

W hen I woke a few hours later, Nathan was gone and a single pink tulip was on the pillow next to me. With the indent of his body still warm. I took a long inhale of the flower and rolled into Nathan's spot, basking in his scent.

I eventually made myself get up and put my clothes back on. Smelling pizza, I realized how hungry I was. I hurried to fix my hair in two long French braids and then headed into the living room. Chloe was sitting on the floor, eating from a pizza box on the coffee table. Two identical redheaded guys were sitting on the couch across from her. They looked up as I entered the room, and both ran their eyes up my body from my toes to my head. Well, OK then. Immediately, I could see why girls flocked to them: dark red hair, long enough to grab ahold of, sapphire blue eyes identical to their sisters, and a smile that could kill.

"Hello, roomie! Pop a squat and eat. These two clowns finally did something right and brought their sweet sister sustenance. Although I think it was a ploy to meet my room-mate." Chloe winked at me slyly.

"Can you blame us?" The twin on the left asked gruffly. "I'm Zeke, by the way."

"It was my idea." The guy on the right hit Zeke on the arm. I assumed he was Zane. (Brilliant deduction, I know.) "We were dying to meet the girl everyone was talking about. My sister can't shut up about Adelaide this blah blah. I'm Reverie's roommate, and we'll be best friends, yada, yada." Zane said in a high-pitched voice, mocking his sister. Chloe threw a pepperoni at him, which he caught with his mouth.

"Impressive," I laughed, clapping my hands.

"Yes, I am," Zane winked.

"You're awful!" Chloe yelled. "I sound nothing like that!" Zeke, Zane, and I died out laughing. "Anyway," Chloe contin-ued, rolling her eyes, "let's dig in." After demolishing the pizza, we all got comfortable and began discussing the initiation.

"Do you know when we can expect to be called up?" I asked the guys.

"It could be at any time." Zeke took a sip of his drink. "We can tell you about ours, but yours will be different."

"It does happen unexpectedly. The lesson they want us to learn is always to be prepared." Zane moved his foot so it was touching my leg under the coffee table. "Some that were lost in our year didn't take it seriously. They thought the tales of past initiations had to be exaggerated." He raised one eyebrow, daring me to move.

Feeling chills spread across my body, I decided to call his bluff. Could I possibly have met more of my Faction already? It just seemed a little too easy, but what did I know? Chloe looked at me and cleared her throat. Oh crap, she must have asked me a question.

"Would you mind repeating that? I didn't hear what you asked." I felt my face get hot and shot Zane a scowl. She gave me a weird look but repeated herself.

"I was just saying how lucky we were to have a family that prepared us. I don't understand why every Aurathion wouldn't do the same for their children?"

"You have to remember that some of these students are from families that were latent for so many generations they didn't even know they were Aurathion. I've heard of students that went in for different medical reasons and due to blood work, Aurathions in the medical profession were able to bring them into the fold." I explained, thinking of how we explained finding Nathan.

"There is a first year, a guy, Nathan Strauss, that literally fits that scenario," Zane said in surprise.

"Ya'll seem to be extremely well informed," I smiled and casually moved my leg over. Sure enough, Zane's foot soon followed. The confidence in this one ran strong.

"It's crazy what a little flirting in the admin office will get you," Zane smirked, having the cojones to rub his foot up and down my leg.

"I bet." I frowned at the thought of him flirting with another woman. Chloe rolled her eyes and shoulder-bumped me.

"These two manwhores are ridiculous. But they do get all the best gossip!"

"I'm not a manwhore." Zeke hurried to say. "I used to be a manwhore, but I'm not anymore." He looked at me pointedly. Chloe stared at them in suspicion and then looked over at me.

Before she could comment, Zane asked, "So, Reverie, do you think you're Nexus or Faction?"

"Hey, moron, you don't just ask that as soon as you meet someone!" Chloe scowled at him.

"I'd like to agree with you, but I think I asked you about them this morning," I smiled, letting her know I didn't mind the question.

Zane bumped knuckles with Zeke.

"She's already asking about us, brother. The Moon twins for the win!"

"More like the I-want-to-moon-them twins," Chloe smirked. I started laughing, and she joined in.

"So, back to the original question, please." Zeke raised his eyebrows. I was surprised at his persistence. He seemed like the more reserved twin.

"I'm not sure yet. I have no preference either way. I can see advantages to both." I obviously couldn't admit to being Nexus, but it felt wrong keeping it from them.

"Well, maybe we can get dinner one night this week and discuss the pros and cons," Zane suggested with a wink.

"Sounds like a p-"

Suddenly I found myself sitting in Precious.

"What the hell?!" I screeched.

Oh no!!!

The power Nathan acquired upon completing the bond must have manifested in me. This wasn't supposed to happen until my Faction was complete. Of course, I would be an exception to the rule. I hoped the Moon siblings were as trustworthy as I thought they were. When they found out Emberhold hadn't taken me to initiation, they would know something was up. It seems like mine and Nathan's bond wasn't through throwing out surprises. I guess I should have expected that after the way it had all begun.

CHAPTER 4
REVERIE

I showed up to prom with the varsity quarterback, hoping this would finally discourage Nathan in his relentless pursuit of me. Nathan hated Dane Taylor as far back as I could remember. They competed for everything, and Nathan usually came up as the winner. Football was the one thing they didn't compete in because Dane was the quarterback and Nathan was a first-team all-district running back. Nathan scored the winning touchdown at state this year, and even though they didn't play the same position, Dane was pissed that Nathan upstaged him and let his displeasure be known far and wide.

Since that first day of kindergarten, Nathan had never hidden how he felt about me—switching tactics from harshly bullying, to sweet cards and gifts. He was a true psychopath. My fathers hated him with a passion. The girls in school could never understand why I wouldn't go out with him. He was the best-looking guy in school — outgoing, cocky, intelligent, every teacher's dream student. I knew the truth, though. He was crazy, and he had no limits. I would have admired that if he had been Aurathion.

Nathan would pull me into the janitor's closet and beg me to *love him. When that didn't work, he would date anyone and everyone to try to make me jealous. Spoiler alert! It worked, but I could never let it show. Once, he even tried to blackmail me by saying he would tell everyone I cheated on the finals. The incident at the beginning of senior year was something I tried to forget. It should have made me hate him, but it had the opposite effect. I was apparently as fucking crazy as he was. Nathan would never accept defeat. Leaving for Emberhold would be my only relief.*

Honestly, I thought I probably loved his crazy ass, but a relationship wasn't possible with a human, no matter how much I wished otherwise. The Aurathion people needed as many strong Factions as possible. I knew where my duty lay, even at the expense of my heart. We had already lost one world, and my people couldn't afford to lose another. I would probably pine for the bastard for the rest of my life.

As we walked into the building, Dane leaned over and whispered in my ear, "As soon as I show Nathan who the best man is, I say we get out of here."

"Sure, we will. Let's find a table and get a drink." I rolled my eyes. Hopefully, somebody spiked the punch, or this night was going to last for fucking ever. I really hoped Nathan appreciated the lengths I would go to save him from heartache. He had also brought a date, but I was pretty sure he was hoping for the opposite result than me.

Dane led me to a table in the front for maximum visibility. I was well-liked at school. My parents encouraged me to participate in everything and enjoy being young. They wanted me to have a wonderful experience before being put in a position of responsibility and possible heartbreak. They knew better than most, the devastation that could happen.

Of course, as soon as we were seated, Nathan led his date to our table.

"Hello Dane. I see you talked Reverie into coming with you. She

must have had a mental breakdown." Nathan sneered. His date giggled like an idiot. Apparently, Nathan's plan was successful. I was jealous, but I couldn't show it for the asshole's own good.

"You're just pissed because she knew I was the superior choice," Dane puffed out his chest and smirked. This guy must have a death wish. Nathan was going to kill him.

"If she's into small-dicked idiots, then yes. She chose correctly," Nathan growled, not caring that he was insulting his date just by having this conversation.

"I should kick your ass," Dane responded, eyeing me for approval.

"I wish you'd try, you piece of shit! I'd wipe the floor with your pansy ass," Nathan spit out.

"Let's go!" Dane growled, trying to look tough. I noticed he wasn't moving to get up.

"That's enough out of both of you! I've made my choice, Nathan. Get over it." I narrowed my eyes at him.

"The fuck you have. There never was a choice. I've just been waiting for you to realize that." Nathan had a crazed look on his face. Just when I started to reply, the principal stepped up to the microphone.

"It's time to announce Prom King and Queen. When your name is announced, please come up on the stage." Mr. Freeman spoke into the microphone. Pausing for maximum effect, he announced, "Your Prom King is Nathan Strauss!" Nathan gave me one more crazy look and then bounded up on stage.

Everyone lost their minds, screaming his name like he was some lead singer in a boy band. After the giggling cheerleader put the crown on his head, Mr. Freeman began speaking again.

"Now to announce our queen." After another ridiculously long pause, he smiled, "Reverie Hawthorne, will you please come up?" Dane half-ass clapped since he was pissed at Nathan for getting king. I walked on the stage, and when the football player started to

crown me, psycho gave him a look. He hesitantly handed the crown to Nathan, and he placed it on my head. He then leaned down and whispered, "See, the whole school thinks we belong together."

"I don't think your date agrees," I whispered back.

"I don't give a shit." He bit out.

The principal broke into our conversation, asking, "Would the royal couple grace us by leading the first dance?"

"Yes, we would," Nathan pulled me onto the floor. Right Here by Staind started playing. How appropriate, I thought. Nathan had to have something to do with it. As we started dancing, Nathan said into my ear, "If you think bringing him to prom means shit to me, you're wrong."

"It had nothing to do with you!" I lied. I hoped convincingly.

"Bullshit! I'll bathe in that motherfucker's blood with a fucking smile on my face if he thinks he's taking you anywhere after prom. Just try me, Reverie." He warned.

"You're crazy," I hissed. I knew I was taking a chance bringing a date. Nathan hadn't responded well in the past when I had threatened him with Dane, and apparently, that hadn't changed. I was running out of ideas, and I didn't know how much longer I could resist him. Why couldn't he just cooperate?

"Yes, I am. And you would do well to remember that." Nathan hissed back. After the dance was over, he dragged me out a side door. Before the door could shut, Dane pushed through. He didn't have time to say a word before Nathan turned, getting in his face, "Get your ass back inside or I'll beat you until you're bleeding out of every opening on your motherfucking body. Then, I'll cut you into pieces and feed you to Mr. Ferguson's hogs."

The crazed look in his eyes must have led Dane to believe him because he turned and went back inside without a word. Nathan jerked me around and smashed his mouth into mine in a violent clashing of lips and teeth. With my training, I could have put him to the ground, but I was so tired of fighting my feelings where

Nathan was concerned. As we kissed, Nathan bit my lip. In the clash of teeth, his tongue must have been cut. When our blood mixed, I felt the ball of power in my chest expanding and the next thing I knew, we were lying across Grumpy's lap on the couch.

"What the actual FUCK?!" He yelled and stood up. Nathan and I spilled onto the coffee table. The table broke, and popcorn and drinks spilled everywhere. Mom ran in from the kitchen with Pop following right behind after Grumpy screamed in a peculiarly high voice, "Adelaide!" Pop never let him forget it. It's been brought up frequently in the months since "the incident," as we're now calling it.

Nathan looked up at me as I lay on top of him. He had liquid dripping down his face and a piece of popcorn sticking to his cheek.

"I think you have some explaining to do."

I couldn't help myself and started laughing hysterically.

Passives find their designation after performing the ritual for the first time. When a Nexus/Faction bond is made, the Faction will immediately develop an ability. Usually, this ability is found in the Nexus family line. Occasionally, if a Faction member had a strong Nexus in their background, they might develop an ability from their line. In most cases, the Nexus doesn't develop any abilities until their Faction is complete. Forming the bond without the ritual was unheard of, but this was getting crazy. I had no idea what the hell was going on. Chloe and her brothers must be losing their minds wondering what happened!

⌁ ⚘ ⌁

C hloe-

We were in chaos.

"What in the actual fuck?! What just happened?" Zane

yelled. We had all jumped to our feet in shock. The coffee table was on its side. Drinks were spilled. I was hyperventilating.

"Calm the hell down!" Zeke shouted. "Just fucking calm down." He walked over to me and put my hand on his chest. "Just feel me breathing, inhale in, exhale out. As my breathing evened out, he said, "There you go, Booger."

"I will junk punch you right now if you call me that hideous nickname again. Then I'll tell Mom." I took a deep breath and narrowed my eyes on the asshole.

Zeke visibly shuddered. "No need to make serious threats like that. I'm just trying to help." Then we realized we hadn't heard from Zane for a few minutes. When I looked over, I saw he'd plopped back down on the couch and was staring into space.

"Hey, are you alright?" I asked him, a little worried because of the look on his face.

"Yep, but I just realized something," he looked at Zeke.

Then they both turned to me in perfect sync and said, "Reverie has a Faction."

I really hated it when they did that.

~ ⚘ ~

Reverie-
I slowly exited my jeep and looked around to ensure nobody saw anything. Luckily for me, it was dark. Also, only incoming first-year classes started tomorrow, so the campus was mostly deserted. Passives were inside preparing for the first full day at Emberhold, thank God.

I tried to remember if Nathan had told me his dorm assignment. The psycho must have left out that important information. Cell phones were useless here, so mine was still in my backpack. Going back in alone was always an option. I felt like I could trust the Moons, but let's face it, I had only just met them today. Nathan was insane, but I never mistook his craziness for stupidity. He was wicked smart, and I needed his input to handle this situation. Since lying to myself was ridiculous, I could admit I wanted to feel his arms around me. I needed his strength and confidence because getting abilities before my Faction was fully formed was insane. Maybe I could reach him through our connection. My parents had been able to do it, but it wasn't reliable anymore since losing two of their Faction members. I shouldn't have been able to do it, but tonight it seemed like anything was possible. I didn't have anything to lose in trying.

Nathan always seemed to know where I was. Maybe it was because of our connection? Or maybe it was because he was a stalker. I may never know the truth. Here goes nothing.

At first, I didn't feel anything. Then slowly, warmth built in my chest. I could see in my mind's eye the well of power that lived there. It was a bright amber ball of light. I was familiar with what it looked like even as a Passive. Mom had taught me to access it through meditation even then. Now, there was a pale green light surrounding it completely. Wow, it was beautiful. I could feel Nathan's essence imbued in it, and when I concentrated on the green ring, I could feel him surrounding me.

Suddenly, I could smell his unique scent and feel his obsession and deep love for me. It brought tears to my eyes. Despite everything we had put each other through, I never had any doubt about his love and devotion.

"Nathan, can you hear me?" I concentrated harder on the

ring that surrounded my power. *"Nathan, hear me!"* I pleaded. *"Hear me!"*

Suddenly, I felt him in my head.

"What is this? Oh, my sweet Nexi! Your mind is such a beautiful, fascinating place to be. I can feel you all over me. Cookies and honeysuckle." He sighed dreamily.

"Nathan! I need your help!" I knew how wonderful it felt, but I wanted him here physically.

"Need me, you say?" he asked, suddenly alert.

"Yes, I need you!" I repeated slowly.

"I just needed to hear it one more time. How may I be of service?" The shithead asked.

"Even in my head, you're an asshole!" I huffed out. *"I'm in the parking lot in my Jeep. I seem to have developed your teleportation power."*

"What? That's awesome! Wait, did anyone see you? Do I need to kill a witness? I've already decided on a plan to dispose of bodies while we're here." Nathan spits out in quick succession.

"No witnesses! No need to dispose of anyone! My roommate and her brothers are the only ones I'll have to answer to. I'm unsure how much we should share with them, but I can already tell they're decent people who'll keep my secret." I hoped so anyway. Strangely, I already felt invested in my friendship with Chloe, and I had a feeling the twins were going to have a vested interest in my safety. Nathan made a grunting noise and spoke.

"I'll be the judge of that when I meet them."

"What's your dorm assignment? We need to decide how we're going to play this."

"It's Dorm A, room 402. But I'm just going to head your way," Nathan said.

"That's OK. I'll just-" I jumped back.

"Too late, I'm here. No way I'm letting you walk in the

dark by yourself." Nathan growled, glancing around the parking lot.

"I hate when you do that!" I snapped, even though I was happy he was here.

"That may be so, but I'm not wasting precious time when you might be in danger." Nathan pulled me into his arms, one of my favorite places to be.

"I love that you want to protect me, even though I've had way more combat training than-" Nathan interrupted me.

"No need to rub it in my Nexi," he frowned. "I may not be on your level yet, but my determination to keep you safe rivals any training you may have had."

I stared at him for a moment. As crazy as he was, that was probably true. I suddenly pictured him being Hannibal Lecter and biting off someone's face.

"OK, point taken. Can we get out of here?" I asked. "My temperature runs hot, but I'm starting to get a little cold in my shorts and T-shirt."

"Absolutely!" He pulled me in close and transported us to his bedroom. "Here we are. Where all your perverted dreams are soon to come true."

"What the actual hell? When did you get that kind of control?!" I was in complete disbelief.

"Just recently. Like as in this exact moment." Nathan smirked as he walked over and fell back onto his bed.

"Are you kidding me?" I tried to keep my train of thought when I saw his shirt ride up as he stretched—that delicious six-pack and the thin trail of hair that led to such a lovely dick. Now, it was my turn to smile dreamily. Looking slowly back up to his face, I saw a devious smirk aimed my way.

"See something you like, my Nexi?" Trying to get back on track, I took a deep breath.

"The last time you successfully teleported two people was

that very first night. After that, you could only teleport yourself. Everything you tried to take with you disintegrated. You
blew up so much fruit, you even made a 'Save the Watermel-
ons' shirt, trying to be funny."

"I wasn't trying to be funny. It was funny. Grumpy just
has no sense of humor." Nathan pouted. "I feel more powerful. I can't explain it, but I knew it wouldn't be a problem."
He looked at me seriously, "I would never chance that beautiful melon of yours exploding." I just stared at him.

"We'll circle back around to that later. How much should
we share with the Moons?" Nathan walked over to me,
picked me up and laid me on his bed. He then plopped down
beside me and rolled me up in his arms.

"About teleporting or us? I also want to point out that I
deserve brownie points for holding in the many jokes going
through my mind about that last name."

I rolled my eyes and looked around his room. The room
had no personality at all. There was just a grey comforter
folded down, black sheets, and two pillows. Nathan had such
a massive presence that I was a little shocked.

"Where is all your stuff?" I asked curiously.

"I didn't bring it." Nathan kissed my head. "I know this
space is only temporary, and as soon as you bring in another
Faction member for me to rule over, we'll be moving to the
housing." I didn't even know where to start with that last
sentence.

"Sure, that makes perfect sense, and exactly what I get for
asking. Back to my original question: what do we share?
Chloe and her brothers were raised in the Aurathion
community, so they're going to realize I'm either Nexus or
Faction."

"Why are her brothers already here? I thought it was just
the first years until after initiation." Nathan started running

his fingers through my hair, removing the hair tie and undoing my braids.

"We didn't have time to get into that before I teleported out." All the tension I'd been holding left my shoulders. The combination of Nathan's presence and the fingers running through my hair was like taking valium. "Mom told me that older students who are teacher's aids come early. Also, some of them come to check out the incoming Passives hoping to find a Nexus or add to their Faction. I'm sure one or both of those apply to them."

"So, we can ditch this place after a couple of years?" I could hear the joy in his voice at the thought.

"Maybe. Depending on the completion of our Faction and how much training we need. My parents can help with some of that, but the academy offers a lot of advanced courses that are important for us to take. We'll have to decide when we get to that point."

"I'll have to decide if any of these Passive wanna-be Faction are good enough for my Nexi," Nathan smiled gleefully. I knew he was looking forward to putting any Passives that wanted to join our Faction through some shit. He truly was a disturbed individual.

"So, back to the Moon issue," I reluctantly sat up and looked at Nathan.

"Well, I trust your instincts, so if you think they're trustworthy, be honest." Nathan lifted his hand and cupped my face tenderly.

"Really? You just said you would need to check them out." I looked at him in surprise.

"Do you think you're going alone to tell them?" He looked at me like I was unhinged. "I'm going to be there and if they do something I don't like, I'll just kill them where they stand." He looked thoughtful, "Do they have pig farms here?

Never mind, I'll stick with my original disposal plan." This was the guy that looked at me like I was unhinged?

"Sometimes I think I'm the crazy one," I stared at him in amazement.

"You're not crazy." He kissed the top of my head. "Your super Nexus powers did pick me, after all." He pulled me back down into his arms. "It stopped me having to go through with my kidnapping plan."

I'd like to say I was shocked by that statement, but nope, it sounded about right. I heard the door open in the living room.

"Oh shit. You have a roommate?" I didn't know why I was surprised. As far as I knew, everyone had at least one.

"Yes. Some massive dude. I mean, I could still kill him, but I'd have to take him by surprise," he said, deepening his already deep voice.

"I never doubted you, psycho." I kissed his cheek, stood up, and pulled him to his feet. "Let's get to it. It's getting late, and we still have some explaining to do." I held out my arms, "I'm ready."

He looked at me in confusion. "Ready for what?"

"To zap out of here. I can't do it yet because I'm not sure how it happened the first time." I was going to have to find a place to practice, for sure.

"Why don't we just walk over?" He looked confused. I stared at him, blinking slowly. It was becoming a habit. But seriously, who could keep up with this guy?

"Okay. Sounds good." I just let it go. Maybe Elsa had it right. "Let's just walk back."

CHAPTER 5
REVERIE

We walked out of the room and into the small living area. The setup was identical to my dorm: the wall color, furniture, and everything. The only difference I could see was the mountain of a man standing in the kitchenette. He managed to make the small space appear even smaller. When he turned, I gasped. Nathan immediately pushed me behind him.

"What is it?" he growled. "What the hell do you see?" Desperately trying to locate the danger. I grabbed his arm, jerked him around, and then punched him in the stomach.

"What the hell was that for?" Nathan wheezed out in complete confusion.

"It was for that stupid sticker you put on my forehead!" I narrowed my eyes at the asshole.

"Why the hell would you think of that now?" He was still trying to catch his breath.

"I think I can answer that." The big guy smirked. "I saw sticker girl this morning while I was picking up my packet and dorm assignment."

"So you two have already met?" Nathan stood up, recovered from the unexpected punch.

"If that's what you call it." I felt my cheeks heat in embarrassment. Nathan started laughing hysterically.

"Since I got a tattoo dedicated to you, I thought you should have something to represent my sacrifice." He cackled, not doing a very good job of hiding our relationship from his roommate.

"And a sticker on my forehead was the answer?" I raised my eyebrows.

"Just a harmless prank, my Ne- Stop hitting me woman or I'm going to assume you want to play," Nathan frowned, trying to block my punches. I was going to kill him. He almost called me Nexi. We already had enough on our plate, having to explain our situation to the Moon siblings. I didn't want to deal with this guy too. The big guy was laughing at our antics.

"So, this the perfect princess you were talking about? I pictured a crown on her head, not a crown sticker on her forehead." *Everyone is a comedian.* I rolled my eyes.

"This is Jet," Nathan smiled. "Although I've taken to calling him Jolly. You know, for the Jolly Green Giant? The vegetable guy?"

"We know who it is, Nathan," I smirked.

Jet just looked at him. Same Jet, same. Seeing someone else stunned by the words coming out of Nathan's mouth felt validating.

"My name is Reverie, definitely not perfect or a princess." I smiled, trying to appear sane after the show we just put on.

"My name is Jet Lockley, definitely not Jolly," he replied with no expression on his face.

"Well, nice to meet you, Jet. We'll talk more later. We've got a previous engagement." I ended the conversation abruptly, dragging Nathan to the door before he said anything else incriminating to this guy. Jet stared at us until we closed the door. I'm sure we both appeared perfectly normal.

Nothing to see here. I rolled my eyes at my own thoughts.

W e arrived back at my dorm and paused in the hallway before entering. I was nervous and just wanted a minute before going in. I hoped this didn't change anything between Chloe and me. We'd hit it off immediately, and I loved the idea of having a friend I could hang out with.

"Let's do this, my Nexi. There's no need to stress about it. If we don't like what happens, I already told you I would take care of it." Nathan reached over and wrapped a lock of midnight hair around his finger.

"I know you did, but I think murder should be our last option." I smiled at him in exasperation. "I'm just nervous it'll change how Chloe looks at me, and I liked the idea of having a best friend."

"I thought I was your best friend. Now I'm thinking murder should be our first choice." The psycho gave the door an evil stare. Before I could respond, the door flew open and Chloe jerked me into her arms. I was so shocked all I could do was stand there with my arms hanging at my sides. Behind her, Nathan mumbled, "Too bad she doesn't have gonads."

"Where the hell have you been? I've been worried sick." Chloe shrieked. Zeke and Zane came running out of the dorm.

"Finally, we thought we were going to have to get in

touch with your family to see if you teleported home!" Zeke grabbed me away from Chloe. Chloe looked as shocked as I was at his action.

"I'm glad you didn't. I'll tell my parents, but maybe not quite yet. I'm sure you have questions and if we can go inside, I'll try to answer to the best of my ability." Nathan jerked me out of Zeke's arms and gave him a narrow-eyed stare. Zeke gave Nathan a cold look in return, but turned and walked into the dorm, and we followed close behind. Chloe and I sat on the couch, but Nathan walked over to pick me up and sat down with me in his lap. I guess someone was feeling a little territorial. "This is Nathan Strauss. We went to High School together and we're a Faction." I rubbed his chest in a calming manner as I spoke. He smiled proudly at my introduction.

"Thank you for not trying to gaslight us." Chloe smiled in appreciation. Zeke and Zane stood side by side with their arms crossed, staring at Nathan.

"Would there be any point? I won't start our friendship by acting like you're stupid." I smiled back at her.

"I appreciate that. But I'm not sure why you wouldn't just tell us when we met. I mean, you must have found your Nexus to be able to access your power." Chloe frowned, "Or you're Nexus, and your Faction is complete but that would be crazy." I glanced over my shoulder at Nathan. He gave me a nod of encouragement.

"Crazy should be his middle name, not mine, but I am Nexus." I reluctantly shared.

"When did you perform the ritual? I bet your mom performed it! She's amazing!" Chloe answered her own question. I sighed in relief. I didn't think we should tell everyone just yet about that little detail, but I didn't want to lie to them. Chloe kept talking, "It would be unusual, but not completely unheard of." She was mumbling to herself at this point. "Nathan must be your only Faction member. That's why you're getting your ability."

"I'm sure that's not the case. My Nexi is way too strong for that. I can feel how powerful she is through our connection." Nathan narrowed his eyes at Chloe like she had insulted me. Zeke and Zane looked relieved at Nathan's statement, but confused at the same time.

"So, if your Faction isn't complete, how in the hell do you have an ability? I've never heard of a Nexus getting access to abilities before completing their Faction, and nothing about this guy looks special." Zeke sneered at Nathan, probably still pissed at how he acted earlier, and a little envious he already had a Faction.

"I most certainly am special. You're just a duplicate. There's nothing unique about *you*," Nathan sneered back at Zeke.

"I'll make sure you're seeing double several times over after I knock the fuck out of you." Zeke growled, balling up his fists.

"Bring it on, bitch!" Nathan growled back. The twins took a step closer to Nathan, and he started to get up. This was getting ridiculous. I put my hand on Nathan's chest to stop him from attacking Zeke.

"I hadn't gained any abilities until tonight. We have no idea what's going on." I said quickly, hoping they didn't question me any further.

"I know we just met, and you know nothing about us, but I promise you we just want to help. We won't tell anybody what happened here," Chloe stated seriously.

"Do you realize how insane this is?" Zane directed the question to me.

"I do. As far as I can remember, nothing like this was in

any of the lessons my parents taught me. Maybe by having access to Emberhold's library, we can figure out what's going on." I looked at Zeke when he cleared his throat to get Nathan's attention.

"Look man, I'm sorry shit got heated, but I was worried about Reverie, and I'm man enough to admit to being a little envious. We've been waiting on our Nexus for a long time." Zeke held his hand out to Nathan.

"Believe me, it's unusual. I'm normally the emotional one." Zane chuckled, trying to lighten the moment further. I frowned at Nathan and waved my hand in a "come on" motion.

"It's all good, dude." He reached out and shook Zeke's hand. "But I do want to reiterate that I am special." He pouted, looking at me for confirmation.

"You're unique alright," I smirked, kissing him sweetly. "I know you won't tell anyone, and I'm truly sorry y'all are getting dragged into our mess. We both have every intention of letting the faculty know about my Nexus status, but we wanted to wait until we've passed initiation." I blew out a breath, relieved everything was out in the open...well almost everything.

"I can speak for both of us when I say we're happy to get dragged into your mess. There is nowhere else we'd want to be." Zane winked at me, continuing his flirting from earlier. I glanced at Nathan and waited for the explosion, but he just looked thoughtful.

"At least, on the bright side, initiation will be easier." Chloe smiled at me.

"How so?" I asked, confused at her reasoning.

"Well, you both will be able to do initiation together," Chloe bounced excitedly.

"I don't think it works that way. My parents said the first

initiation is solely to prove your worth as an individual." I told her, hoping I was wrong.

"That's the norm, but has anyone ever formed a Faction before initiation? If so, I haven't heard of it." Zeke ran his fingers through his hair, still appearing agitated.

"If there's the slightest chance you think it might be possible to go together, I'll take it. It's killing me to think about her going it alone." Nathan squeezed me tightly.

"Your parents are right. The academy has never let two people go through it together. Although, as Zeke said, I've never heard of anyone being Faction before initiation. Who knows what Emberhold will do?" Zane said, eyeing Nathan's arms that were still wrapped tightly around me. Zeke seemed hesitant, but began speaking, looking Nathan in the eye.

"I just want you to know that we're here for you both. We only met Reverie tonight, but the devastation I felt seeing her disappear is unlike anything I've ever experienced and frankly, shouldn't have, since we just met. I'm sorry to lay this on you, but you're being honest and I wanted to return the favor." He paused, taking a deep breath, "We'll be part of your Faction, and the ritual will be just a formality." Zeke moved his gaze to me, his sincerity and adoration obvious.

"I feel the same exact way. I've never felt anything like it before." Zane agreed, eyeing Nathan like he was a ticking time bomb.

"I understand how you're feeling because I felt the same way as soon as I saw her." Nathan nodded his head knowingly, looking surprisingly at ease. I stared at Nathan in amazement. When we were in school, if he noticed anyone looking my way in class or anywhere, for that matter, he would threaten them with death. The fact that Dane survived prom was a smooth miracle. Lucky for him, Nathan manifested his power and its fallout probably saved his life. Nathan noticed the amazement on my face, "I was pissed when he jerked you into his arms without my permission. Him not acknowledging how special I am was harsh too, but they seem like all-right guys and the fact they noticed how amazing you are earns them points. Plus, for some reason, I don't mind them looking." Nathan appeared a little puzzled at this.

Zeke and Zane both looked at each other with giant smiles on their faces. Then turned in unison to stare at me with so much heat in their eyes I started sweating. Chloe jumped up and down, screaming in excitement. Nathan looked at her with annoyance.

"What the hell is all that about? Just because I don't especially want to murder them doesn't mean that I believe they have souls or anything." Nathan grunted, speaking with his usual flair.

"This is going to be fun," Zane laughed evilly.

"What's going to be fun?" Nathan narrowed his eyes in suspicion. I just stared at them all, feeling a little shell shocked.

"Hell, yes, it is!" Chloe fist pumped.

I got up from the couch and excused myself to the restroom. I quietly shut the door and then leaned back against it. Closing my eyes, I took a deep breath. I just needed a moment. Nathan was already such a part of me it should have been hard to imagine the twins in my life in the same way. It wasn't. Remembering all the things Mom had told me over the years brought me some measure of comfort.

⁓⚜⁓

Mom and I sat on the front porch swing, enjoying the evening breeze. My daddies were cleaning up the kitchen because I heard Mommy say that she might be too tired to wrestle with my daddies later if she had to do it. I wasn't sure what she meant because it was almost bedtime.

"Mommy, how did you meet my daddies?" I asked her in my tiny five-year-old voice.

"Well, baby, I met your Grumpy and Pop first. I was at Ember-hold and stayed after class to speak to one of my professors. I was running late for my next class, so I rushed down the hallway, not looking where I was going. Out of nowhere, this giant wall appeared. I hit it and then fell to the ground. As I looked up, I got super scared because I thought I may have gotten a concussion," Mommy laughed.

"Why, Mommy?" I scrunched up my nose.

"Because I was seeing double," Mommy grinned.

"Double trouble!" I giggled.

"Exactly. Double trouble indeed." Mommy said with a dreamy look in her eyes.

"Was you in love at first light?" I waited excitedly for her answer.

"It's 'love at first sight', precious girl." Mommy laughed. "It wasn't exactly love. More like tingles at first sight."

"I felt tingles when Nathan held my hand yesterday at school." I was excited to have something in common with my mommy.

Mom looked at me strangely. "You did? Maybe you were just cold."

"No, Mommy, it felt like ants crawling on my arm, but in a good way," I snuggled closer to her.

A plate crashed, and Mommy got up and ran inside. I heard Pop and Grumpy arguing about whose fault it was and Mommy saying something about knowing bullshit when she heard it.

Grumpy hated when Mommy said bad words. I thought she sounded tough and wanted to be just like her.

∽ ⚭ ∾

T he memory calmed me, and I was able to breathe. I splashed water on my face and returned to the living room. Walking in, I heard the guys talking about football as they sipped a beer. Wow, it looked like they were already bonding. Poor Nathan was new to this world and had no idea what this meant. Everyone loved him in school, but he never had any close friends. I didn't think he was ever that interested in having them.

I joined Chloe in the kitchenette as she cleaned up. All the guys' eyes followed me as I walked across the room, never breaking from their conversation.

"Feeling better?" Chloe asked me in concern.

"I just needed a moment. I wasn't expecting to add to my Faction so soon." I sighed, then smiled. "Having a complete Faction does take the pressure off."

"What makes you think you're done?" Chloe jabbed me with her elbow and grinned.

"Don't even imply that there'll be more. Three is average and those men in the living room are probably going to feel like six." Chloe laughed at that. "Plus, that's the most common number in most Factions." I said, totally ignoring the way I felt meeting Jolly...I mean, Jet. Damn Nathan and his nicknames.

"Your mom got four," Chloe's grin got bigger.

"That doesn't prove anything. Mom is the strongest Nexus I've ever heard of." I shoulder bumped Chloe back.

"Maybe that was just until her daughter came along," Chloe jabbed me again.

"You, my friend, are a handful." I thumped Chloe on the forehead. "We better kick the guys out and go to bed. Tomorrow is going to be crazy. I sincerely hope we don't get called up for initiation." I yawned, "Staying up this late isn't going to do us any favors." She flicked me with bubbles from the dishwater and we both started giggling.

CHAPTER 6
REVERIE

My alarm went off at 5:30. Even though we'd been up late, I didn't want my fitness to fall by the wayside. I could hear Grumpy's voice in my head, "Conditioning is your friend." I grinned, missing him already. I jumped out of bed, threw my long hair into a ponytail, and pulled on black shorts, a sports bra, and a red razorback tank.

I walked down the hallway, stopping at Chloe's door, but didn't hear anything. Heading to the kitchenette, I made a pot of coffee using the beautiful coffee maker my parents were kind enough to buy. Chloe had been amazing to me, so making coffee for her seemed like the least I could do. I just might stop by Java and Jam and bring her some jelly donuts too. I wouldn't mind a little sugar after our late night, either.

Quietly shutting the door behind me, I turned and ran directly into a hard chest. I looked up and saw one of the twins standing there. I was pretty sure it was Zeke. I'd noticed when we met he had gold flecks in his eyes, while Zane's were a clear blue.

"Good morning, Reverie." He smiled.

"What are you doing here so early, Zeke?" I couldn't imagine he was here to see his sister this time of the morning.

"You can tell us apart?" He grinned, puffing his chest out.

"It's in the eyes," I smiled, feeling a little shy after his declaration last night. His grin got bigger.

"Nathan told us you usually ran in the morning. Full disclosure, I didn't sleep at all last night. I thought, why not snag a little alone time to get to know each other better?"

"I didn't sleep that great either. Between meeting these two amazing guys last night and my first day at the academy, my mind wouldn't settle." Look at me, managing to flirt at 5:30 in the morning. "I'd love to have a running buddy this morning. Let's get started because I want a shower before class." I held up my knuckles. Damn I'm lame, I thought to myself.

He didn't respond, crap he must think I'm lame too. This was getting awkward. A full minute had passed, and he still hadn't said anything.

"Zeke," I snapped my fingers in front of his face, starting to get a little worried. "Earth to Zeke!" He jumped, then looked down at me and blushed.

"Sorry, I suddenly got a mental picture of you in the shower, and I didn't want to return to reality." He ducked his head and rubbed the back of his neck. "That was probably an over-share." He chuckled at his own expense.

I rolled my eyes and busted out laughing. He was adorable. Hooking our arms together, I pulled him toward the stairs. At least I never had to worry about Zeke's honesty.

Walking out of the building, I inhaled the crisp, cool air. It was just the kind of weather I enjoyed on a run. Back home, we didn't experience weather like this until November, if we were lucky.

We set off at a good pace, running in perfect sync like we'd been doing it for years. The first path we came to wound through the woods, past the training facilities, and behind the academy, ending back at my dorm. The route was about four miles. I usually ran at least eight, so I was going to have to run it twice or explore longer trails. As we caught our breath, I turned to Zeke, "I'm going to head to Java and Jam and get breakfast for me and Chloe. Do you want to go?" His eyes lit up.

"Absolutely, I would." As we headed that way, Zeke moved in closer and grabbed my hand. Threading his fingers through mine, he looked at me shyly. "Is this ok?"

I squeezed his hand, smiled and nodded my head. I couldn't believe how natural it all felt. With Nathan, it could've been like this if I had known he had Aurathion ancestry. In fact, it was like this, until I got old enough to know that friendship wasn't all I felt for him.

"So, how was it growing up away from the Aurathion people?" Zeke asked as we walked along the path. The sun just starting to come up over the horizon.

"It was alright. I wasn't completely secluded. The council visited often, much more than my parents would have liked, and we went to the occasional gathering during the Aurathion holidays. When my mom lost Rue and Sly, it was tough for my family. Mom told me when I got older that it felt like she wasn't a complete person anymore. I would see her staring into space with a sad expression on her face many, many times. My fathers would immediately do something outrageous to distract her or take her upstairs when she got like that." After bonding with Nathan, I admired her even more. She had the strength to be an amazing mom to me, even with the horrible pain she must have felt every day.

"That's so sad," Zeke frowned, stopping and pulling me in for a hug.

"It really is. Unfortunately, I never got to know them. They both died toward the end of the war. My mom didn't know she was pregnant with me until a few weeks later. My pop told me that he thought I saved my mom's life and helped the family heal. Even though I know they never recovered completely, my parents always ensured there was plenty of love in our house." I smiled softly, knowing how lucky I am. "What was your childhood like?"

"We grew up close to Cleveland, Ohio, in a small Aurathion settlement. My parents were a big part of the community. My dad, Mark, is Nexus. He runs a mechanic shop with my poppa, Michael. Meredith, my mom, teaches kindergarten at our small school. We call them the triple M's," Zeke laughed. I was glad they had a nice childhood. I hated to ruin the moment, but I had to know.

"I feel a little awkward asking you this, but Chloe told me about Kristine. Are y'all still involved with her? No pressure. I just don't want to start the academy and immediately make an enemy."

Zeke winced, "No, not romantically, but we still hang out now and then. We've known her family since we were kids." He stopped walking and turned to grab both of my hands. "We should never have attempted the ritual with her. Our parents and Chloe warned us against it, but we didn't listen. Now, after meeting you, I know how ridiculous it was. She sometimes grabs lunch with us on campus, but we won't do that anymore if it makes you uncomfortable."

I hated how timid he sounded. I knew he and his brother had been looking for a Faction for a long time. Now that it was a possibility, he didn't want to do anything to upset or offend me.

"I would never ask you to give up a friend. I'm just a little leery because Chloe doesn't seem to like her *at all*. I don't want to worry about drama while trying to prepare for whatever Emberhold throws at me for initiation." I smiled softly, hoping I wasn't coming off as an asshole.

"I get that. Chloe and Kristine had a falling out. We asked Chloe about it, but she wouldn't tell us what happened. Kristine just said she was being ridiculous. Zane and I decided to stay out of it. I'm not going to lie to you, we hooked up occasionally but, when the ritual didn't work we decided to just be friends." Zeke squeezed my hands again. I could tell he was nervous. "I don't think Kristine was entirely on board with that. But we were still looking for a Faction and didn't want to muddy the waters. I'm so glad the looking is behind us now."

He leaned down like he was going to kiss me. Just then, we heard someone running up behind us. Turning, we saw Zane coming up the sidewalk.

"Hey, Reverie, why are you out with the uglier version of me?" Zane joked, pulling me in for a hug. Zeke frowned at Zane for the interruption.

"You wish. Everyone knows that you're just a shittier version of the original."

"Eleven minutes, asswipe, just eleven stinking minutes!" Zane stuck his tongue out at Zeke.

"You two remind me of my fathers. Always arguing over who's the better-looking twin." I laughed at them both.

Zane waggled his eyebrows at me. "You can call me Daddy."

Oh, lord! These two were going to fit right in. Grumpy

and Pop were going to love dealing with three guys. I smirked imagining the smack talk.

We walked into Java and Jam, and I went to the counter to order mine and Chloe's breakfast. A good-looking guy came up to take my order. He had short brown hair, green eyes, and a nice smile. His eyes zeroed in on my breasts and slowly rose to my face. That would have been a loss of points if I had been the least bit interested. Which I wasn't.

"Hey, sexy Snow White, what can I get you to eat?" he winked at me.

"That's a new one." I hoped if I ignored his flirting, he would get the hint. "I'll take two chocolate donuts and two with jelly." When I turned to ask Zeke and Zane if they wanted anything, they were both glaring at the counter guy with deadly intent. Granted, Zeke and Nathan had not hit it off immediately, but Zeke had been the first to try to resolve their issue. The menacing way they were looking at the counter guy gave me chills. There was a lot more than met the eye with these two.

"Do you see us standing here? Did you just call her sexy while we are standing right...fucking...here?" Zane growled menacingly.

"I think he did," Zeke narrowed his eyes.

"Do you want me to pluck out your eyes and feed them to you?" Zane asked with an insane smile on his face.

The Joker didn't have shit on him. What the actual hell was going on right now? They went from zero to sixty in point two seconds. The poor counter guy looked like he was going to shit himself. Did I get triple Nathans?!

"Guys, please stop. I'm sure he was just being nice." I smiled reassuringly at the counter guy. "I'm so sorry, can I just get my donuts so we can leave?" I continued smiling, but checked nervously over my shoulder, making sure the twins weren't going to attack. He quickly packed my donuts, and we turned to leave.

Right before the guys walked out the door, he decided to sack up and shouted, "You should keep them on a leash." I cringed, this idiot deserved whatever he got for being this stupid.

Zeke turned around and walked back, grabbed his shirt, pulling him partially over the counter. He leaned right in his face and then barked in a low, threatening way several times. The counter guy pissed himself, then Zeke slowly lowered him to his feet. Turning to me, he gently reached down and grabbed my hand. Zane opened the door for us, smiling sweetly.

"Let's go, honeybuns. Assembly is starting soon."

I walked out the door with a stunned look on my face. I didn't know what to think of the twins' Dr. Jekyll and Mr. Hyde personalities. It seemed that my Faction may have been the teeniest bit insane.

⮞ ⚜ ⮜

I entered my dorm and saw Chloe making two to-go cups of coffee in the kitchen. "I knew I loved you." I smiled in appreciation, "Let me grab a shower and we can walk to the assembly together."

"No worries. We still have about thirty minutes to spare. Where are my brothers? I thought I heard them outside the door." Chloe added three spoons of sugar to one of the coffees.

"They were, but they had to return to their dorm and get dressed for class. Did you know they were both crazy?" I asked, tongue in cheek.

Chloe looked at me puzzled while adding three more spoonfuls to the same cup. I laughed, "I'll explain on our way if you don't go into a diabetic coma before we can leave." Chloe gave me the finger.

"How do you think I stay so sweet? Are those donuts for me?"

"Yep, enjoy," I laughed as I walked out of the room. After showering, I looked in my closet, trying to decide what to wear. We didn't get uniforms until after initiation. I guessed there was no point in the expense until the Council knew if you were going to live or not. What a bunch of dickweeds.

I decided on ripped bootcut jeans, and a pink button-down shirt partially tucked in, with my western belt. The belt had a large buckle made of rose gold with my initials in the center. The buckle had been a gift from my mom for Christmas last year. I left the first three buttons undone and wore a rose gold chain Nathan bought me that had a pink glittery "N" charm that stood for Nexi, of course. Leaving my long black hair down to dry in waves, I swiped on some mascara and a little lip gloss. I sat on the bed, reaching for the drawer in my bedside table. I pulled out my holster, wrapped it around my ankle, and slipped my knife inside. I slipped on my shit-kickers, grabbed my backpack, and headed into the living room.

"Well, don't you look like a little Texas heartbreaker?" Chloe grinned. She was wearing jeans and a mint green sweater with knee-high black boots. "I take it pink is your color?"

"A girl can never have too much pink." I smiled, thinking of my mom. "You're looking good yourself, like a beautiful Irish rose."

"Since you started your Faction, I figured it couldn't hurt

to throw out some bait and see if I get any bites." Chloe sassed, striking a pose.

"Looking like that, I'm sure several Passives will be inspired to take a nibble." I smiled at her antics.

Students were to report to the assembly hall this morning before class. As we headed that way, we compared schedules and saw we had three classes together. Aurathion history, Biology, and Battle Strategies. Other than lunch, the rest of our day would be spent conditioning and preparing for initiation.

The second, third, and fourth years, depending on whether you'd found your Faction, had classes about their abilities and how to use them. They then spent the entire second half of the day learning to fight together. Students that hadn't found their Faction helped with classes for the younger students, in the hope that they'd find their Faction before the four years were up and they had to return to the outside world as a Passive.

The assembly hall was a vast room. The setup was like a basketball stadium. Students entered from the top, and the faculty members came through a door at floor level. The giant domed ceiling was made entirely of stained glass with different nature scenes and animals from our home world. The beautiful reds, lavenders, and oranges contrasted sharply with the gothic feel of the massive room. The floor was made of black polished stone with prominent white veins running through it. It almost had the effect of cracked glass. There were several oversized chairs, with the middle chair looking like a giant throne, all made of the Aurathion stone that ran throughout the building. A large podium was at the front of the stage.

I saw Nathan and the twins standing at the entrance. A beautiful brunette stood close to them, trying to get Nathan's attention. While she talked, she kept touching Nathan's arm and standing as close to him as she could.

"Looks like the wicked bitch of the west found another guy to try to sink her claws into. You better get over there before she fools him with her lies and little innocent act." Chloe sneered.

"That's not going to happen. Just keep watching. My psycho is not anything she's ever dealt with." I smiled evilly.

No sooner than the words left my mouth, Nathan glanced down as she grabbed his arm. He took hold of her hand gently, and she smiled at him. Suddenly, he twisted her arm behind her back and had her standing on the tips of her toes, trying to keep the pressure off her shoulder. He leaned down and whispered something in her ear, and her face lost all color.

The twins looked stunned and just stood there in shock. Nathan released her, and she stumbled forward. Walking some distance away, she turned and gave him the finger. Nathan just laughed.

"Well, I'll be damned," Chloe smiled. I gave her a smug look that had Chloe laughing.

"I told you so."

About that time, Nathan saw us standing there and walked over. Grabbing my cheeks and giving me a big wet kiss, he smiled, leaned down and whispered in my ear,

"You ready to find a seat and get this over with, my Nexi?" I should have been annoyed at him kissing me so openly but screw it. After that display of loyalty, I didn't care.

"Absolutely, my sweet psycho." I smiled dreamily. He had done some terrible things in the years we'd known each other, but his love and loyalty for me was never a question in my mind. The minute we bonded, he became the person he was before I ended our friendship. The way he looked at me never failed to give me goosebumps. That was part of the reason my parents had reluctantly accepted him. The love and devotion he felt for me was written all over his face. Nathan linked our fingers together and we headed into the room, followed closely by the three siblings.

"I never thought I would meet someone crazier than the Moon twins, but here we are," Chloe said, raising her eyebrows at her brothers.

"No shit!" Zane laughed. While Zeke nodded his head in agreement.

CHAPTER 7
REVERIE

We walked into the assembly hall and found seats close to the top. As usual, Nathan pulled me onto his lap instead of letting me have my own seat. Zane sat beside Nathan, leaned down and pulled my feet, boots and all, onto his lap. Then Nathan and Zane proceeded to stare at each other.

I glanced at Nathan and then looked back at Zane. I had no idea how this was going to turn out. Zeke took the seat on Nathan's other side, grabbed my hand, and weaved our fingers together. Nathan turned and looked at Zeke. I was starting to feel like I was participating in a game of Twister.

The way they kept staring at each other was making me nervous. I tried getting up and pulling free of them because I didn't want to put on a show for everyone. But not one of them would let go.

After the long stare down, Nathan calmly turned his head and faced forward like nothing had ever happened. Zeke and Zane smiled at each other and relaxed their shoulders.

I took a deep breath and whispered to the guys, "I thought we would just stay friends until after initiation?"

"Friends do this," Zeke whispered.

Nathan put his lips to my other ear, "The closer the friends, the deeper in."

Zane started cackling, glancing at Nathan and said, "We're going to get along just fine."

Well then. I guessed that was that. I was sure the blood ritual was in my future sooner rather than later. These three were clearly unhinged and here to fuck shit up.

"I guess I'll just sit way over here, away from my bestie. Unless Nathan will let me sit on Reverie's lap." Chloe gave Nathan doe eyes.

"No," Nathan said and scowled. "Stop saying you're her best friend. You're a friend, not the best friend." He gave her the evil eye.

I elbowed him for looking at my new friend like that, but as much as I wanted to disagree with him and be all "sisters before misters," the truth is that I knew in the deepest recesses of my heart nothing would pry Nathan from my side or from having my back. I'd just met Chloe and hoped for a lifetime friendship, but my parents had taught me that friendships took time, and actions spoke louder than words. Zeke and Zane being part of my Faction, and what I knew of Chloe so far gave me hope, but only time would tell.

Feeling eyes burning a hole in my head, I turned and saw Kristine and three other girls walking into the assembly hall. Kristine narrowed her eyes at me and whispered something to the tall blonde beside her. The blonde sneered at me and the guys and whispered back into Kristine's ear.

The girls took seats across the aisle from us, continuing to whisper amongst themselves and glancing back at our group occasionally. I knew they would be a problem, precisely what I didn't want to deal with right before initiation.

A large door opened, and the Aurathion Council filed in, with Council President Randell Hunter stopping to sit on the throne-like chair in the middle. Everyone got quiet and trained their attention to the hall floor. The dean of Ember-hold Academy walked up to the podium.

"Hello Aurathions! I'm so glad to see a full assembly hall on this first day of learning. I'm Dean Mathews. My staff and I have worked tirelessly to make this new year a productive one. Our numbers have been down in the last few years. We hope that, with the number of Passives that registered, more Aurathions will find their Faction. Thus, helping us to defend this new world we have integrated into." He took a sip of water and then continued.

"Most of you come from families that remember the war and fought for our world. But it excites me to tell you that in the last few years, the Council has conducted extensive searches for Passive families that came to this world years before the war. Some had no memory or idea that their ancestors hailed from another world. It is my pleasure and great privilege to welcome our Council and ask our Council President, Randall Hunter, to step up to the podium." Dean Mathews gave him a welcoming smile.

The Council President was a tall, distinguished man. He had dark hair cut short, a neatly trimmed beard, and wore a suit with a tie. I'd always thought he was a handsome man. I had met him many times over the years. Mr. Hunter had been a friend to my parents. He had fought closely with them in the war. Unfortunately, their friendship had taken a beating after he started pressuring my mom to seek out other Passives for her Faction.

I know the divide between my family and Mr. Hunter's

family had upset Mom. Mr. Hunter had three Faction, Mary-lynn, Helen, and Joan. All three of the women had been super close to Mom. Their support after losing Sly and Rue had been invaluable to her. Mom had felt betrayed, especially because Randall had been close to my father, Sly. They were distant cousins and had grown up together. I'd heard Grumpy talking to Mom several times about Mr. Hunter and how he thought he wanted the best for his people. But, after losing the war and fleeing their world, he became obsessed with transforming more Passives into Faction.

They understood what he was trying to do. More powerful Factions were needed to defend our new home. But, trying to force Passives into Faction just hit a little too close to what the leader of the Dark Faction had done. The blood ritual rarely worked unless the Passive and the Nexus had that beautiful mystical connection, and when it did, some gained weak abilities and even worse, no abilities at all.

"Hello Aurathions! I'm honored to welcome you to the most critical years in our people's journey to defend and thrive in our new home. The threat from the Dark Nexus and his perverted Faction caused us to have to flee our precious home and seek sanctuary in this new world." He spoke in an impassioned voice. "The program we have implemented to find Passive families has been wildly successful. Over seventy-five new hopefuls will be starting at Emberhold this year. We are sure that expanding the number of Passives will lead to more Factions being formed. I send many good wishes in the hope that every one of you passes the initiation Emberhold Academy has in store. Thank you for your service and may the ancestors of the past be with you on your journey toward the future."

The Council stood and applauded, along with the student

body. President Hunter bowed his head and then returned to his seat. Dean Mathews approached the podium once again.

"Students, please head to your first block. After today, if you want to change your schedules or think you have met fellow Passives who might be Faction members, please report it to me or my staff. The latter only applies to incoming students after initiation. Good luck."

As we all got up and filed out, Nathan stepped to the side, pulling me into an alcove off the hallway, and the twins followed. "This looks like a Faction thing, so I'll see you in class. This time, I control the seating order." Chloe said, sticking out her tongue in Nathan's direction before she walked off.

I laughed, "OK, I'll be there shortly."

Nathan watched Chloe walk away with zero expression and turned back to me. "I'm not sure I'm enjoying you having friends. It seems like sharing you with other Faction should be enough."

"I need some female friends to complain to about y'all. It'll make our relationship healthier." I grinned.

"I'll set up a complaint box in my bedroom and you can drop all the complaints there." He gave me an innocent look.

"That's an excuse to get our Nexus into your room," Zeke smirked.

"First of all, she's not your Nexus. She's just mine. And-" Zane interrupted Nathan.

"Yet. She's not our Nexus yet. But she will be."

"Maybe, maybe not. It depends on whether I approve of you or not. And if you keep interrupting me, your chances are getting slimmer." Nathan narrowed his eyes.

"That's not the way it works, asshole," Zane narrowed his eyes.

Nathan stepped up to Zane, getting in his face. Zeke stepped up to his brother's side. Then the stare-down commenced.

"Okay, I've seen enough! Was there a point to this meeting or are you three just going to throw down and get it over with?" These men were about to get a beat down. I was getting tired of their shit.

The stares transferred to me. Unfortunately for them, Adelaide had raised me and they didn't intimidate me at all. Tapping my foot, I gave them my best I-mean-business look. "Well, time is wasting away. What did you want, Nathan?"

A little shocked by my nonchalant attitude. The twins relaxed their stance and stepped back a little. Nathan, not shocked at all, just walked over and kissed my forehead, then adjusted his pants.

"You know when you get cocky, it makes my cock want to rise to the occasion," he winked at me. Zeke and Zane both burst out laughing, and Nathan joined in. It was like their standoff didn't happen and now they were the best of friends. Guys were dumb.

I pouted at Nathan and walked closer. "You're such a big, strong man and I love when your cock rises to the occasion." I ran my hand down his chest in the direction of his dick. Zeke and Zane were watching us with heated eyes. Nathan, for his part, was looking at me with suspicion... smart man. Moving my hand to his crotch, I thumped the cock he was so proud of. Side note: he had a reason to be proud.

"Hey!" Nathan screamed in a high-pitched voice. "You don't want to damage Big John." I looked at him in shock.

"You do know that's my Grumpy's name, right?"

"Yeah, so?" He raised his brow.

"So, you better name it something else or you'll never enter my love castle again." I narrowed my eyes.

"Love castle?" Zeke questioned, looking at Zane.

"I've always wanted to be a knight rescuing the princess. Maybe I can bring my battering ram to break into the gates?" Zane looked hopeful.

"I think we've gotten a little off topic. What was so important you risked making us late for class?" I asked, giving Zane the side-eye. Battering ram, what the actual hell?

"I didn't know the soulless wonders would join us." Nathan eyed the twins. "I just wanted to ask you when we would report our Faction status to the dean?"

Was this fool serious? So far, I hadn't actually lied to the twins about not needing the ritual. But if I publicly claimed Nathan, the Council would know we'd never registered to perform the ritual. Not to mention, we would never have been permitted to do it until after initiation. I would eventually have to come clean with the twins because Nathan and I would have to do the blood ritual to confirm him as Faction to the Council. We needed to discuss when we wanted to tell them.

Zeke rolled his eyes at Nathan, "Firstly, of course, we would join you. We expect to be full members of this Faction soon, with or without your approval. Secondly, you aren't going to be able to do that yet."

"Why the fuck not?" Nathan glowered at Zeke.

"It's unheard of for there to be a partially formed Faction before initiation. Also, I'm pretty sure the Hawthorne Faction didn't get permission to perform the ritual, if that's what happened." Zeke glanced at me as if he would find the answers on my face. Apparently, he didn't buy in to the conclusions Chloe had come to. "Drawing the Council's attention wouldn't be a great idea. In fact, after initiation, it might be better for us to do the ritual first."

"The hell you say? I'll be damned if you two become official Faction before I do." Nathan bit out.

"Calm down, psycho," I stepped up to Nathan and hugged him, "He does have a point. Especially when it wouldn't take too much digging to find out about our relationship. My parents have enough issues with the Council that I wouldn't want to add to it. There is no question that we'll wait until after initiation. Then I'll request that we perform it together." Turning to the twins, I gave them a stern look, "That goes for both of y'all, too. No stirring up trouble. We'll just carry on like we're exploring our options."

"We just want to get to know you better and show you what we bring to this Faction. You are the most beautiful, incredible Nexus anyone has ever had, and we're fortunate to call you ours." Zane lifted my hand and brought it to his lips, kissing it gently. He then turned to Nathan. "Look, man, we aren't your enemy. We grew up in this world, and I know it's all new to you, and parts of it will seem strange or hard to accept. We want to get to know you too and answer any questions you might have from a male's perspective." Nathan gave the guys a cool nod.

"I did feel strangely accepting of you both right from the start. This world is different and finding out I'm Aurathion has been crazy. I'm letting y'all know from the beginning I'll do anything for Reverie." He pulled me into his arms. "Anything. I've loved her for years, so I'm on board with whatever needs to happen to make me stronger for her." He narrowed his eyes, "But let me be clear. If either of you does one thing to hurt her. I'll put you in an unmarked grave. Well, what's left of you after the pigs have had their fill."

I leaned up and kissed his cheek. My psycho was one of a kind. I was super proud of him for accepting this new culture and always putting my feelings first. I felt my heart overflow seeing all the guys coming together.

"Nice to know murder and crazy behavior get rewarded. I think we're going to fit right in." Zane grinned, letting the crazy from the coffee shop show in his eyes briefly.

OK, maybe they were three of a kind.

"Let's get to class while y'all are still being nice to each other," I smirked and led the way with my men following right behind. I put a little extra sway in my step. Hearing a whistle and then a slap, I burst out laughing.

"We are three lucky guys," Zeke groaned, never taking his eyes off my ass.

I turned and winked at him over my shoulder and walked off into the sunset like the badass bitch I am.

I then stepped on a pencil someone dropped and stumbled, caught myself, felt my face get hot, then resumed my ass swaying prowl down the hallway.

Fake it till you make it, baby.

"You got that right, brother," Zane whistled again, dodging Nathan's hand this time. "Shake that groove thing, Rev!" He yelled, ignoring my stumble. They're not the only lucky ones. Clearly, I was too.

"What the actual Fuck? And who the fuck is Rev? That's a stupid nickname." Nathan scowled.

"Just trying out some options," Zane smirked, then walked away whistling.

"Is he whistling, 'My Milkshakes bring all the Boys to the Yard?'" Nathan narrowed his eyes on Zane's back.

"I think he might be." We looked at each other and started laughing. These two Moon boys were perfect for me, and I hated to see what them and Nathan got up to in the future. I grabbed Nathan's hand and pulled him in the direction of our classroom.

"Come on, crazy. I don't want to be late." Per our entire relationship, Nathan followed right by my side. Before we entered the classroom, I stopped him and narrowed my eyes. "I meant it about you renaming your penis. Why in the world would you think it would be sexy to call it Big John?"

"Just trying out some options," he winked at me, mocking Zane.

"You're absolutely ridiculous, and you'd better hope Grumpy never finds out," I gave him the side-eye.

"He should be flattered. My penis is big and gorgeous." Nathan smiled, showing all his teeth.

I just stared at him, speechless. Somehow, I didn't think Grumpy would take it as a compliment. On the other hand, Pop would love it.

We walked into history class just in time to sit in the seats Chloe saved for us. Jet was seated at the desk directly behind me. The professor entered right after the bell rang and stood behind the podium. He was average height, with short silver hair.

"Hello, class. My name is Professor Austin. Welcome to Aurathion History. I can't wait to begin teaching you about your heritage. For those Passives who have just found out about their lineage, I will be assigning you a tutor. This will be one of our upperclassmen."

Walking to his desk, he grabbed some papers and asked a girl in the front to pass them out. "This is a little pop quiz to see how much information you have and if it's correct. Newly found Passives, answer as much as you can. This will help me assess how much help you need," he explained.

Nathan leaned over and whispered in my ear, "I won't be tutored by anyone other than you. Let's hope Big John and Little Jesse taught me enough."

"Are you fucking kidding me right now? At this rate, we

may never have sex again." I looked at him in astonishment. "And I'm telling Pop you called him 'Little Jesse'. I'm sure y'all can work it out on the mats." I could swear I heard Jet chuckle. Turning my head to check, I found him as stoic as ever.

"Damn N- Reverie, no need to go full-out Beth Dutton on my ass. Nobody can take a joke anymore." Nathan winced, knowing he almost messed up and called me Nexi.

"Well, bless your little psycho heart," I smiled sweetly. "Now pay attention and use that sharp mind for something other than torturing me."

Nathan grumbled under his breath about mean southern women but looked down at his test and got started.

I knew all the questions, I hoped correctly, and turned in my test first. Directly behind me was Jet. We both returned to our desks and waited for the rest of the class to finish. Class ended about twenty minutes later with one poor guy turning in his test right before the bell rang.

"How did you do?" I asked Nathan.

"I think I did well. Your Grumpy would shoot me with his airsoft gun every time I got a question wrong." He grumbled, "I became extremely motivated to study."

"He did what?" Chloe laughed.

Jet followed close behind us and once again, I thought I heard him chuckling. But when I looked at him, his face was utterly expressionless.

I grinned at Chloe and leaned close, not wanting Jet to hear. "Grumpy had a lot of aggression to work out when Nathan became my Faction. To say he had to warm up to him is putting it mildly."

Walking down the hall, I felt eyes on me and saw Kristine marching toward us with her band of girls from the auditorium. Walking straight up to Nathan, she pouted, "I don't know what little Moon here told you about me, but I'm no threat to you. I thought we could get to know each other if I tutored you. I'm extremely knowledgeable, and not just in history." She fluttered her eyelashes at him.

In the most high-pitched voice I'd ever heard, Blondie stepped up next to Nathan, "Chloe's always been jealous of her brother's time and attention. That's the only reason she doesn't like Kristine."

What the actual fuck? This girl must have a death wish. What was the deal with Blondie? Was she some kind of ambassador for Kristine?

Nathan moved closer to me and put his arm around my waist. "I don't give a single fuck about getting to know you. Reverie is the only tutor I need, so kindly fuck right off," he said, mean mugging the fuck out of her.

"Who is Reverie?" Kristine pouted, looking directly at me.

"Well, aren't you just cute as a bug?" I smiled sweetly.

Nathan looked at Chloe and whispered, "Slowly back away."

"Why?" Chloe frowned.

"'Cause shit is about to get real." He backed up to stand next to Jet.

Kristine looked confused by this point, but was unwilling to back down. "I asked you a question, Chloe," she said sharply. Blondie stepped up and nodded her head in Chloe's direction in a get-to-it gesture.

I know this bitch isn't talking to my new friend like that. I'm about to go straight up western on her ass. I stepped closer to Kristine. "My name is Reverie Hawthorne. Are we going to have a problem?"

Kristine wrinkled her nose like she smelled something bad.

"A Hawthorne? I've heard of you. Your mom didn't do her

duty and bring more Passives into her Faction." She looked at me like I was gum on her shoe, then said in a haughty voice, "She should have been grateful they requested it of her after there were rumors your dad Rue was involved with the Dark Factions."

I pulled back my fist and punched her right in the nose.

That's how I ended up in the dean's office on my first full day of classes at Emberhold Academy.

CHAPTER 8
ZANE

I got comfortable at my desk in the corner of the large classroom. The room was set up with a row of seats starting at floor level and rising from there so that everyone had a good view of the podium. Professor York's ability to create and project illusions made him perfect for this profession. When giving his lecture, he was able to produce images that better helped his students understand and process what he was saying. The professor walked in, surprised to see me already at my desk.

"Good morning, you're here early. As a student, you barely made it in before the bell rang."

"I wanted to be a better aide than I was a student," I smiled, knowing Reverie was the reason I was early.

I didn't give two shits about being an aide. I was finding it hard to let her out of my sight and who could blame me? The girl was beyond gorgeous and sassy as fuck. I was becoming slightly obsessed.

"You were an excellent student, just not very punctual." Professor York put his briefcase on his desk, cleaned off his glasses and put them on. "I'm glad you're in early. This class is the largest yet, and we must try to stay on top of everything."

"I'm your guy, Professor York," I smiled, wondering why he wore glasses when Aurathions didn't need them. Maybe he thought they made him look more competent. Who knew?

Students started filing into class. I was anxious to see Reverie, all that raven hair and those beautiful amber eyes. I loved it when she smiled and those two dimples appeared on her cheeks.

My Nexus was perfect. Zeke and I had to be the two dumbest bastards on earth to try the ritual with Kristine. When it was real, there was *no* doubt. *She* was my Nexus. I could feel it in my soul.

Kristine had talked us into the ritual. To be fair, it didn't take much convincing. We had been desperate to find a Faction. I had seen what happens to Aurathions that remained Passives. Some made a good life, but most became bitter, more than a few committing suicide. I didn't want that for me or my brother. Now knowing what it felt like to have a true connection, I knew I was a damn fool.

I came alive the moment I met her. My blood sang in recognition.

Performing the ritual with her was just a formality. I didn't doubt that Reverie was my Nexus. The minute she entered the living room, I felt tingles all over my body and I couldn't take my eyes off her. When I glanced at my brother, he was the same. I felt such joy in that moment knowing we would get our wish to be in the same Faction.

With Kristine, we were desperate to get our abilities and be in a Faction together. She was convinced that she was Nexus. We'd slept together occasionally. She was fun and adequate in bed. We thought deeper feelings would grow in time. Meeting Reverie, I knew how juvenile that was.

I would give up my ability just to be with her. Becoming Faction was a bonus, but not my focus. Reverie's safety and happiness was all that concerned me.

The door shut, interrupting my musings. I looked up into the seats to try to spot the face fast becoming the most important in my world. I saw Chloe sitting alone—no sign of Reverie.

Just then, Professor York addressed the class.

"Hello Aurathions. Welcome to Biology. My class will begin by teaching the basic anatomy and reproductive systems of Aurathion's and how it differs from humans." He glanced down at his roster. "We seem to be missing three of our students. Does anyone know where Reverie Hawthorne, Jet Lockley, and Nathan Strauss are?" Chloe raised her hand, Professor York nodded his head "Yes, Ms. Moon?"

"Reverie had to visit Dean Mathews's office, and Nathan insisted on going with her." Chloe glanced in my direction. "Jet also accompanied them."

What the fuck? Why in the hell did she have to visit the dean? I stood up and headed toward the door.

"Where are you going, Mr. Moon?" the professor asked.

I kept walking, ignoring his question. Nothing was more important than getting to my Nexus. What if she needed me? I picked up the pace, wanting to get to her as soon as possible.

When I got to the office, Zeke was already there, sitting next to a massive guy. It wasn't often that my brother and I felt small, but Zeke looked average size sitting next to this guy. Nathan sat across from them with a murderous gaze trained on Kristine, who was sitting a few empty seats down from Zeke, holding an icepack to her nose. Kristine was surrounded by the Bitch Brigade, tittering over her injury and shooting dirty looks Nathan's way.

"What the hell is going on?" I demanded, looking around the room and seeing no sign of Reverie.

"The little bitch you're all so fascinated with hit me. I told you both that you shouldn't be associating with her. She's trash, just like her disloyal mother." Kristine said in a nasally voice.

"She hit Kristine for absolutely no reason. Kristine was just offering to tutor Nathan and help him catch up." Kristine's friend chimed in, I think her name was Sophie. I'd always avoided hanging out with Kristine when her friends were around. They were all annoying as fuck. She flinched when Nathan jumped up.

Anticipating the move, Zeke rose quickly and grabbed his arm. "They're not worth it, man. Just ignore the toxic bitches."

Kristine looked hurt. "I can't believe you said that. I've been friends with you guys for years."

"We were friends with your brother for years, before he turned into such an asshole. We just became friendly with you last year. Apparently, we should've paid closer attention to what kind of person you are," Zeke barked out.

"I haven't been very impressed with you two assholes. Now I'm questioning your intelligence. Anyone with half a brain can see she's toxic," Nathan snarled at Zeke. "Don't ever grab me again. I won't have her talking about my Reverie like that."

Zeke glared at Nathan, not the least bit intimidated, "There are more subtle ways to deal with a problem. Use your brain."

Kristine was starting to look a little more cautiously at the guys. Maybe the dumb cunt realized she had fucked up. I hated to agree with Nathan, but perhaps my brother and I were dumbasses.

I was surprised to hear Nathan using Reverie's name and not Nexi. It just showed how vital her safety was to him. The guy was rough around the edges, but I would be proud to have him as my Faction brother. We just had a few minor kinks to work out.

"Going back to my original question, what the hell happened?" I was getting impatient.

"This girl was too stupid to take a hint and approached me again. Then had the bright idea to insult Reverie's parents." Nathan grinned widely. "Reverie helped her see the error of her ways by reconstructing her nose. I'm just sorry it'll heal quickly." Nathan gave Kristine a menacing stare.

I couldn't keep the smile off my face, "Reverie is a little spicy, I guess you got a sample of that." I laughed at Kristine. Before she could respond, the dean's door opened, and Reverie walked out with Dean Mathews directly behind her.

"Ladies and gentlemen, you need to get to class. This doesn't concern all of you. Kristine, come, let's get your side of the story." Dean Mathews escorted her into his office.

The Bitch Brigade grumbled but got up and left. Sophie flipped us off before she closed the door. That bitch better watch it, or she would get to know the real me.

Nathan jumped up and pulled Reverie in his arms. "Are you okay, my sweet Reverie?"

Looking up at him, she said, "Better than OK. I got to practice my swing while punching the face of an actual tampon-sucking, asslicking, douche guzzling, shit stain." Reverie tilted her head up and kissed his cheek.

I couldn't wait until she felt that comfortable with me.

"Damn Reverie, you sure have a way with words," Zeke chuckled.

"You ain't heard nothing yet. Wait until poker night. She's a sore loser." Nathan smiled, in a much better mood now that Reverie was in his arms.

"I haven't lost to your ass at Texas Hold'em yet!" Reverie punched his arm.

"She seems like the kind to cheat," the big guy said, speaking for the first time.

Reverie turned and mean-mugged the shit out of him.

I was confused at his presence, "Why are you here?"

"I'm a witness," he said in a deep voice. "What's it to you?"

I scowled at him, "I tell you what it is to me, bitc-." Nathan interrupted.

"This is Jet. We share a dorm."

Of course, the two nutjobs shared a dorm. If he didn't watch how he talked to me, I'd slice his big ass. I'd have to catch him while he slept and probably bring Zeke with me, but it could be done.

The more I watched his eyes, the less I believed he was here for any of the reasons given. His eyes only left Reverie reluctantly. Just great, another one.

Walking over to Reverie, I pulled her away from Nathan and into my arms. Nathan was so surprised he released her without a fight. When he realized what happened, he scowled at me.

"What did the dean say?" I brushed back her hair, releasing a wave of her honeysuckle scent.

Looking slightly surprised at my show of affection, she said, "He was just disappointed in me for not taking the high road. Especially knowing who my parents are. I told him he must not know them very well because they would be proud of me for not putting up with her shit."

I chuckled and squeezed her a little tighter. This was the first time I'd gotten this close, and I was taking advantage of it. Was it weird if I sniffed her hair? Did I care? Apparently not, because I leaned down and rubbed my face on the top of her head, inhaling deeply as I did. I closed my eyes and breathed in the smell of honeysuckle and cookies. I felt my cock jump and goosebumps break out all over my body at the scent.

The big guy stood up and casually bumped into me, causing me to let go of Reverie and stumble back. What the hell? I narrowed my eyes at him. I fucking knew it, the jealous twat.

"So, do you need me here? Cause if not, I'm going to head out." Jet growled out in his freakishly deep voice.

"I don't think so," Reverie frowned. "After the bullshit comment, he told me that he would contact my parents. It all seems ridiculous when you realize we're over eighteen and could die during initiation."

I nodded absently in agreement. Fucking Jet. Now Nathan had pulled Reverie back into his arms. The fool stuck his tongue out and flipped me off behind her back.

I turned and looked at Jet, narrowing my eyes at him. It was that asshole's fault for bumping into me. Jet just stared innocently back. I used my middle finger and pointer finger to point at my eyes then Jet's, in the universal symbol for I'm watching you.

Jet might be joining us, eventually. I noticed Reverie watching him almost as much as he watched her. I need to find out more about him. Right now, I wasn't too thrilled at the idea. He seemed like a cockblock to me, and Nathan was going to be bad enough.

I felt like Zeke and I needed to spend time with Nathan to start building a relationship. It wasn't going to be easy since asshole was Nathan's default personality. But working together as a cohesive unit was extremely important to the safety of our Nexus. I felt the power inside Reverie, and it would take more than a few Faction to protect and fight beside her, so we needed to get on the same page.

"Are you headed back to class?" Zeke asked Reverie. I needed to talk to him about improving our game. I wanted our relationship cemented ASAP. We had an advantage over this dude. Every girl fantasized about a twin sandwich, didn't they?

"I guess so. I think battle tactics start in about ten minutes. Who teaches that class?" Reverie asked.

"Professor Lee," Jet smiled, showing the dimple on his cheek. "I've met him several times. Let's head that way and I'll tell you about him." Holding out his arm to Reverie.

Was this fucker serious? Flashing that fucking dimple at my Nexus? If he thought for one second he was jumping in line, that fucker was dead wrong. I looked over and saw Nathan giving him the evil eye. Zeke was frowning in Jet's direction as well, probably because he'd stolen Reverie's attention.

Well, well. It looked like Nathan, Zeke and I had something to bond over.

Reverie walked over to him, put her arm through his, and they headed out of the office. Nathan followed immediately, still staring a hole in the back of Jet's head. Well, maybe his upper back. The fucker was huge.

Zeke left with them and I was right behind. I damn sure didn't want to be here when Kristine came out. Zeke and I were helping with conditioning after lunch, so we would be able to look out for Reverie. Unfortunately, Oren Storm was the instructor of fighting techniques and conditioning. My brother and I used to be best friends with him. Oren was a badass, there were no two ways about it. Hence, why he was offered the position at such a young age. He was two years older than us, and our families spent a lot of time together. After Oren finished his fourth year without finding his Faction, he stopped spending time with us and became belligerent. We felt terrible for him but couldn't deal with the constant hostility, so we lost touch.

I really didn't want to be the one to tell Reverie that Oren was also Kristine's stepbrother.

We left Reverie, Nathan, and dimple boy in their classroom and headed toward the gymnasium and workout room.

Zeke looked at me. "Are you telling Reverie about Oren, or am I?"

"I think it should be you," I smiled innocently.

"Why the hell should it be me?" Zeke frowned.

"Because you're the oldest, so it's clearly your responsibility." He wanted to brag about those eleven minutes, now he could sack up.

"Are you serious right now? You're always bitching about it just being eleven minutes." Zeke said in disbelief.

"But you're the one always bringing it up. Time to use that maturity and wisdom, and man the fuck up." I crossed my eyes and stuck out my tongue.

"You are a fucking idiot," Zeke growled at me. "I'll tell her, but you're going to owe me one... and I will collect."

"You got it! Now, on to the next business. Did you notice that dude Jet staring at Reverie when she wasn't looking?" I growled out.

"What is his deal? I noticed him flashing that damn dimple. I wasn't amused." Zeke ran his hand through his hair, frowning.

"I think he might be another candidate for Reverie's faction. I'm not sure she's aware of it, though. She watched him when he wasn't looking and didn't hesitate to take his arm when he offered it. So, we need to check into him." I narrowed my eyes. If he wasn't a good candidate, he might just disappear. Everyone would just assume he didn't survive initiation.

"I've never heard of him. Which, isn't unusual since he's a found Passive. But if he's a possible Faction brother, doing some digging would be worth it." Zeke agreed.

I nodded, "Let me check in at the office and see if I can get any information."

"Are you really going to flirt the information out of Frances knowing you've found your Nexus?" Zeke said disapprovingly.

"I'm so good I can *not* flirt, and girls still think I'm flirting." I winked.

"What the fuck did you just say?" Zeke squinted at me in confusion.

"As my twin, I should never need to explain myself," I smirked at my brother. "Seriously, you know that Reverie will never have to question my loyalty to her. I was so scared this day would never come for us or that we would be separated. I wouldn't do a damn thing to jeopardize that."

"Me too, brother. Me too." Zeke agreed, hugging me and patting my back. "Let's see if we can gauge Oren's mood. I'd hate for Nathan to try and kill the asshole on his first day at the Academy."

I was excited for this new chapter in our lives. We had lucked out and got the most beautiful and powerful Nexus anyone could ask for, and we got to stay together. No matter how much work it would take, it was all worth it.

"Let's go. He's an asshole, but as our soon-to-be Faction brother, it's our duty to look out for him."

CHAPTER 9
REVERIE

Heading into class, I saw Chloe waving at me from the middle row. As I made my way over, I glanced to the front of the class and noticed a tall Asian man staring at me.

Jet leaned down and whispered in my ear, "That's Professor Lee. He was a Major in the war because of his ability."

Trying to hide my shiver in response to his warm breath in my ear, I asked, "What's his power?"

"He's a precog specializing in strategy," Jet told me. "I think the war would have ended differently if he had joined sooner."

"Why didn't he?" I moved over slightly. If he whispered that close to my ear again, I might embarrass myself.

"He didn't find his Faction until several years after it started. By the time he mastered his power, the war was almost over. It's said that he is the one who told the general they needed to leave our world and travel to this dimension." Jet told me.

The events of the day had apparently frazzled my mind. "Mom did mention him. He was friends with my dad, Sly, back in the day." I tilted my head in thought, "She told me he'd written a note and gave it to them to put in a safe place." I stopped talking. Why did I just tell him that? I'd only met him recently, and he sure as hell didn't need to know things about my family. Also, why did he know so much about our history, being a found Passive?

"That's interesting," Jet smiled slightly and flashed that damn dimple again. "When I discovered I was Aurathion, I studied everything I could get my hands on so I wouldn't show up to Emberhold completely ignorant. But if I need any help, I'm coming to you. It sounds like your parents are exceptionally knowledgeable."

"I'd be glad to help." Nope. I was going to avoid this guy. I had enough on my plate with Nathan and the twins. I wasn't ready to admit Jet was most likely my Faction too.

Reaching Chloe, I sat down and tried to recenter. The day had been a clusterfuck, and it wasn't even lunch yet. Jet started to sit beside me until Nathan cleared his throat loudly. I thought for a moment Jet was going to ignore him, but he took a seat next to Chloe.

Sitting beside me, Nathan grumbled, "Jolly and I are going to have a little talk when we get back to our dorm."

I rolled my eyes, "He was just telling me about our professor. No need to get pissy."

Nathan slid his hand under my desktop and palmed the crotch of my jeans. I could feel the warmth of his hand through the denim, and my panties dampened immediately.

"I saw him flash that fucking dimple again, so don't give me that." I heard his deep voice in my head. *"It seems that you're the one getting pissy. You seem a little tense after everything that's happened today. Do you need me to relax you?"*

"No, I do not!"

I looked around the classroom, but everyone was listening to the professor review the syllabus. Nathan was facing forward, doing an excellent job of pretending he was paying attention—the reprobate. The bottom of my shirt was covering what he was doing with his hand.

I grabbed his arm and tried to pull it away from me, but I couldn't budge it. Then I didn't want to. He was rubbing the seam of my jeans right over my clit, and it felt amazing. Even though I was sure my face was glowing red and I was scared someone would see what he was doing to me (thank God Chloe was a good student), it felt too good to make him stop. I wasn't entirely sure that was even possible. His firm but small movements kept us from being seen, but I needed more. I leaned closer to him so he would have better access.

"Open those beautiful eyes, my Nexi. You don't want anyone to guess what's going on."

I heard in a tone that had me obeying instantly. I opened my eyes but couldn't comprehend anything the professor was saying. I felt myself getting wetter and knew Nathan could feel it through the denim. He slid his hand up higher and undid my jeans, sliding his fingers into my pants.

"So wet, my naughty Nexi," he moaned, then started rubbing my clit gently with his thumb. He used just enough pressure to keep stoking the burn even higher without letting me tumble off the edge. If this was his way of relaxing me, he was doing a piss-poor job of it. I didn't know how much more I could take, and feeling the trembling of his thigh, that I was gripping with my hand, I wondered if he felt the same. Just when I thought the pleasure couldn't get more intense, he suddenly plunged two of his fingers deep inside me. It was almost too much—the things my psycho did to me.

My breathing became labored, and I was desperately trying not to close my eyes in pleasure. Being able to feel how turned on Nathan was on top of my own desire was profound. He sped up the motion, plunging his fingers in and out as he started rubbing my clit faster. I whispered his name, not having the concentration to communicate mentally, I heard Nathan give a low moan. At that moment, I knew I was going to come. I rolled my head to the left and was suddenly caught in Jet's molten gaze. Everything became too much, and I couldn't hold back any longer. I closed my eyes, and my toes curled as the intense orgasm washed over me. Just when I thought it was over, Nathan groaned, pumping his fingers faster, and I experienced his pleasure, which threw me into a second orgasm.

I felt Nathan move his hand from under my shirt. Opening my eyes, I saw him licking his fingers clean.

"Pure sweetness." He had to be one of the sexiest men on earth, my lips parted slightly, and I took a calming breath. He leaned over and kissed me gently. *"Now my Nexi should be in a better mood. I know I am."* I glanced down and saw a massive wet spot on Nathan's jeans.

"Shit, how are we getting out of here without anybody seeing that."

Nathan glanced down and then over at me, *"I don't give a damn who sees. It's like a badge of honor, showing how desirable my Nexi is."*

I heard nothing the professor said for the rest of class. This man was unbelievable, and he was all mine. What was I going to do with three of them? Maybe, I'd be the most satisfied Nexus on earth. I smiled dreamily at the thought.

True to his word, when class was over, Nathan casually got up, took my hand and headed to the cafeteria for lunch. I avoided looking at Jet because I knew my skin was still glowing. Partly in embarrassment and partly in satisfaction.

"Hey, wait for your bestie!" Chloe yelled, running to catch up.

"If she keeps calling you her bestie, I'm going to need a little hand action in our next class to relieve *my* stress," Nathan scowled in Chloe's direction. I rolled my eyes but was too relaxed to respond.

Chloe pulled even with us. "That was interesting. I found that class intense at first, then strangely relaxing at the end. What did you think?" she innocently looked at me with a twinkle in her eye.

Damn. I felt my face grow hot once again. I thought she was too distracted to realize what we had been up to. I had a feeling it would be a while before I heard the end of it.

We entered the cafeteria. It was a large room with cream-colored walls and large black sconces spread every few feet. The tables were of different sizes and shapes, made of the same stone used throughout Emberhold. I was happy I didn't have to move them. Hopefully, whoever did, had an established Faction. There were long windows on one wall made of stained glass with the Aurathion triquetra on the middle panel, the outer panels had animals and plants from our home world like the ones in the assembly hall.

The food was arranged in a buffet-style spread for self-service and there was a vast salad bar. Various vending machines were lined up against one wall, with a variety of drinks and sweets offered.

Nathan led me to a long table close to the windows. I was surprised at that, I figured he would sit at a smaller table with room for no more than three or four.

"We might as well sit at a large table since you keep collecting people," Nathan joked, and pulled me onto his lap.

Chloe stuck her tongue out at him as she sat opposite the seat, that would've been mine, if not for possessive Faction. Jet followed behind her and took the seat across from us.

I kept my gaze focused on Chloe, no way did I want to look at Jet. I'm sure my face was still glowing red. The more I tried not to look at him, the more I felt my eyes stray his way. I couldn't believe I had let Nathan finger me in class. I was such a hoe. I smiled in remembrance, but an extremely satisfied one. Feeling eyes burning into my forehead, I couldn't resist glancing Jet's way. He was staring directly at me.

"Do you want to *come* to our dorm later and study? I'm sure Nathan won't care if you *come*. If you don't want to *come* tonight, you can *come* tomorrow."

I stared at him, not amused at all.

Nathan started laughing, "I don't care when you *come*, just as long as you do." Giving zero fucks who knew what we had done.

Chloe died laughing, pointing at Nathan. "Where can I find one?"

"You can't. I'm one of a kind, baby Moon." Nathan gave her a cocky grin. "See, my sweet, how fortunate you are." He smirked and squeezed my thigh. I turned and kissed his cheek.

"I never doubted that." I couldn't imagine my life without this man in it. Zeke and Zane showed up, pulled out a seat, and sat down.

"Hello, sweet Reverie of mine. How was Battle Strategies?" Zane smiled.

"I think she was delighted at having the opportunity to *come* and hear the lecture," Jet looked innocently over at Zane.

"Who knew you had such a sense of humor, Jolly," Nathan grinned. "I might let some of your past behavior slide."

"I feel like we're missing something," Zeke looked at all of them suspiciously.

"You definitely are." Chloe cackled. "I would tell you, but I'm trying to solidify my best friend status."

"There is no solidifying that. I hold that position and every other position of importance." Nathan scowled at her, losing his grin.

"I've decided to take the best friend status. My personality fits her much better." Zane stared at Nathan in challenge.

"The hell you say? Everything I've got fits her." Nathan hissed at Zane. "Some things are a little tight, but we make it work."

I face-palmed, groaning in embarrassment. These men were going to be the death of me. I was tired of their shit and moved to my own chair, giving Nathan the evil eye. Zeke and Jet left the table, presumedly to get food.

"Sure, they are," Zane held his finger and thumb about an inch apart.

"Reverie, tell him that's not true!" Nathan demanded. "It's about ten of those. Add that up if you can, you soulless ginger!"

"If you want to see a ginger snap, keep calling me soulless. I'm full of fucking soul! I know the words to every song Muddy Waters ever sang," Zane snapped at Nathan.

I sighed, and looked at Chloe "Let's go get some food. The big dick energy in here is smothering me."

"Sounds like a plan. I'm starving, and they aren't showing signs of stopping." Chloe rolled her eyes.

"That confirms it, B-I-G D-I-C-K energy!" Nathan spelled out like a cheerleader at a pep rally, smirking at Zane.

I shook my head and turned to leave, bumping into Zeke who had plates for me and Chloe.

"No need to go anywhere. I brought food for my two favorite ladies." He slid a plate of spaghetti and meatballs with garlic bread in front of Chloe and a massive plate of food in front of me. "I just put a little of everything on your plate, since I wasn't sure what you liked."

Looking down at my plate, I saw a piece of pizza, a small steak, a baked potato loaded, some asparagus, an egg roll, and a small salad with ranch. I looked at Zeke and smiled, "Thank you. I like almost everything. You might have to help me finish all of this, though."

He looked back at me and smiled shyly, "I'll help you with whatever you need." Did he mean that like it sounded? I blushed once again.

Damn my fair skin!

"Too late," Chloe smirked, wagging her eyebrows. I was going to kill this girl. I hope she found her Faction soon so I could get a little payback.

Giving Chloe a puzzled look, he turned back to me, "I also got you a glass of sweet tea. I thought since you were from Texas, you'd like it."

"You thought right," I winked at him, shooting Chloe the bird.

"Damn, Bro, you're killing it!" Chloe high-fived him, still laughing at me.

Nathan looked at Zeke and sulked, "I'm the one that has to approve you. You should've brought me a plate." Standing up, he headed to the buffet. We watched him leave and then busted out laughing. He was something else, and I wouldn't change a thing about him. Except maybe for his ability to be discreet, thank goodness Jet hadn't returned to our table yet.

Jet and Nathan returned to the table with plates heaped full. Everyone dug in and ate like their life depended on it.

Chloe sat back patting her flat stomach, "I'm dreading these next classes, they're going to be intense. Instructor Storm is a real bastard and doesn't care if you pass or fail. I guess the whole family is full of assholes." She turned to her brothers and asked, "Why did you two quit hanging out with him?"

Instead of answering Chloe, Zane gave Zeke a look and nodded his head toward me. Zeke just kept staring at him. Zane gestured with his head again and raised his eyebrows. What the hell was wrong with these two? Zeke rolled his eyes and gave a long-suffering sigh.

"Reverie, can I talk to you after lunch? We can walk to the gym together," he asked quietly.

"Sure, is everything OK?" I was puzzled by their actions.

"I hope so." He mumbled.

Nathan put his arm around her, "I'm coming with her." I don't think anyone was surprised by his statement.

"You probably need to hear it too," Zane took a big bite of his burger. Seeming happy now that his brother asked to talk to me.

"I'm coming too," Chloe pouted.

"It looks like we're all coming," Zeke said, exasperated with the whole thing.

Jet started laughing so loudly that everyone in the cafeteria looked over at us. I stared at him in shock. I didn't think he had it in him to be this jubilant. When he could catch his breath, he grinned at me. "You're not leaving me out this time. I want to *come* too."

I rolled my eyes and stood up. Everyone was a damn comedian.

Walking outside, I noticed Professor Lee standing at the

side of the building, watching me. I hoped it didn't have anything to do with what Nathan and I had been up to in class. If he told my parents, I would never be able to go home again. We left the building and walked down the path, headed to the gym. Zeke walked beside me and grabbed my hand, stopping me before we entered.

"The instructor's name is Oren Storm. He was a pretty good friend to us in the past, but after he graduated from Emberhold and still hadn't found his Faction, he started acting weird. He disappeared for a while, and when he returned, he was different. He was angry and more psycho than usual. We tried to talk to him, but he wasn't having it."

"I hate y'all lost a good friend, but what does that have to do with me?" I asked, confused.

"I bet I can answer that question," Chloe winced. "I don't think anyone has mentioned it before, but Kristine's last name is Storm. Oren is her stepbrother, and you rearranged his baby sister's nose."

Well, shit. This ought to be good.

CHAPTER 10

OREN

I was sitting in my office in the gymnasium, the only modern building on campus. The gym was massive, half of the building was dedicated to conditioning with a fighting ring, climbing walls, workout apparatus, uneven bars, and various other equipment. Separated by a large wall that didn't quite make it to the ceiling, were insane obstacle courses that would help prepare the Passives for initiation. Even as an instructor, I didn't know what the academy had planned for the initiates.

I didn't have to worry about a training regimen. The academy changed the obstacle courses from year to year, sometimes even day to day. No one knew when Emberhold would take each Passive to initiation. Fortunately, the academy cared enough to try to prepare them. I usually didn't give a shit, I had enough on my plate. But this year was different.

Some Passives were ahead of the curve because their families started training them at a young age. The unlucky were the students new to the Aurathion culture. The ones who thought they were completely human until the Council began actively looking for those with Aurathion ancestry. The Council members were patting themselves on the back at the success of their little program. I bet they changed their tune after they were all killed during initiation.

I remembered my initiation. It was amazing. I was thrown into a dimension where even the plants would try to kill you. The extreme heat drained my energy, and I fought creatures I could never have imagined. I loved it when the odds were stacked against me. It was rare I was actually challenged by anything.

I grinned, thinking about the look on my professors' faces when I appeared back at the academy. My body had been entirely black from the blood of the creatures I killed, only the whites of my eyes showed. I thought the massive smile on my face probably threw them for a loop. If I were allowed to experience it all again, I would. It wasn't often that causing death and destruction was allowed.

I still had hope then. I knew that every skill I developed would protect my Faction. I was proud of what I brought to the table and was excited to be part of something bigger than me. A found family, because my own was fucked.

I had always been a little unstable. I never cared about friendships or making alliances like the rest of my family. The only friends I'd ever had were the Moon twins. They hid it well, but they were almost as unhinged as I am. I had a grin on my face, thinking about the shit we got up to when we first started attending Emberhold. Things even *I* shook my head at now.

I decided to end the friendship when I became aware of the things brewing in my future. I hated it, but there were moves I needed to make and things I needed to keep hidden until I was ready. I'd noticed in the last year that they were

getting desperate. They even tried the ritual with my stepsister, dodging a bullet with that one. I'd attempted the ritual
myself early on with several girls who were hungry for my
dick. Luckily, it didn't take, or I would have had a life full of
regret. That's a lie. More than likely, they would have met
with an unfortunate accident. I wasn't one for sacrificing my
happiness because of one little mistake.

Suddenly, my door opened so forcibly that it bounced off
the wall. Looking up, I raised my hands, and sparks came to
my fingertips. Seeing it was my stepsister, Kristine, I quickly
lowered my hands. She was holding an ice pack to her nose
and had medical tape on it to hold it straight.

"You need to do something about the bitch that did this,"
she dropped into one of the chairs in front of my desk.

"I don't have to do shit about anything. Your problems
aren't mine." I yawned in boredom. I was familiar with her
dramatics. She was exactly like her mother. When Diane
joined my father's Faction after the loss of my mom in the
war, she brought all the drama and none of the substance. I
wasn't sure the Faction had a peaceful day since.

Changing her tactics, she whined, "But she hit me for no
reason. I was talking to one of the found Passives, and she
took offense."

"I hate to repeat myself, but I don't give a shit. So, take
your ass wherever it is you're supposed to go. I don't have
time for your preschool drama." I twirled around in my
chair, demonstrating clearly I had the time but not the
desire.

Kristine smiled slightly and said, "It was the Hawthorne
girl that hit me."

Well, that changed things. The Hawthorne family had
pissed a lot of Aurathions off by not replacing their lost
Faction. Aurathions with less power were forced by the

Council to replace members lost to the war. I'd heard a lot of grumbling at the different gatherings I had attended, unhappy with this. Even though it was 17 years in the past, a lot of the Factions were in turmoil due to the Council's mandate. So, to say they were pissed that the more powerful Factions refused the mandate, was putting it mildly.

I lost my mother when I was four. The Storm family did their duty and started going through the process of looking for a Passive to fill her place. My father interviewed several Passives until they decided on Diane. She was a daughter of a prominent Faction who had strong abilities. Diane had never found a Nexus and, at thirty, hadn't expected to. She had a daughter and was married to a fellow Passive. She left his ass in the dust when the opportunity arose to become Faction and access her abilities. That says everything about her character, so she fit right in with my father's Faction. Diane was tied to the Storm Faction when the blood ritual was performed, and she was compatible. Her ability turned out to be fire, so she was an excellent addition. Most of the Storm Faction had developed elemental power in one way or another.

I wasn't fond of Diane. My childhood was shit because of the conniving bitch, not to mention the conniving bitch she produced. Father dearest loved to talk far and wide about following the rule of the Council, even though his Faction was only surpassed in power by the Hawthorne Faction. He was the one that passed the mandate, so I didn't find his actions noble.

"I saw her name on the roster. I already have an addition to her first obstacle course planned. Let's see if she can live up to her mother's abilities." I smiled in anticipation.

Kristine was almost bouncing in her seat with excitement. "I think I'm going to hang out here and watch."

"I don't give a fuck what you do. I'm not doing any of this for you," I sneered, standing up to leave the room.

Entering the gym, I leaned against a wall partially hidden in the shadows. I wanted to have a good view as the students started filing in.

The Passive students walked into the gym. Most had looks ranging from caution to outright fear. Then, a group strolled in with the Moon twins. My gaze honed in on the raven-haired girl directly in the middle. I was stunned at her beauty. Those eyes looked like polished gold. I saw her laughing at something the guy next to her said, both dimples were on full display. The guy put his arm around her, looking like your typical boy next door, high school prom king all the way. What a fucking douche.

The twins' eyes were laser-focused on her. I wondered if they were going to attempt the ritual with her—poor, desperate bastards. The guy behind her was a massive moth-erfucker. His hands were twice the size of mine, and I wasn't small. Coming in at 6'5", I didn't look up at many men, but this dude had me by at least a couple of inches. Bouncing behind them was the twins' annoyingly hyper sister, Chloe.

Well, it looks like she didn't wait long to surround herself with allies. It wouldn't do her any good. I planned on testing her strength, and none of the bitches surrounding her would be able to do shit about it. Her beauty had left me stunned for a moment, but it wouldn't change anything. Let's see what she was made of. Waiting until everyone was seated in the stands. I walked out of the shadows to address the class.

"Hello Passives, my name is Oren Storm, and I'm here to ensure you survive the initiation. Some of you are new to our culture. You have no idea what's coming for you, and it's my job to see that you're prepared. I will do my best to give you a chance, but it's your job to pay attention and make the most of what I teach you. I won't repeat myself or hold your hand through any of this. At the end of the day, it's your life on the line, not mine. Honestly, I don't expect most of you to make it." I smiled at the terror on their faces. What a bunch of little bitches.

Looking directly at Reverie, I smirked, "We'll begin with obstacle courses. I incorporated a few surprises, but Emberhold created them. I have no idea what the academy will throw at you because it's different every year. You will perform these alone, just like your initiation." Damn, I loved making this speech every year. There was nothing like the scent of terror in the air.

Was that stupid girl smirking at me? I frowned. That just wouldn't do, she must be taught a lesson. Her ridiculous family probably put her on a pedestal and never made her train at all. My father had always said the Hawthornes thought they deserved special treatment. I was about to show one member of their family that I didn't abide by that bullshit. You couldn't survive in our world without putting in the work.

The Moon twins made their way out of the stands to go to the stations I had assigned them. It was apparent that neither wanted to leave Reverie's side. Those two fuckwits weren't doing her any favors by coddling her. Zeke and Zane were known for their ruthlessness, but it looked like it didn't extend to her. More's the pity.

Unlike Zeke and Zane, I wouldn't be coddling anyone. I truly didn't give a fuck about most of the Passive's survival. Training to pass initiation was a personal responsibility and if you didn't have the sense to recognize this, the Aurathions didn't need you. Staying at the academy was of utmost importance to me, so I had to fake it occasionally. I'm not sure the dean was fooled but, my ruthlessness had saved more Passives than it hurt.

Looking at my roster, I started putting the Passives in groups. Little Hawthorne just happened to find her way into mine. I noticed Prom King had a mini breakdown when placed in Zeke's group. Zeke leaned close to him and said something that had him relaxing his posture and losing his attitude. Very interesting. They looked to be forming a friendship. Some would even say bonding. Hmmm, I wonder why that was.

We had about thirty Passives to a group. There were two classes: Group One trained for the first two hours after lunch, then switched with Group Two and went to conditioning. I was the instructor of both, lucky them.

Looking over my group, I could pick out the newly found Passives. Some looked like they'd been training, some looked like they had never trained a day in their ridiculous lives. I bet most wouldn't make it through my training, much less initiation.

"Okay, let's get started."

Behind me stood a course with a series of obstacles. The course started with students scaling up to a narrow beam several feet in the air, where the Passives had to keep their balance until they came to a series of climbing walls that got progressively larger, followed by an extremely tight maze with many twists and turns. Darts were shot out at different points, leaving glowing marks on the students on impact. The course ended with the Passive going through a dark, narrow tunnel that was deceptively simple. Emberhold Academy imbued it with the ability to expose them to their worst fear. Some didn't make it out of training completely sane. I personally believed you couldn't be completely sane if you made it through.

Passives from past groups that barely made it through had chosen to leave Emberhold and integrate back into human society, giving up any chance of coming into their abilities. I guess their thought process was, if they couldn't survive training, they couldn't survive initiation. Spoiler alert: they were right.

"Aren't we going to change into workout clothes?" a cocky-looking guy in the back asked. I loved this part.

I smiled, "Do you think the academy will give you time to change before throwing you into your initiation? I've seen Emberhold pull guys standing at a urinal pissing. If you feel it's important to be in workout clothes, I suggest you wear them morning, noon, and night."

"This first attempt won't be timed. Starting tomorrow, that will change and every attempt should get better. Then we'll move on to the next course. These courses will get more challenging as soon as you master them. Emberhold makes damn sure of that."

"What if we still can't do it?" A tall, extremely slim, blonde girl in the back asked. She was biting her nails, and her face was flushed in unattractive red blotches. I would bet my left nut she was going to find out.

Checking my list, I saw her name was Cassandra Silt. "Then you better hope you get the chance to drop out before the academy decides to start your initiation." I had no sympathy for her. She should have prepared better. "Those new to our culture will find we like to weed out the unworthy. There's not enough Nexus to bring out our abilities. We don't need Passives who are weak, blocking the line." Good riddance to any Passive that were as pitiful as this girl. We didn't need Factions made up of weak cowards. Her ability would probably end up being able to tell a person's name by smelling their ass.

I couldn't wait to see how Reverie handled the special surprise I had in store for her. If she made it out, nothing was guaranteed. Her last name meant shit to me. Making it through my tests and the academies was going to be based on her ability and nothing else. I wanted to rub my hands together and laugh evilly, like a super villain.

I had brought a little something special back from our home world. My pride and joy, Pantar. His name meant midnight in the Aurathion language, and I loved the vicious, blood-thirsty Fellat. I'd found him as a cub and brought him back to raise. The beast was more of a friend than a pet. He usually came and went as he pleased, and since he chose to remain invisible most of the time, no one had found out about him yet.

Unfortunately, I could only see Pantar when the big Fellat chose. Fellats only bonded with Nexus. Faction members gained the ability through them. I had looked forward to bonding with my beloved friend, so when it never happened, I assumed that I was destined to be Faction.

I had noticed Pantar hanging around the gym and my office all day. As soon as the Passives filed in, he settled near the stands, becoming invisible. The Fellat were an intelligent species. They had many abilities, some Pantar had been willing to share. They could be extremely vicious and cunning, sometimes hunting for fun and not just to eat. My Pantar was especially fearsome, and that's why we made such perfect companions.

Fellats resembled a panther but were the size of a small horse. They ranged in many colors not found in this world. The beautiful animals all had massive, serrated teeth with two large incisors; it was a mix between a shark and a saber-toothed tiger. Two massive fur-covered tentacles were just below the shoulder muscles. Instead of suckers, they had small spikes that they used to kill their prey and hold them while they feasted.

Pantar was solid black except for his two front legs, which were covered in fur and shimmered with a dark amber hue. He was beautiful and majestic, and loved nothing more than the taste of fresh blood. Apparently, not being raised in the wild didn't reduce his violent nature.

Fellats had been a big part of the Factions of old. They would bond with the Nexus first and guard them until their Faction was complete and they could access their power. There was not as much mystery involved with finding out your designation before our world went to shit. One of the many things the Aurathion people lost because of the war. Or so the Council wanted us to think.

No matter, it was time to put the Hawthorne girl to the test. I'm sure that the academy had some special surprises to go along with what I had planned. Reverie better hope that she inherited her family's talents because her life might depend on it. This was going to be fun.

CHAPTER 11

REVERIE

I walked into the gym, dreading what was coming. I had seen Kristine come out of a doorway near the stands. She walked by and made a point of looking up at me with a malicious smirk. Her friend Sophie joined her, and they sat in the stands, putting their heads close together and whispering back and forth.

Just great. The bitch ran right to her brother. Well, fuck them both. I wasn't scared of him or the bow-legged bitch. My parents had taught me the importance of standing up for myself, and I had no problem showing the Storm siblings what an open can of whoop ass looked like—Texas style.

A large man walked out of the shadows and came to stand in front of them. I felt goosebumps all over my body, and my stomach bottomed out. I closed my eyes briefly, willing the sensation away. No way was it what I thought it was. He was good-looking. He had beautiful dark brown hair, and his eyes were a striking seafoam green. His hair reached his shoulders, and he had the middle pulled back with a piece of leather. A close-cropped beard and full lips completed the devastating picture. He was taller than the Moon twins but shorter than Jet. His brown leather pants were well worn and paired with a short-sleeved black shirt and tall black boots. Was he going to a cosplay event after class? I smirked thinking of him posing for pictures at Ren Fest.

All Aurathions were attractive, but it felt like every guy I'd met at the Academy was next level. Then he began to speak and became a lot less pretty. You could tell that he gave no shits about any of the Passives gathered here.

Staring directly at me, he narrowed his eyes. "We will begin with obstacle courses blah, blah, I'm an asshole, blah." Or something like that. I zoned out after he began talking in his evil villain voice. I bet he went through breath mints like no other with all the shit that was coming out of his mouth.

I saw Kristine smiling evilly in my direction. It didn't carry the sting I'm sure she was hoping for with the medical tape on her nose. Focusing back on the asshole, I saw him frowning at me. Way to go, Reverie. Good job pissing him off even more.

Oren started separating us into groups, and with zero surprises, I was put in his.

"Fuck this shit," Nathan growled. "You're not dealing with him by yourself."

"Do you not think I can handle him?" I widened my eyes at Nathan. Nathan was no fool.

"Of course you can, but you shouldn't have to with me here." He grumped.

"Go catch up with Zeke. I've got this. If I need help, you know I have no problem asking, but I feel like he'll underestimate me, and that will work in my favor." Blowing him a kiss, I followed my group, to what was beginning to look like my own personal ShitStorm.

After listening to more crap come out of his mouth (I especially loved it when he said he didn't need weak Passives blocking the line), his status was confirmed as a giant bag of dicks. This was going to be fun.

"OK, first up, Cassandra Silt. Step to the front and begin when you're ready." When no one immediately walked up, ShitStorm narrowed his eyes. "Silt, you better get your ass up here, or I'm sending you back to your family. I don't have time for cowards."

The slim blonde girl, that had found the courage to ask a question earlier, stepped up to the front. Storm motioned for her to enter the course. She walked up the steps leading to the beam, looking completely terrified. I felt sorry for her because it was apparent she hadn't been prepared well. Why would the Council send these poor Passives directly to the academy without training? It was like sending lambs to slaughter.

The girl turned and gave Oren a pleading look, but he impatiently waved her on. The poor thing was wearing a dress with ballet flats. The shoes would be fine, but I hoped she had shorts on under her dress. As she climbed higher, it became apparent that was a no.

The boys started laughing and yelling at her, acting like complete morons. Didn't they understand every move was life or death here? Surprising me, Oren spoke in a harsh voice,

"Shut the fuck up. As weak as you all look, I'd be more worried about my turn instead of looking up girls' skirts like virgins who had never seen a pair of panties in their lives."

When the morons showed enough sense to shut up, I looked back at Cassandra. She was balancing precariously on the beam, looking like a drunk sailor on leave. You could see the sweat running down her face, cheeks red from exertion.

Finely crossing the beam, she came to the first climbing wall. This wall was reasonably easy because the hand and foot holds were spaced close. Cassandra tentatively grabbed the first hold and started to climb. She was having difficulty with her skirt. The length was causing her trouble when she needed to bend her legs.

"Tie your skirt above your knees!" I yelled. The fashion choices a lot of us had made today were going to get us killed, me included. It was a stupid mistake that I wouldn't make again. The morons below started yelling in excitement again, and this time, Storm let them be. "Ignore them and do what I said, or you won't make it over the next one," I urged the terrified girl.

Cassandra looked down at me and nodded her head. Climbing the rest of the way to the top, she sat on the wall and slowly pulled her skirt up, tying it in a large knot at her upper thigh. Looking down at me, she gave a thumbs up. I returned the thumbs up.

"You got this!" I hoped she had this.

"This isn't a sporting event, Miss Hawthorne," ShitStorm said in a pissy voice. "Keep your mouth shut and wait for your turn."

"Absolutely, instructor Shi- I mean Instructor Storm." I smirked. He frowned at me, looking confused. He knew I was insulting him but unsure how.

Turning back to Cassandra, I saw that she had completed the first climbing wall and was starting to ascend the next. This one, more difficult because the hand and footholds were much further apart. Luckily, she was tall and had no difficulty getting to the top. As she threw her leg over and started to climb down, water began slowly dripping from the top down the sides in slow rivulets. Oh shit, the level of difficulty was about to get a whole lot harder. Cassandra lost the confident look on her face and glanced at me in panic. Completely ignoring what ShitStorm had said, I gave her a big smile and a thumbs up.

"You can do this!"

Instructor Storm turned to me. "If you yell one more thing, I'll make her do this course twice. That's assuming she even makes it out this time." I nodded at the dick and turned my attention back to Cassandra once more. Cassandra took a deep breath and started climbing down.

The water sped up considerably and ran down in streams. Her foot slipped. Letting out a scream, she scrambled to find another foothold before she lost her grip and fell to the bottom. She was able to get the tip of her toe on the next hold and, slipping and sliding, finally reached the bottom.

I released the breath I had been holding, but wanted to start biting my nails when I looked at the next wall. The hand and footholds were spaced so far apart that you had to push off with your foot to get enough height to grab the next handhold. If that wasn't bad enough, they were positioned where you had to climb the wall in a zigzag pattern. It would take much longer to get to the top of this wall, and upper body strength would come into play.

As Cassandra stepped up to start her climb, water began dripping from the top of this wall, too. Taking a deep breath, she stepped onto the first hold. Pushing off, she grabbed the next hold and carefully pulled herself up until she could place her foot on the hold to the right, stretching her legs to their limit. Even though she had tied her skirt up, it was still impeding her movements. I heard a crackling noise and looked up. I couldn't believe what I was seeing. The water was slowly freezing into sheets of ice. Looking back at Cassandra, I saw her face lose all color. Fuck! This was crazy. I was scared to see what the academy threw out next.

"Did you Passives really believe the academy would make it easy for you?" Instructor Storm laughed. "Emberhold has all kinds of surprises to test your mettle and ensure you're worthy of being part of a Faction."

Cassandra had come to a complete halt. She was too terrified to move. This rock wall was probably about 30 feet tall, so she had a way to go. Hearing laughter and jeering coming from the stands, I saw the Bitch Brigade had joined Kristine and Sophie.

"What a fucking idiot. This dumbass hasn't spent any time training. She needs to fall already and let the next Passive go." Sophie started laughing loudly, encouraging the other girls to join in. I hoped Instructor Storm would put an end to it.

"You better get moving, girl. I don't think Emberhold will allow you to just hang there like a piece of meat." His smile looked identical to the Grinch's after he ruined Christmas. What a taint-licking asshole.

I opened my mouth to encourage Cassandra, but no sound came out. Trying again, it felt like my throat had closed. I turned to look at Instructor Storm, he winked at me. What the fuck? Was he doing this? But how? He wasn't part of a Faction.

Trying not to panic, I looked up and saw Cassandra had started moving again and made it about halfway. I felt the hold on my voice release and glanced back at Storm, but he wasn't paying me any attention. Hearing gasps all around me, I looked up just in time to see Cassandra's holds disappear and her falling swiftly through the air. Right when she should have hit the ground, the gym floor opened, and Cassandra disappeared through it.

What in the fucking, fuck just happened?!

"Well, it seems that Emberhold felt like it was a good time for Cassandra Silt to be initiated," Oren laughed maliciously. "I have serious doubts that we'll be seeing her again."

I saw panic on the faces around me and heard sobbing. A few Passives started running for the doors. Hearing my name yelled, I saw Nathan running in my direction. When he was almost to me, Oren stepped into his path. Nathan started to shove him out of the way, but right before he made contact, he fell onto his back like he had ran into a brick wall.

"I guess you're not as strong as you think you are. You better start working out, or you'll be following right behind Miss Silt." Storm smirked.

Nathan looked stunned but flipped from his back to his feet instantly. I was ninety-nine percent sure Nathan had never made contact with him, so how had he fallen? Nathan walked up to Oren and reached into his pocket.

I yelled, "Don't, Nathan. I'm okay. Go back to your group."

Nathan halted his hand and gazed around Oren. "Are you sure, Reverie? I will slit this asshole's throat if you need me to," he narrowed his eyes at Storm.

"I'd like to see you fucking try Passive," Storm smiled in challenge.

"You're a Passive too, motherfucker, and I don't need special powers to beat your ass," Nathan gritted his teeth, stepping closer to Storm.

"Try me, boy. I dare you." Storm was still smiling, but his right eye started twitching. Nathan had that effect on people.

"Yes, I'm sure. Please go." I begged. Using our connection, I told Nathan, *"We must be careful with him. Something's not right."*

He stared at me for a moment, but nodded slightly in

agreement. Both twins had walked up behind him and were staring at Oren in confusion. Reluctantly, Nathan turned and walked back to his group.

Zeke and Zane looked at me in concern, but when I gave them a nod, they turned and followed Nathan. Of course, Nathan had to turn around and give ShitStorm the finger. I shouldn't have expected any less.

"Your boyfriend better be glad you talked him into leaving. Any aggression perpetrated against a professor leads to instant expulsion and no chance of becoming Faction." Storm told me in a bored voice.

Speaking to him with more caution than before, I said, "Nathan is a hothead, but he won't cause any trouble." I didn't know what was going on, but I was determined to find out. Until then, I needed to be careful of antagonizing the dick.

"He better not, because I'll be watching closely. It would be a real shame if I had to report him before his initiation." Winking at me, he called the next student to the course. The fool thought that Nathan was the threat. He had no idea I was the real danger. As much as my psycho loved me, I returned those feelings twofold and wouldn't tolerate any menace directed his way.

The next several Passives made it through the course. Barely, and not without trauma. These Passives had grown up in the Aurathion culture and had training. When they emerged from the tunnel, some had tears running down their faces, and some were so terrified that they had trouble speaking. But they did make it.

Several found Passives opted to drop out and had returned to their dorms to pack. I'd be surprised if they were allowed to leave that easily after the Council had gone to so much trouble to find them. Emberhold hadn't taken anyone else to initiation, but each Passive knew it was only a matter of time.

Instructor Storm faced me. "It's your turn, Hawthorne. I hope you inherited some talent from your famous mother. You're going to need it." Letting my temper get the best of me, I flipped him off. I knew he had left me last to build the anticipation and try to get in my head. "Temper, temper. I'd hate to see you fail spectacularly in front of your boy toys." He smiled mockingly in the direction of the Moon twins and Nathan. All three had walked closer. The twins looked worried, but Nathan was smiling in anticipation. He knew what I was capable of.

The other two groups had finished with just four Passives failing to complete their obstacle course. It made sense that Instructor ShitStorm would oversee the more difficult one. He was a dick like that.

Staring him dead in the eyes, I started taking off my boots, unstrapping the holster around my ankle containing my knife and unbuttoning my pants. Other Passives had adjusted their wardrobe, but I was the first to strip down to my skivvies. I didn't just want to complete the course, I wanted to make it my bitch.

"What the hell are you doing?" Storm raised his brows.

"Is there a rule about doing the obstacle course in your underwear?" I raised one eyebrow.

"No, you can do it buck naked if you want. It's your funeral." He smirked.

I continued to pull my jeans down, took my shirt off, calmly folded both, took the hair tie off my wrist and threw my hair up in a messy bun. Looking up at the course, I took a deep breath.

The bitches in the stands started criticizing my body like I gave a tinker's damn what they thought.

"Look at those hips. I can't believe I saw her eating that huge plate of food in the cafeteria. She should be eating nothing but salad." a redheaded girl, sitting behind Kristine said.

"Check out those tits. They look saggy, even in a bra. Gross." Sophie fake gagged.

Nathan turned and started laughing at them. They looked stunned at his amusement, clearly hoping to get a different reaction.

"If all y'all can do is throw insults at her body, you girls are bigger dumbasses than I thought. She is perfection in human form. Anybody with half a brain can see that. Like her or not, that's just fact."

"No shit. These bitches would give both tits to look in the mirror and see a body like that reflected back at them." Zane laughed along with Nathan.

Turning red in anger and embarrassment, they quieted down, but the whispering started back up. I had a feeling they weren't done with their shit and were just regrouping. No matter, I put my focus back on what was important.

I couldn't believe I didn't think about initiation when dressing this morning. My parents stressed that you could be pulled away at any time. I couldn't afford these kinds of mistakes. Bought wits are the best kind, and I wouldn't forget it again. I didn't need to do it naked, but I had more movement without my jeans. Lucky for me, I had my boy shorts on and a decent bra that wasn't overly skimpy, so it was no different than wearing a bikini. I just wished I weren't so into Minions.

Suddenly, I heard Nathan say in my head dreamily, *"So fluffy."* I rolled my eyes.

"Any day now, Miss Hawthorne." Oren tried sounding impatient, but his voice was a little hoarse and shaky. I stretched, making sure to arch my back so he could get a good look. Take that dickhead!

Nathan spoke to me through our connection, *"Storm seems to be having trouble keeping his eyes off you."* He chuckled evilly. *"You've got this, my Nexi. Show this ballsack just how amazing you are."*

Smiling, I started to climb.

CHAPTER 12

OREN

Was swallowing your tongue possible? I hoped not because when Hawthorne dropped her pants, I thought I might be in danger of choking on mine.

Those moronic friends of Kristine's were trying to make fun of her body and calling her tits saggy. Those girls sounded ridiculous, when anybody with eyes could see she was perfection. Reverie's tits looked like two perfect plump melons, and that ass. I was an asshole, but I wasn't ignorant enough to try and insult a body built to make a man lose his mind.

Damn, this girl was fine. How could someone so short have legs that looked like they went on for miles? Was her skin glowing? That midnight hair hanging down her back against all that pale skin was striking. I didn't think it could get any better. Then she put it up and her neck's beautiful lines were displayed. I would fantasize about biting it for weeks.

Minions? What the actual fuck?! Would I ever be able to

watch my favorite little yellow buddies without a hard-on? This was getting ridiculous.

I discreetly felt to make sure I wasn't drooling and put my bitch face back on. I hoped she had trouble with the course because if she didn't, she was damn near the perfect woman.

I couldn't believe my eyes when I came out of my thoughts and saw she was already past the beam and climbing the first wall, scaling it like a monkey. When she reached the top, she stood up and leaped to the next wall.

What the fuck?! That was the only phrase that came to mind as I watched the most amazing, sexy, badass I had ever seen go through this obstacle course.

Landing in a crouch, she paused and eyed the third wall. It was significantly taller than the wall she was on.

"Hot Damn girl, you can move! I'm in love and don't care who knows it!" Zane yelled, but ended in a gasp when Nathan punched him in the stomach.

"Don't distract her! I love you, my Reverie!" Nathan yelled.

"How in the hell is that different from what Zane did?" Zeke asked in confusion.

Zane was still trying to breathe, but it looked like he wanted to ask the same question. What a trio of dumbasses. This was who she chose to spend time with?

"It's coming from me," Nathan said, completely serious. I couldn't believe these idiots. If they ended up in the same Faction, it would be fucked.

Hearing a grunt, I looked back at Hawthorne and saw that she had made the jump and was holding onto the ledge of the last wall by her fingertips. It would be too bad for her when it started to ice over. Then I could see what she was really made of.

Just before the ice coated the top of the wall, she used her upper body strength to pull herself up. Looking over at me, she stuck her tongue out and dropped, going so fast down the wall that she used every other hold.

What kind of training did this girl have? If her parents were responsible, then all the hype about the Hawthorne family must be true. Coming to the maze entrance, she paused momentarily to catch her breath. Watching this reminded me to breathe. I had apparently been holding my breath when she started her descent.

No way would she make it through unscathed. Every student in my group had come out covered in glowing marks from the darts. They better hope they took advantage of the conditioning and became quicker on their feet. If not, initiation was going to be impossible for most of them.

Hawthorne entered the maze. On average, Passives took about ten minutes to complete this section. I was curious to see how long it would take her and how many darts she would be hit by.

I looked at my watch, it was just hitting the five-minute mark when she came out and headed for the tunnel. I couldn't believe my eyes. The only mark on her was her upper arm, and I didn't see any others. She was amazing. This wasn't going as planned.

I was curious to find what the academy would deem her greatest fear. She better hope she recovered enough to find a way around my precious pet. Pantar would be waiting for her at the end of the tunnel, and I had encouraged him to be as vicious as he wanted. Seeing all that pale, glowing skin shredded would be a shame. I resisted the sudden need to stop her from entering, she needed to be tested.

As a small child, I had to deal with a new addition to my father's Faction, a raging bitch at that. The Hawthorne family was no better than us, nor was their little princess. I wasn't cutting her any slack.

There were strategically placed cameras throughout the maze so that I could watch later and see what each Passive needed to work on. I couldn't wait to see how she made it out so fast. I hated to admit it, even to myself, but Hawthorne was incredible. She had to be Nexus. What abilities would she bring out in her Faction? She might end up even stronger than her mother.

The three guys had moved closer to me. The twins looked terrified, but the newly found Passive Nathan didn't look worried in the least. I needed to look a little deeper into that. Next class, I would be sure he was in my group.

Zeke approached me, "How long did the other Passives take to get through the tunnel?"

"The time differs depending on what Emberhold throws at them. You just witnessed their different reactions," I said, looking at Zeke like he was an idiot. "Damn man, find your balls. The way you're worrying about her is disgusting." I completely ignored the feelings I had experienced earlier. I was a hypocrite, so what?

"Go fuck yourself, Storm." Zeke growled, "You've really turned into a sadistic asshole."

"She's probably going to come out crying for her mommy," I smirked, just to rile him up. "There's no telling what the academy has in store. I hope it's tough, it seems like she needs to be brought down a peg or two. I doubt a princess that's been coddled as much as she has can make it."

"Reverie will make it. She isn't scared of shit. I bet she comes out of that tunnel with a smile and her middle finger up." The annoying as fuck, Nathan smiled like he knew something the rest of us didn't.

"You are an idiot," I said snidely. "Let's make a wager. I bet she comes out bleeding and sobbing, if she comes out at all. If I win, you must leave the academy and remain a Passive bitch forever." Let's see if his balls have dropped.

"Don't worry, Nathan," Kristine called from the stands. "I'll let you perform the ritual and join my Faction." All the girls around her started tittering in glee. Nathan just gave her the finger.

Zeke warned in a gruff voice, "Watch your mouth about Reverie. She's exceptional, and you'll regret being such an evil bastard one day." Turning to look at Nathan, he said, "Just ignore him. He used to be a decent person, but now he acts like a cunt."

"No, Zeke. I'll take his wager. If I win, which is a foregone conclusion, you have to wear a shirt to class all week that says 'Reverie's Bitch' on it." Nathan smiled evilly.

This motherfucker was crazy. After seeing her wreck the obstacle course, I'd be hesitant to take that kind of bet, but I knew Pantar waited at the end of the tunnel and he was a vicious, bloodthirsty beast.

"I'll take that bet. I can't wait for you to leave your 'precious love' here, alone. Who knows, I may take pity on her and fuck her over my desk." I taunted him.

Zane jumped in front of Nathan before he could attack me, holding him back. He should have grabbed Zeke too. Before I could react, Zeke had punched me directly in the face and I was looking up at the gym ceiling.

"I told you to watch your fucking mouth. Unlike Nathan, you can't do shit to me, and you know exactly what I'm capable of," Zeke said in a spine-chilling voice.

People thought Zeke was an easygoing guy who disliked making waves. Zeke made sure he was perceived as such. He liked to watch his target and plot his moves. He was the kind of guy who befriended the person he wanted to hurt, learned everything about them, and then quietly made them disappear. He loved nothing better than stalking and hunting his prey.

Fortunately for me, I was just as cold-blooded as Zeke, with a little something extra the Moons knew nothing about. I would take on Zeke if I had to. But I didn't want to. Zeke was the kind of stone-cold to be very wary of, Passive or not. Getting up and wiping the blood off my face, I nodded to Zeke.

"I'll give you that one. I may have been slightly out of line. But if you do it again, I will retaliate."

Zeke nodded back. "I would expect no less."

Hearing clapping coming from the course, we all turned and saw Reverie headed in our direction. She looked at Zeke and smiled. "Zeke, you have one hell of a right hook."

I couldn't believe what I was seeing. She had dried tear marks running down her face, and it was apparent she hadn't come out completely unaffected. But there wasn't a mark on her, and my beloved pet was walking behind her, nuzzling his nose in her hair, giving her an adoring look.

Kristine and her friends were utterly silent. This was unbelievable, and even they knew something special had just happened. Zeke and Zane looked as stunned as I was. Nathan, on the other hand, looked terrified.

"What the fuck is that?!"

Well, well. A change of plans might be in order. It seemed like Miss Hawthorne was stronger than I expected. The next few months at the academy were going to be very interesting.

CHAPTER 13

JET

I was put with Zane's group. The obstacle course I had to deal with was challenging, but nothing like Reverie would face in Instructor Storm's group. That course was the most difficult to complete. It was the only one with the tunnel of fear, as the Passives were calling it. We would switch up every day, and I was told after everyone attempted all three, Emberhold would make the courses even more brutal. The academy wanted us to survive. Otherwise, all of this would be easier.

I was disappointed in my performance. I finished at the top but not without some bloodshed. With all my training and experience, I held myself up to high standards. If I was honest with myself, my human training wasn't up to par with the Passives raised in the Aurathion culture. That scared the shit out of me because my training was some of the most elite the United States had to offer.

Baby Moon finished right behind me. Her performance impressed me, and you could see the pride on her brothers' faces. Chloe was the real deal; I was glad Reverie had been paired with her. They could help each other through the trials to come.

I heard all the screaming from Reverie's group and felt my heart drop when the twins and Nathan ran that way. I had to fight my desperate need to go to her. Everything in me, every instinct I had, urged me to her side.

I had feelings for her that I didn't understand. I'd only known her for one day. How was it possible to become so fascinated in such a short time? Seeing her fall apart for Nathan in class was next level. I didn't know if my hard-on would ever completely go away. Why didn't I want to kill Nathan? Did I belong to her too? Was this what it felt like to be Faction? The answer to those questions didn't matter. It couldn't happen. I had a mission to complete.

Thankfully, Reverie was ok. The cause of all the screaming was another girl that Emberhold had taken to initiation. The thought of her being harmed or not making it through initiation was too painful to contemplate. Luckily, she and her family were part of my mission, so I had an excuse to watch her. After finishing, Zane instructed me to head to conditioning. I wasn't going to do that. Slipping behind the wall separating the obstacle courses from the conditioning area, I stayed to watch Reverie run her course.

When she started stripping, I was impressed. I was always taught to be prepared, so I had questioned some clothing choices I'd seen today. It looked like my Reverie had smartened up while waiting for her turn.

Dammit! She wasn't mine!

I needed to stop thinking like that. Mind on the mission, Jet! I still needed to observe her, but maybe from a distance.

Wait! Was that a Minion's bra and boy shorts combo? My boy Kevin was the shit! This girl! How was I supposed to concentrate when I was exposed to fuckery like this? I took a deep breath.

The way she went through the obstacles was mind-blowing. This girl was next fucking level. "Oorah," I thought, smiling widely. She was everything I wanted in a woman: beautiful, athletic, and with a hell of a left hook. This was going to be a problem. I needed to back off and reassess.

Instructor Storm was a complete dick and seeing Zeke punch that fucker in the face was fan-fucking-tastic. A little fucking scary, but awesome. I couldn't hear everything they were saying, but it was apparent I needed to study Zeke a little closer.

Hearing clapping, I looked back toward the obstacle course and saw Reverie with some monstrous-looking panther thing. It was nuzzling her fucking hair, those razor-sharp teeth on display. I instinctually felt for my sidearm and remembered I didn't have it. I couldn't believe my eyes. Were those fucking tentacles coming out of its back? What the fuck? This would have to be reported immediately.

Reverie was smiling and petting the freaky-looking thing. I relaxed, realizing she wasn't scared of the animal at all. Damn, what in the hell would I see next? This shit was crazy. My superiors were going to shit a brick when I updated them. Maybe their fear was warranted. How could my world hope to defend against these people? I prayed it wouldn't ever be necessary.

I slipped out of the shadows and headed to the equipment to begin conditioning. I would have to up my game to survive initiation and complete my mission. Aurathions were here to stay, I just hoped they were content with the status quo. If they ever decided to take over, I feared there wasn't much we could do to stop them.

CHAPTER 14
REVERIE

I flew through the obstacle course. I was pissed that I didn't dodge the dart that got me in the shoulder. I had let my concentration slip for one second because I stepped on something sharp.

Damn it! My clothing choices had come back to bite me in the ass. My parents would be so disappointed in me. I wouldn't make that mistake again and would ensure that Nathan and none of my new friends would either.

Taking a deep breath, I headed into the tunnel. I had heard about this from my parents. Pop said it was one of the most challenging parts of the training. The tunnel of fear.

∽☖∼

Fourteen-year-old me was sitting in my yard petting a Bat-Eared Fox. Things like this happened all the time at my house. My Grumpy's power seemed to call animals from every-where. I had no idea how he got here, but the species were native to

Southern Africa. I had researched it when he first showed up, curious about the little guy.

Stroking his ears seemed to soothe me as much as it did him. I had a tough day at school. There was a dance this weekend, and I'd been so excited about going. My good friend Marcus was on the cheerleading squad with me and we were going together. Marcus was gay and made no bones about it. Even for a guy so young, he was comfortable in his skin. Mom talked to me a year ago about not forming romantic relationships. I knew I would leave for Emberhold in four short years, and I understood that my parents didn't want my heart to break. Marcus asking me to the dance was awesome because we were just friends, and there was no chance of anything romantic.

Per usual, Nathan ruined it for me.

I was putting books up in my locker when Marcus approached me and said he wasn't going to the dance. When I asked him why, he gave a lame excuse about forgetting a project he had due on Monday. I knew it was all bullshit because Nathan was standing a few lockers down, staring at me with a smile on his face. I was so tired of his crap. Fighting my feelings for him was exhausting. Especially since I had to fight both of our feelings. Nathan had upped his campaign at the beginning of the year and hadn't let up. I hated school now. I had friends, but they didn't understand why I wouldn't date Nathan. Some of them were downright assholes about it. I knew it was jealousy since they would give anything to have his attention.

Hearing the door to the house shut, I looked up and saw Pop heading my way. Sitting beside me, he asked, "What's wrong, Tater Tot?"

"I was going to the dance tomorrow, and once again, Nathan ruined it." I sighed. "I know it's silly compared to everything all of you deal with, but I just wanted to experience things like a normal human."

"It's not silly. You're allowed to have ordinary experiences. I need to visit this kid, maybe as a Siberian Tiger." He transformed just his face and let out a roar.

I started laughing. "I would love to see that. He would shit his pants."

"Reverie Cleopatra Hawthorne!" Pop frowned, trying his best to look stern. He failed miserably. "Your mother has much to answer for where your language is concerned."

I just rolled my eyes. My middle name was ridiculous. Mom told me Cleopatra was Aurathion and a distant relative. I knew bullshit when I heard it. Knowing Pop wasn't nearly as offended as he tried to act, I ignored his outrage.

"I'm just afraid of losing my friends, of never getting to experience everyday human things, disappointing y'all at Emberhold, giving in to Nathan, and being heartbroken when I leave. Sometimes, I want to hide under my bed and never come out."

"Honey, you must face what scares you. Fix the things you can and accept what you can't. Every person you know fears something." He smiled softly.

"That's not true. You, Grumpy, and Mom aren't scared of anything." I said in a quiet voice.

"It is true. I hate to break it to you, kid, but we're scared of many things. One of the obstacles we had to defeat at Emberhold made us face our fears. The academy makes you face and understand what you fear to help you through initiation. I found it to be the most challenging thing I had to do up to that point." Pop frowned, obviously thinking about losing two Faction members.

"What did the academy show you?" I questioned.

"What my life would be like if I never found a Faction." Pop pulled me into a hug.

"That was your greatest fear?" I leaned my head on his shoulder.

"At the time, yes. Both of my parents were Passive since they *never found a Nexus. They loved each other deeply but never got to experience their power. The thought of that terrified me." He grimaced.*

"How did you get through it?" I asked softly.

"I realized that being afraid won't help change the outcome of anything. If I stayed Passive, I could help our people in other ways. It didn't mean giving up our culture. I had to realize that fixing the things I could and accepting what I couldn't was the only way to deal with my fear."

"Luckily, you found Mom," I smiled.

"Exactly. I was worrying about something that hadn't even happened yet. I was fortunate that Adelaide always ran late and crashed into your Grumpy in the hallway. When she looked up at us, I knew we had found our Nexus. Her only fault was and still is her foul mouth." He said with a twinkle in his eye.

"Mom has told me that story so many times," I said dreamily. "It's so romantic."

"Not long after, we met your other fathers, Sly and Rue, and our Faction was complete." He smiled in remembrance.

I pondered my solution out loud. "Well, I can't appease my friends, but I guess if they don't respect my decisions, they aren't my friends anyway. I can act by going to the dance and having a good time with my real friends," I said hesitantly, looking at Pops. He smiled at me encouragingly. "And I'm going to put in the work so I can kill it at Emberhold. Lastly, I can't control Nathan's actions, so I'm just going to roll with it as they come."

"You never need to worry about disappointing us. We'll be proud of you if you put forth your best effort. We all love you very much, Tater Tot."

"I love y'all too." I replied, so happy I had been gifted my wonderful parents.

～♠～

The darkness was absolute. I couldn't see anything. Moving carefully forward, using my other senses, I could hear water dripping and feel cool air blowing on my face. The farther I walked, the lighter it became until I could make out shapes.

Suddenly, I heard Nathan calling for me in a frantic voice. I panicked and started running in the direction his voice was coming from. How in the world did he get in here without ShitStorm seeing him?

"Reverie, hurry!" Nathan yelled, sounding pained.

I felt like I was flying, moving so fast I could barely see my feet. Coming into a large, cavernous room, I saw Nathan being held between several robed figures. The robes looked like the ones worn by the Council during ceremonies.

"Let go of him!" I demanded. This couldn't possibly be real. It had to be an illusion. The figures holding Nathan pushed him to his knees. Oh shit, the Council must have found out the truth about Nathan and that we formed a Faction without the ritual.

"Please don't hurt him. It was an accident." I pleaded.

Just then, I heard my mom say, "It's okay, sweetheart. They were bound to find out the truth. We'll never regret covering for you."

I saw two more robed figures standing next to my parents, who were in chains. My fathers were struggling, trying to reach my mom.

A booming voice from one of the robed figures said, "You are all found guilty of perpetuating a lie and keeping vital information from your people."

"No, they aren't at fault. It was all me! Please let them go!" I begged.

This had to be the academy. Fight this Reverie. It's not real, I kept chanting. Squeezing my eyes shut, I tried blocking it all out. Hearing footsteps, I opened my eyes.

One of the dark figures stepped up, and flames shot from his hands, disintegrating my mom on the spot. My fathers started screaming and fighting the men holding them, trying to get to me. The men pulled out knives and slit both of their throats simultaneously. Blood began gushing out onto the floor and running toward my bare feet.

Nathan broke free, running in my direction. The man who could wield fire turned to him, and flames shot out again, turning my beloved psycho into ashes.

The heat from the flames and the smell of burnt flesh was overpowering. I could smell the coppery scent of my fathers' blood, feel how sticky it was coating my feet. This wasn't an illusion! It had to be real. All my five senses confirmed it. I fell to my knees sobbing, closing my eyes tightly so I couldn't see the bodies of my fathers and what was left of my sweet mother and the man I loved.

Suddenly, I felt a rough tongue lick my face, from chin to forehead. Opening my eyes, I saw a creature I had only heard about in stories.

Seeing a Fellat shocked me so much that I snapped out of my grief and realized it had been Emberhold all along. The smell and feel of the blood disappeared, and the illusion was broken. My greatest fear was the Council discovering my secrets and taking the ones I loved from me.

Feeling the great beast snuffling my hair brought me back to reality. What in the hell was he doing here? Where did he come from?

"I'm here because I felt you calling me, Nexus." Looking around to see where the voice was coming from, I realized it was just me and the Fellat here. *"My name is Pantar, so you can stop referring to me as the Fellat."* How in the hell was he speaking to me telepathically? I thought frantically. That was Grumpy's ability. *"Calm down, Nexus. I can speak to you because you have the ability inside to communicate with animals. It can be found in your ancestry."*

This was incredible. "How are you here? I thought your entire species was all killed during the war." I couldn't believe this. Using his tentacles, he helped me to stand.

"Nexus shouldn't lower themselves so." He took me to task, *"especially one such as you."* Answering my question, he said, *"Most of my kind were killed trying to defend the Nexus we had bonded with during the war. Luckily, my Dam hadn't found a Nexus worthy; already bred and close to giving birth, she found a safe place deep in the Cimarron Forest. We stayed there until we were old enough to venture out on our own."*

"But how are you here at the academy?" I asked.

"I felt you. Your power is incredible. I deeply regret not finding you before you started your Faction." Pantar replied without completely answering my question.

Still shocked at this turn of events and the illusion I had experienced fresh on my mind, I begged, "Please, you can't say anything. Nobody knows!"

"Silly Nexus, I can't communicate with just any Aurathions," he rolled his eyes. *"And I am insulted that you would think I would betray you."*

I sighed at my stupidity. "That's true, I suppose, and I'm sorry." He was so beautiful, and his fur looked so soft. I hesitantly reached up to touch him, and he lowered his great head so I would have better access. His back leg started tapping when I scratched behind his ears. Seeing such a vicious-looking animal looking so adorable made my heart melt, and a smile come to my face.

He shook his great head and said, *"Okay, enough of that. We need to get you out of here, and I would like to make our bonding official."*

"How do we do that? My mom had a Fellat, but it was killed defending her Faction. She doesn't talk about her, and since we thought your kind extinct, there was no need to discuss the bonding process." I was excited and scared all at the same time.

"That is understandable. The process is quite simple. All it takes is a small bite, and the bond snaps into place."

I winced looking at Pantar's sharp teeth, but the honor of bonding with this great beast made me push the fear to the back of my mind.

"I'm honored you chose me, and I'm ready when you are," I told Pantar.

Leaning down, he took my wrist delicately between his teeth and bit down gently.

I felt the bond snap in place immediately. It was like a warm balm to my soul. I felt a burning between my breasts and a swelling of power in my gut. Pantar bent his front legs and bowed his head like I was royalty.

"I am honored to bond with you, Nexus, and will protect you and yours all the days of my life."

"I accept your vow and promise to honor you and your kind until my last breath," I said. Not knowing where the words came from, but needing to say them.

Standing, Pantar decreed, *"It is done. Now, let us leave this place."*

Coming out of the tunnel, I saw Zeke hit Instructor Storm and knock him on his ass. I couldn't help clapping at the fantastic sight. I don't know what he did to piss Zeke off, but whatever it was, I'm glad I didn't miss the awesome sight of that bag of dicks laying on the ground bleeding.

The guys turned to look at me, and their mouths dropped open in shock. I guess it wasn't every day they saw someone walking around with a giant, tentacled beast at their back.

Things were about to get real. There would be no doubt about my Nexus status now. The time had come to own my shit, and I was ready for it.

With Pantar by my side and my Faction coming together, I was going to be just fine.

CHAPTER 15
REVERIE

Walking up to the guys, I channeled my inner cocky bitch. I had defeated this obstacle course and left with a legendary companion. The first anyone had seen in years. I deserved to have a little strut in my step.

"What the fuck is that, Reverie Cleopatra?" Nathan asked, as if I had done something wrong.

"Did you just middle name me, dickface?" I questioned in my not-to-be-fucked-with voice. Being extremely familiar with the voice, Nathan changed his tone.

"I would appreciate it if you would step away from the large animal until we know what it is and if it's dangerous."

"Your middle name is Cleopatra? And you're a Minion fan?" Zane asked, looking me up and down with raised eyebrows.

"Forget the middle name. Nathan will be punished later for blurting that out. And everyone loves Minions." I dared him to prove me wrong.

"I never have, but I'm starting to see the appeal," Zeke grinned at me.

"I'll take my punishment like the strong, secure man I am. Now get over here and away from the giant panther, alien thingy. Right fucking now!" Nathan growled while stomping his foot.

"It's a Fellat, you dumb motherfucker!" Oren yelled at Nathan. "Fuck, you need to study if you're this clueless about the Aurathion culture."

Nathan took a big step and punched Oren in the mouth in such a quick, smooth motion that there was no defending against it.

It didn't seem like he tried to hide the extra strength he had gained since becoming Faction, either. "Looks like this dumb motherfucker just knocked you on your ass."

Zeke leaned down to help Oren up, "You had that coming. If you try to report him to the dean, you'll regret it."

Wiping the blood from his nose, Oren growled out, "I'm not reporting shit, but the next motherfucker that punches me is getting fucked up. I don't give a fuck who you are. Just try me."

I walked in the direction of my clothes. I was physically and emotionally exhausted and didn't have the time or inclination to referee these fools. Though I was getting a thrill at seeing ShitStorm knocked on his ass so many times.

I rubbed between my breasts; it was stinging unmercifully. I glanced down, lifting my bra slightly. I didn't see anything.

Pantar stayed near me, never taking his eyes off the guys. *I don't disapprove of your first Faction member. The other potentials need to prove themselves before performing the ritual.*

I looked at him and gave a small nod. I didn't want anyone to know about my newfound ability. I would later let

Pantar know that Oren was certainly not a potential candidate for my Faction. I was still in shock that I could communicate with the Fellat. Getting a new ability without adding another Faction member was unheard of. I really needed to talk to my parents. Maybe they could help me figure out what was going on. Honestly, I needed to see them and make sure they were alright after that horrible illusion I had just experienced.

Stopping to get dressed, the twins and Nathan headed my way. Pantar let Nathan pass, but stepped between me and the twins. Zane frowned at him and made a shooing motion with his hands.

"What the hell are you doing?" Zeke asked incredulously.

"Trying to get him to move," Zane continued shooing the giant animal out of the way.

Pantar stared Zane in the eyes, then slowly sat back on his haunches.

"I think he has zero intentions of moving until she's changed. Apparently, you must be Faction to have the privilege of standing close to her," Nathan smiled smugly.

"You better enjoy being the single member now. Cause I think we'll get to join you sooner than expected, possibly before initiation, in fact. It would have been feasible to wait until after, for Reverie to emerge as Nexus, but now I think the three-hundred-pound cat is out of the bag," Zeke said to Nathan while staring at Pantar in awe.

"I think he's right." I finished dressing and slipped my boots on. "I'm going straight to Dean Mathew's office. There's no way I want ShitStorm to tell him first." I absently rubbed at the spot between my breasts again. It had stopped stinging but was still a little painful.

"ShitStorm?" Zeke asked, smirking in Oren's direction.

The man in question was standing next to the obstacle course, watching us.

"Makes complete sense to me," Nathan and Zane said in unison.

Zeke started laughing, and before long, everyone joined in. I was overjoyed to see them getting along. This was what a Faction was supposed to look like.

Looking past the guys, I saw Oren looking between Pantar and me in contemplation.

What was that asshole cooking up? I wondered nervously. No matter, I'd deal with it as it came.

Heading toward the Dean's office, Pantar didn't attempt to hide his presence. He stood directly behind me, allowing only Nathan to walk by my side. The twins followed as close as he would allow.

People in the hallway were looking on in shock. I'd never seen a Fellat, and most Aurathions had only seen them in books. So, the reaction was to be expected. The attention was a little unnerving, but I held my shoulders back and stood tall. I'd just decided to own my shit, and that's exactly what I did.

Professor Lee stood at the end of the hallway, staring in our direction. He bowed his head reverently to me when I walked by. It was odd. I needed to remember to ask my parents about the letter he had given them.

I leaned close to Nathan. "You can't go with me to the office."

"Why the hell not?" He frowned.

"I don't want to hide what we are to each other, but no one can know about our bond until we do the ritual, and no rituals will be performed until after initiation is complete. Unless this changes things." I glanced at Pantar.

"Okay, my Nexi. I'll wait for you in my dorm. Let me

know if anything goes wrong, and I do mean any little thing." Turning to give the twins a look, he let go of my hand and reluctantly headed outside.

The twins continued to follow me. When I looked at them in question, Zeke motioned for me to keep walking. Trusting they knew what they were doing, I continued heading toward the front office. Dean Mathews was headed out by the time I reached the office. Stopping, he looked at Pantar in amazement.

"I was just coming to look for you. I've had no less than twenty students and ten professors come here to tell me about the Fellat in the hallway. I had to confirm it with my own eyes."

"I came straight here, Dean Mathews. I thought it impor- tant to let you know and possibly get permission to contact my parents." I said in a respectful tone. I wasn't sure he even heard me. He couldn't take his eyes off Pantar.

"Where did he come from?" he asked reverently. "How did this happen?"

Suddenly, out of nowhere, Instructor Storm appeared from behind the dean. How in the hell did he get here so quickly?

"I'm curious about that as well. How did this happen, Miss Hawthorne? Is your family somehow involved in this?" Storm smiled, with what looked like mischief.

What a fucking asshole. Trying to involve my family, the nickname ShitStorm genuinely fits him. "I was in the tunnel confronting what Emberhold deemed my greatest fear and out of nowhere, the Fellat appeared. I don't know any more than you do." I said to him sincerely, ignoring Storm.

"I think we need to call Callum of the Rossi Faction. He'll know if she's telling the truth." Storm said, still standing behind the Dean. He then winked at me like this was all in fun. What fuckery was this?

"I'm not sure that action is necessary. Let's head to my office and discuss this without an audience." Dean Mathews glanced up, noticing the crowd gathered in the hallway for the first time.

When Zeke and Zane started to follow, the dean stopped them, "I don't think your presence is needed. Instructor Storm was leading her group and should be able to answer all my questions."

Zane frowned, "We were there when the Fellat came out with Miss Hawthorne. My brother and I would be more than happy to give an accounting from our perspective."

"It's not needed at this time. I'm sure Instructor Storm will have all the insight I need." The Dean said sternly.

I saw ShitStorm smile smugly at the twins. When the Dean turned to walk into his office, Zane flipped him off. Hopefully, I'd get to see Zane knock him on his ass in the near future.

Smiling reassuringly at the guys, I entered the Dean's office with Pantar right behind me. The Dean sat at his desk with me and Storm taking the chairs in front. Pantar prowled around the room, sniffing various objects. I was thankful the office was large. Otherwise, it would be a tight fit. Pantar was a massive Fellat.

"Thank you, Nexus. I am exceptional, that is true." The giant beast preened.

"I need an accounting of the events that start with you entering the tunnel." The Dean said, still spellbound by Pantar's every move.

"Well, as I explained, I was confronting the scenario that Emberhold had shown me, and Pantar just appeared and snapped me out of my fear. I have no idea where he came from." I explained.

"Are we really expected to believe that?" ShitStorm asked. "How does she know the Fellat's name?" He smirked at me. God, I hated his stupid face.

Pantar forced himself between me and Storm's chairs. Then looked down on Storm and growled in a low, threatening manner. Take that dick!

Storm looked shocked and strangely hurt by this and leaned away from Pantar. I tried my best not to show any amusement, but from the way Storm glared at me, I wasn't sure I succeeded.

"When we bonded, his name just came to me," I replied to Dean Mathews. No way was I going to say the beautiful beast told me himself.

"You've already bonded?" The Dean asked in amazement.

"Yes, we bonded while still in the tunnel." I showed him the bite marks around my wrist that were already starting to heal. I rubbed my chest, but stopped when I noticed Storm staring at the motion.

Storm leaned closer, like he was trying to see through my shirt. Pantar blocked him and lifted a massive paw, knocking him from his chair and to the floor. This was the third time today I had seen him on the ground. I really hoped it would trend. #ShitStormonhisassonceagain. I lifted my hand to cover the smile on my face at the thought.

Oren jumped to his feet, glaring at Pantar. I thought it odd that he hadn't shown any fear of the Fellat thus far, my Pantar was extremely fearsome.

"He isn't too bright, but he would make a brave faction member," Pantar spoke, surprising me with his comment.

"I didn't think you liked him," I said, finding it much easier

to speak to the Fellat this way than when I communicated with Nathan.

"He needs to remove his head from his ass, but he does have good qualities that would enhance your Faction." He yawned, showing all his teeth.

"I haven't seen any proof of them yet." I looked again at the dean, who had pushed his chair as far away from the Fellat as he could.

Storm scowled at them both and said to the dean, "She shouldn't be allowed to keep him at the academy. It could pose a danger to the other students. I would be glad to keep the Fellat with me."

Pantar began growling again. The dean stared at him fearfully. "You know as well as I that a Fellat will not be separated from their Nexus after they have bonded, which brings us to the following matter. Even though you haven't performed any rituals, you are obviously Nexus. It's highly unusual, but do you already have potential Faction members in mind?"

I needed to be extremely cautious here. Bonding with Pantar was strange enough without the Dean finding out about Nathan becoming my Faction with a simple blood exchange—no ritual needed.

"There are a few Passives I've felt a connection with. Of course, I have no intentions of getting serious about it until after initiation." I told him.

"Zeke and Zane seemed upset when they couldn't attend this meeting. That Nathan fellow, who I believe is from your human school, has also been rather invested in you since you arrived. Going so far as insulting my dear sister in a perceived slight against you. Seems serious to me." Shit-Storm looked down his nose at me. I hoped to have the opportunity to knock him on his ass soon. Maybe even start a club. I bet there would be plenty of Passives wanting to join.

Dean Mathews looked a little bewildered by Storm's hostile tone. "There was a mishap with your sister, but it was cleared up—just a tiny misunderstanding. I'm surprised at your hostility, Instructor Storm. This is a fascinating development and a chance for our Passive students to become Faction."

"I apologize if you felt like I was being harsh, Miss Hawthorne." Storm said in a fake-as-shit, apologetic voice. He turned to the dean. "I just wanted to point out she may have led some of our Passives to believe they would be first in line to perform the ritual. It's unfair to make them think that if she's not really interested."

"Nexi, are you alright? I can feel your anger. Do you need me?" Nathan suddenly asked.

"No, ShitStorm just really pisses me off." I replied.

"I'm here and waiting. Let me know as soon as you get out of there." My psycho said sternly.

"I will." Oh, how I loved that man.

"Well, be that as it may, with so few Nexus, all Passives should expect a little competition. My dear nephew hasn't found a Nexus yet, so I must introduce you." Dean Mathews said casually.

I heard a growling noise coming from Storm, it must have been in annoyance at the dean's fawning. Glancing at Pantar, I saw him watching Oren with an expression that seemed almost smug. I wondered what that was all about.

That's why it felt like Dean Mathews was catering to me. Absolutely ridiculous. My mother never let anyone dictate to her about faction choices, and I damn sure wouldn't either.

"I want to follow up with you directly after your initiation. It is astounding to have a Nexus revealed so soon, and it happened due to bonding with an animal we thought was eradicated because of the war. Simply amazing! I can't wait to inform Councilman Hunter of these developments," the Dean seemed almost euphoric. I saw Storm roll his eyes, but he said nothing further.

"May I speak to my parents?" I inquired.

"In our history, it was told that Fellat had the power to create portals. Maybe your new companion would like to help with your request?" The Dean turned to Pantar in hopeful, expectation. Pantar looked around the room in boredom, not acknowledging him at all. "Or maybe not." Annoyance showed briefly through his friendly demeanor.

"I'll open a portal for you to visit. But I expect you back within the next couple of hours. There will be another portal waiting in the exact place you appear." Dean Mathews gave me what I was sure he thought was a kind smile. To me, he just looked constipated. Oren looked pissed at this turn of events, but said nothing. Doing us all a favor and keeping his mouth shut for once.

The dean opened the portal; it would be nice if everyone had that ability. He then motioned Oren to follow him out of the office.

"The dean has allowed me to use a portal to talk to my parents. Please let the twins and Chloe know what's going on. When I get back, I'm going straight to my dorm because I'm exhausted." I spoke to Nathan.

He answered me immediately, *"I'll let everyone know. I hate that I won't see the shock on their faces, but you can describe it to me in detail tomorrow. I love you, my sweet Nexi. Get some rest, and I'll see you in the morning."*

Surprised at getting no argument, I replied, *"I love you too."*

I looked at Pantar. *"Are you ready? I'm excited to see my parents, even if it's only been a few days."*

"Let's go Nexus. I, too, am excited to meet the parents of the one I've bonded." Pantar extended a tentacle to me to hold while going through the portal.

We both stepped through and came out near the barn. I started walking toward the house. It was supper time, so my parents should be there. I stopped when two large grey wolves came out of the barn and growled at Pantar. I forgot about Grumpy's natural defense system.

"Your home is interesting, Nexus." Pantar showed no fear of the wolves and why would he? The wolves, on the other hand, had never seen anything like him. *"Why don't you tell them I mean no harm?"* He asked.

Holy shit, that's right, I can communicate with animals now! Not wanting to wait another second, I scrunched my eyes up and concentrated hard, but nothing happened.

"Just let it come. There should be no effort involved. Let the words flow and direct it their way." Pantar encouraged.

Taking his advice, I took a deep breath and tried again. "He means you no harm. If you're good, I'll have Grumpy bring you a treat later tonight." I heard a series of growls and grunts in my head, but knew that they were agreeing. Jumping up and down, I hugged Pantar. "I can speak to animals!"

"I know this my, Nexus. Now let us go and speak to your parents." He turned and walked in the direction of the house. I had a massive grin on my face and was almost skipping as I followed behind him.

When I entered, I could smell cream cheese chicken enchiladas, and my mouth immediately began to water.

"Mom, I'm home." I yelled, entering the dining room.

My parents looked at me in surprise, which quickly turned to shock when they spotted Pantar behind me.

"Holy shit!" Mom shouted.

In shock, Grumpy said absently, "Watch your mouth, Adelaide."

Pop got up from the table and pulled me into a hug. Looking at Pantar in awe.

"It's an honor to meet you," Grumpy told Pantar. I was in complete shock. I could hear what Grumpy had just said.

"Holy shit!" I blurted out.

Grumpy glared at me and then pointed to Mom. "Like mother, like daughter."

"The honor is all mine." Pantar replied to Grumpy. *"My Nexus is shocked that she can hear you communicating with me."*

"Holy shit!" Grumpy exclaimed. Everyone looked at him in astonishment, and I started laughing. I wasn't the only one that picked up Mom's bad habits.

CHAPTER 16

REVERIE

Once their shock faded, Pop made Pantar a bowl of water, and Mom pulled a roast from the refrigerator she was going to cook the next night. Putting it in a pan, she brought it out for Pantar to eat. When everyone was settled and I had served myself a massive plate of enchiladas, the questions began.

"How did you get here?" Grumpy wanted to know, petting Rubbish who had somehow ended up on his lap.

"Dean Mathews used his ability to create a portal. I think he was accommodating because I'm Nexus. He mentioned introducing his nephew to me after initiation." I replied with a mouthful of my mom's delicious enchiladas.

"He always was a self-serving prick," Mom rolled her eyes.

"Not even three days you've been gone, and you return with Pantar, an animal most Aurathions believed extinct because of the war. We always knew you would make a splash, but this is a tidal wave." Pop laughed.

"How did you acquire Pantar?" Mom asked, staring at the

Fellat in adoration. Her eyes had barely left him since I walked in the door.

"I was being shown my deepest fear and not dealing very well with it. Suddenly, Pantar showed up and snapped me out of it. I have no idea how he got there, and he hasn't said." I looked at Pantar as I spoke, but he never stopped eating.

"Other than your wonderful fathers, having my Mira was the greatest part of being Nexus." My mom said with tears in her eyes. "Our connection was so strong she gave her life defending my loves." Mom looked at me with tear-filled eyes.

Grumpy got up from his chair, pulled her into his arms, and sat back down with her in his lap. The way my fathers loved my mother was something special to behold. They showed it every day in their every action.

"Mira is the reason I'm still here today. The reason all three of us are." Grumpy's expression was full of remembered pain.

"I don't care how he came to be at the academy, I'm just glad you have him," Mom sniffled. "Nothing reassures me more than knowing you have his protection."

"Anything else happen that we should know about?" Pop asked.

Mouth full, I winced and mumbled, "I seem to have already developed Nathan's ability."

"Did you say you already gained Nathan's abilities?" Grumpy gasped incredulously.

I nodded my head without looking up, absently rubbing the spot between my breasts that had started stinging again. I noticed Mom watching me intently.

"Are you absolutely sure?" Pop had a look of amazement on his face.

I swallowed and nodded my head again. "If you don't believe me, I have three eyewitnesses." I laughed, remembering the panic the Moons were in when I returned to the dorm.

"Of course, we believe you, Tater Tot. I'm just in shock." Pop rushed to say.

"Eyewitnesses? Who are they? More importantly, will they keep their mouths shut? Tell us exactly what happened," Grumpy said in rapid succession.

"Take a breath, John." Turning to me, Mom smiled in reassurance. "Explain what happened before your father loses it."

"I was in my dorm eating pizza with my roommate and her brothers. Suddenly, I felt a tingle in my stomach and was in my Jeep." I lowered my head, peering up at Mom through my lashes. "Nathan discovered he could communicate mentally with me. When I teleported, I was so freaked out, I thought I would try to contact him for help. It took a minute, but I could. Have you ever heard of anything like that happening?"

"Not unless your Faction is whole." Grumpy jumped to his feet and started pacing. "Is there anything else?"

"I might have found two more Faction...my roommate's brothers," I whispered.

Grumpy sat back down, leaned his head back, and closed his eyes wearily, "Anything else?"

"Let me think. Punching a bit- girl in the face," I decided Grumpy had just about reached his limit, so I changed my word choice, "teleporting, telepathy, communicating with animals, gaining a Fellat. Yep, I think that's it."

"Brat," Pop laughed, despite the situation.

"And yes, my roommate and her brothers can be trusted." Trying to lighten the mood, I said, "the brothers are identical twins."

"I highly recommend twins." Mom wiggled her eyebrows. "Double the trouble, but double the love, if you get my drift."

"Adelaide Ophelia, that is our daughter you're talking to!" Grumpy said in a stern voice with a blush rising on his face. Pop died laughing. Mom tried but failed to look innocent.

"She's almost nineteen and already has one Faction member. She knows what sex is." For once, it was my Pop and Grumpy making gagging noises. I was laughing too hard to be grossed out. "What are their names?" Mom asked.

"Chloe, Zeke, and Zane Moon, they're from Ohio, and I think they're all amazing," I smiled. "I felt a connection to the twins as soon as I met them."

Mom smiled at me fondly, "I'm so happy you're already forming a support system." She looked at me with caution and asked, "Why are you rubbing your chest?"

"Ever since I bonded with Pantar, it's been bothering me." I felt the stinging again and brought my hand back to rub the spot.

"Can I look at it?" Mom asked, getting up out of Grumpy's lap.

"Yes." I dutifully got up, and she followed me into the downstairs bathroom. Mom came in behind me and shut the door. I unbuttoned my shirt and pulled down my bra. I heard Mom let out a gasp behind me but was too amazed by the sight in the mirror to turn around.

"What the hell is that?" I finally pried my gaze away from the glowing triquetra now tattooed between my breasts and looked at my mom's stunned reflection behind me.

"That's the mark of a Nexus, but I've never seen one quite like that." She had a look of awe on her face.

I turned back to the mirror and admired the silver lines that formed the triquetra, there was a circle interwoven to form six spaces the top space had an oak or ash tree with widespread branches in glowing amber, in the space slightly below it to the right, was a dagger in emerald, green, the remaining four spaces were empty. Between the lines forming the circle were the words: Exordium, Inter and Exitus.

Mom held up her wrist, so it was reflected in the mirror. I used to trace it with my finger when I was a child. It was a triquetra with an ash tree in the center surrounded by flames. Nowhere near as detailed as mine, no words and no extra symbols like the dagger. The four extra spaces that looked like they were waiting to be filled was unique too.

"Sweet baby girl, I knew you were special the minute you took your first breath." She turned to me, straightening my clothes. "The mark usually shows up after you've bonded with your Fellat. I never told you any of this because I thought all the Fellats had died out. No one has gotten the mark in over twenty years." Mom pulled me into a tight hug, "Let's go back out and join your fathers. I'll try to research this and see what all of it means."

Grumpy and Pop were looking at us in question when we walked into the dining room.

"She's gained her Nexus mark, but it has symbols and words that I've never seen appear in a mark before." Mom sat in Pop's lap this time. Both of my fathers looked at me in amazement.

"This is unbelievable!" Grumpy sounded excited and scared all at the same time.

"Not so unbelievable. She is special and called to me before ever entering Emberhold." Pantar spoke to me and Grumpy.

Grumpy nodded in agreement, then looked at me, "Don't let anyone but Nathan see it. There are too many things stacking up. If the Council finds out about this, I'm scared of what their reaction will be."

Hearing Grumpy sound so worried was freaking me the hell out. Pantar prowled over to me and nuzzled my hair in comfort. It was becoming our thing.

"Finish your food, Tater Tot, we'll figure this all out in time." Pop smiled. "Back to what you were saying before—"

Grumpy interrupted, "Who did you punch in the face?"

"A girl who had a thing with the twins last year. She had it coming, though." I grinned. Trying to hide the worry I still felt.

"Why did you punch her?" Pop asked, looking inappropriately proud. Mom was watching him with a disapproving look on her face.

"She insulted y'all, and it pissed me off. Unfortunately, her brother is my fighting instructor, so you can imagine how that went. His name is Oren ShitStorm.... It's Storm, but my name fits him better." I continued stuffing my face. After eating my last enchilada, I realized my parents had gone completely quiet. Looking up, I saw grim expressions on their faces. "What? Why are y'all so quiet?"

"There are a few things we never told you for the safety of you and our Faction. You know about the testing that was done on embryos?" Grumpy sighed.

"Yes," I murmured.

"Every Aurathion was excited to see what would come of it, and with our technology, we were able to test on synthetic embryos, not live subjects. What isn't widely known is that the experiments Rue conducted weren't just on the embryos. Most Aurathions have no idea that there were older test subjects."

"I remember hearing a little about that." It was a fascinating subject but obviously, painful for my family.

"The testing involving the embryos was very successful, and Rue was so excited. Then, the Council became involved.

Some members had siblings and children who had never found a Nexus. They wanted Rue to begin giving them the same serum he had given to the embryos." Grumpy frowned.

"We knew so many wonderful Passives who deserved to experience what it means to be Faction. Rue was wary of giving the serum to older subjects." Mom said quietly. "I think he was skeptical of it working, but he wanted all Aurathions to experience what we had: longer lifespans, fantastic abilities, the connection to each other."

Grumpy rose from his chair, took Mom from Pop, and sat back down with her on his lap. I knew how much talking about the past could upset her.

"The suicide rate had skyrocketed over the years for Passives who hadn't found their Faction. Even though we're hard to kill, there were plants in our world that were highly lethal and would do the job. Many saw them as inferior, and Rue hoped to find a solution. We found out later that the only Passives that had been given the opportunity to try the serum were related to the Council or upper-class Aurathions that the Council chose." Grumpy spoke in a sad voice.

"The Storm Faction's Nexus, Remus, was on the Council then and campaigned heavily to start experimenting on adult Passives. He had a younger brother, Trent, who'd remained Passive, they didn't like the stigma attached to that. Rue said that Trent was one of his most successful test subjects. Several Passives had gained abilities and seemed completely normal, but Trent's abilities appeared quicker and were stronger. Oddly, he disappeared a few weeks before the war. No one has heard from him since," Pop explained.

"So other subjects had side effects from the serum?" I asked.

"Rue came home many nights and barely spoke, even to me. Then, one night, he came in late. He was upset and woke us up. He said several of his Passive subjects had gained abilities over the last few weeks but showed weird behavioral changes. Some test subjects initially had mild, easygoing personalities, but after a few weeks, that changed. Extreme aggression, moody, indifferent emotionally. It seemed to be getting progressively worse." Grumpy rubbed Mom's back as she talked. "Earlier that night, one of his subjects murdered his wife. The Council enforcers brought him into the lab. They didn't want the public to know. When confronted, the subject kept screaming that his wife wasn't Nexus. He had to kill her so his Nexus would come. Rue concluded that not having a Nexus to center the power drove many older subjects insane. Rue wanted to stop the testing immediately, but Remus Storm wouldn't hear it."

"Were the Storm Faction ever questioned about him? Why weren't they ever investigated?" I scrunched up my face in confusion.

"The other Council members did inquire several times, but Remus said that the Dark Factions must have captured him. He sponsored several missions to look for and retrieve him. We could never prove Remus was involved, and even though he isn't on the Council anymore, his Faction is still powerful." Grumpy grimaced.

"I'm confused. The test subjects started gaining abilities without a Nexus? Didn't other Aurathions become suspicious? And why did they assume Trent had been captured when he disappeared before the war?" I frowned.

"Trent disappearing before the war was a sticking point for Sly. He always felt that Remus was hiding something." Grumpy kissed the top of Mom's head.

"People see what they want to see, and they had no idea that the serum had been given to adults. It's still believed that the war was caused by power hungry Factions that wanted total control, and that's not completely wrong. The power-hungry Factions just happened to have been brought into their abilities by Rue's serum. After Rue and Sly were killed, we tried bringing the experiments to the public's attention. Things got dicey between the Storm Faction and ours. We would have carried it further, but not long after, we found out we were going to have a baby, and we couldn't risk it." Pop said in apology.

"You must understand, Reverie, you were all we had left of Rue and Sly. I couldn't take the chance of losing you." Mom started sobbing. Pop got up, kneeling in front of Grumpy's chair. He put his arms around them both. Pantar went around the table to rub his cheek against the top of Mom's head. Pop held out an arm for me, and I joined the group hug.

"We'll figure it all out, Tater Tot. Together, we're unstoppable."

After helping my parents clear the table, Mom walked with me and Pantar back to the barn. It was almost time for the portal to appear. As we walked arm in arm, I thought about how lucky I was and how very much I loved my parents. They had always supported me and been there no matter what.

"How are you and Nathan doing?" Mom asked.

"We're amazing. It's truly unbelievable how our relationship has changed since we bonded. There were times over the years when I thought I hated him. Now, the thought of being without him is unbearable." I couldn't keep a smile off my face just thinking about my psycho. Looking over at Mom and seeing the agony on her face, I immediately apologized, "I'm so sorry I wasn't thinking." Turning, I pulled her into a fierce hug.

Mom rubbed my back. "It's alright, sweet girl. I'll miss

Rue and Sly until my dying breath, but seeing them in you gives me comfort."

"I wish I could have known them. Is it weird to miss someone you've never met?" I sighed wistfully.

"No, it's not. They'd have loved you so much. Rue was brilliant. He would've loved teaching you about any and everything. My Sly was fierce. Nathan wouldn't have lived past junior high if he'd been here." Mom laughed.

"He's lucky because it was touch and go a few times with Grumpy and Pop." I laughed in remembrance.

"It was," Mom agreed, laughing with me. "We'll get this all figured out. You concentrate on getting through initiation." Walking up to Pantar, Mom put her arms around his neck and hugged him. "Keep our girl safe and make sure the Passives wanting admittance to her Faction are worthy."

Pantar gave a regal nod, then leaned down and licked her face from chin to forehead.

"Nexus, tell your mother it will be my privilege," Pantar growled out in my head.

"He said it would be his privilege," I told Mom, laughing as she used her shirt to wipe the drool from her face.

Just then, the portal appeared. Pantar extended his tentacle to me. I kissed Mom's cheek (the one with no drool), and Pantar and I stepped through.

CHAPTER 17

REVERIE

The weeks flew by as I attended classes and tried to keep a low profile. It was easier said than done when I was followed everywhere by a giant Fellat. Pantar wasn't fond of anyone that wasn't me or Nathan. He allowed Chloe to pet him, but that was it. Zeke and Zane tried to get close to him, but Pantar told me he was waiting for them to prove themselves to him. Whatever that meant.

Since bonding with Pantar, the Passives all knew about my Nexus status. So far, none had approached me, primarily due to the shadow of initiation looming over them and the guys running interference. I'm sure Pantar flashing his teeth at everyone as we walked down the hallway was also a factor.

Instructor Storm liked to torture me daily, and his dickish behavior didn't go unnoticed by Nathan and the twins. Nathan took every opportunity to fuck with him. He even went so far as giving Oren a t-shirt that had 'Reverie's Bitch' on it. Apparently, Storm lost a bet. He tore it up on the spot and told Nathan to go fuck himself.Fun times.

Zane had found a clearing deep in the forest behind

Emberhold for me to practice teleporting. I had improved enough that I wasn't afraid of any accidents happening in front of anyone. Nathan wanted us to try teleporting home, but I didn't want to take the chance of alerting the dean of our absence, and my ability.

Several Passives had been taken for initiation. One guy disappeared while eating lunch, and another girl was taken just as she came out of the bathroom stall. Unfortunately, Cassandra never came back, another found Passive among several who lost their life. The level of stress everyone was under was tremendous.

Kristine apparently had no other purpose but to torture me. She was pissed about Pantar and constantly made comments to whoever would listen that me and my family didn't deserve such an honor. Acting like I was the one who chose Pantar when it was the other way around. She was a bitter, want-to-be Nexus, bitch. That's how Chloe called it, anyway. Her Bitch Brigade backed her up and tried to approach Nathan and the twins at every opportunity. I'm not sure they had a single brain cell between them.

I hadn't heard from my family, but I felt sure they would have found a way to contact me if they'd found any answers. Hopefully, they'll have more information soon. I was keeping my tattoo hidden from everyone but Nathan. Nathan was pissed that he hadn't gotten one and made me inspect him all over to make sure. I was annoyed at first, but Nathan made it worth my while.

I was bothered that I hadn't confided in the Moons about all my abilities, but the time hadn't felt right. I needed to ask Pantar if he was okay with me sharing our ability to communicate. His decision would be the deciding factor.

Getting out of bed, I pulled on my black cargo pants with a lightweight, white cotton shirt and threw my hair up in a messy bun. Sitting down, I put on my brand-new combat boots. They were hot pink, a gift from Zeke after he had noticed my love for all things pink. Fitting my boot knife in its sheath, I turned and grabbed my backpack. I had learned my lesson that first day when Cassandra was taken to initiation. I opened it and ensured it was stocked with water and granola bars that would last a few days. I hoped that I could catch enough to eat if I was gone longer than that.

I threw my pack over my shoulder and looked at Pantar, lying on my bed. "Hey, lazybones, are you coming with me or hanging out here?" I scratched him under his chin.

"I'm coming with you, Nexus. If you are pulled away to initiation, I won't be left behind." Pantar yawned, looking like a giant housecat.

"Do you think the academy is going to allow that?" I asked.

"There is no allowing. We are a package deal since the bonding. Where you go, I go. There is no alternative." He leaped off the bed and stretched.

It was crazy to think I'd only had him for a short while and loved him as much as I did. I couldn't imagine my life without him. I always knew my mom was strong but, after bonding with Nathan and Pantar, I knew how much strength it must have taken for her not to give up.

"You are correct, Nexus, and I love you too." Pantar grinned, showing all those deadly teeth.

Opening my door, I smelled the aroma of coffee. Walking into the small living area, I saw Zane sitting on the couch with a giant to-go cup in his hand.

"Is that for me?" I asked, grabbing the cup and taking a big sip before he could answer me.

"Well, I hope so, piglet. Now, it has your Nexus cooties all over it." He smiled in amusement.

"Nexus cooties?" Chloe asked in puzzlement, walking into the room. "Is that a thing?"

"If it is, I'm going to roll around in her sheets," Zane looked at me with heat in his eyes.

I blushed and hid my grin behind my coffee cup. My relationship with the twins had been coming along nicely. Neither one had made any serious moves yet, but I thought that was mainly due to Pantar, who rarely left my side. Deciding to try my hand at flirting, I said, "As good as you smell this morning, I wouldn't mind." Zane looked slightly stunned for a second, and then one side of his mouth rose in a cocky grin.

"You think I smell good, Nexi?"

Nathan appeared in our living room at precisely that moment and slapped Zane in the head. Zane fell off the couch onto the small coffee table. The table broke, and he rolled into Chloe, who fell sideways into me, thus spilling my coffee. I slowly raised my head from the mess on the floor and looked at Nathan.

"Did you just cause me to spill my coffee?"

"Oh shit, your ass is in trouble now!" Chloe pointed at Nathan and laughed.

Zane got up off the floor, "I was going to fuck you up, but I'll leave that to my N-E-X-I." He slowly spelled it out, looking Nathan dead in the face.

Nathan did not look amused. "I'll get to you in a minute." Walking up to me, he dropped to his knees, wrapped his arms around my waist, and started his elaborate apology. "Please forgive me, *my* Nexi." He side-eyed Zane. "It will never happen again. I will walk on my knees to every class I have today to show just how much I regret the spilling of the most essential first cup of morning coffee. I will give up my pride. I will provide the first cup of coffee every day for the rest of my life. These things I pledge if you will only forgive me."

Chloe, Zane and I looked at him in stunned disbelief. Nathan just continued to kneel at my feet, showing no signs of moving.

"I assume you aren't getting up until I forgive you," I asked, still trying to digest that elaborate apology.

"*My* Nexi," he side-eyed Zane again, "is so intelligent, not to mention unbelievably beautiful."

"Get off the floor, psycho." I couldn't help but laugh. He was adorable. (I was probably the only one who thought so.)

"Not until I hear the words of forgiveness spilling from those plump, gorgeous lips." He hugged me, and even on his knees he was able to lay his head on my breasts.

"I forgive you, crazy. Just get up!" I had a hard time staying mad at him, and he knew it.

"I'll see you two soon, when you're not so overdressed." Nathan said to my breasts. He rose to his feet. "I will now run, not walk, to replace this inferior coffee with a cup that will be much more palatable to your taste buds." Before leaving, he turned to Zane. "We'll be having a conversation later."

Zane didn't respond. I think he was trying to process what he'd just witnessed.

"Where in the hell can I get one of those?" Chloe asked, still stunned by Nathan's crazy apology.

"He can be a little extra." I smiled, thinking of some of his past exploits.

"I bet everything is extra, and I can get behind that, or in front, maybe laying on my side," Chloe said, still staring at the doorway that Nathan just passed through.

Zane started gagging as I cracked up laughing all over again. "Please shut up. Seeing that look on your face makes me sick."

"I'd like to make him throw up from his little head," Chloe said longingly. Just fucking with Zane now.

"It's not little," I smirked.

"Really, bestie? Now you're just being mean. You shouldn't rub that in a girl's face who hasn't gotten laid since she got to the academy."

"What the fuck, Chloe? Are you trying to make me sick? Between you and that sickening display my soon-to-be Faction brother put on, I'm feeling extremely nauseous. I'm leaving before I lose it." He approached me and whispered, "My second head is pretty impressive, too." He then turned and strutted out the door.

Well damn, I just bet it was. Hopefully, it wouldn't be long before I found out.

❧

Walking down the hallway to class was an experience all on its own. Pantar stayed directly behind me and Chloe. Even though it had been weeks, the students still stopped to stare. Thank goodness the academy was massive, or he would never have been able to go with me everywhere.

"Yes, I would, Nexus. Reducing my size would solve that problem." Pantar communicated, then growled at a guy that walked closer to us than he liked.

"Reduce your size? I didn't know that was possible." I was amazed at this piece of information.

"As a superior Fellat, all things are possible." He licked the side of my head.

Wow, Pantar was just as arrogant as all the other males in my life. Why was I not surprised?

Entering the classroom, I saw an empty seat beside Jet

and headed in his direction. He had been elusive the last few weeks. I saw him in class, but usually, he sat surrounded by females. Sophie was stuck to his side like a leech most days, elbowing the other girls out of the way. I was sure they were hoping he was Nexus. He was a good-looking guy and built like a brick shithouse, so I wasn't surprised by the attention he was getting. Jet was in all my classes, but these days he avoided me and the guys. It was odd, considering he was always lurking in the background during my first few weeks at Emberhold.

"Is this seat taken?" I asked him.

"Not yet." He replied in his no-nonsense way.

I sat as Chloe took the seat next to me. Pantar regally lowered himself in the aisle beside Chloe. He growled and flashed his teeth at any students that got too close.

"We haven't seen much of you lately. How have you been?" Chloe leaned up and asked Jet.

"Good." He pulled his notebook out for class. A man of few words, as usual.

"I'm glad. I saw your performance on the obstacle course the other day. It was extremely impressive. What did you do before you discovered your Aurathion heritage?" I asked casually. I was curious about Jet and how he felt about Emberhold and the Aurathion culture in general. I also felt a pull to him, which I was trying to ignore at present.

"I was a bouncer. Keeping in shape was part of the job, so luckily, I was somewhat prepared for life here at the academy." Jet faced forward, clearly done with the conversation. Just as I was about to ask him another question (whether he liked it or not), Nathan entered the classroom holding a massive coffee in one hand and a thermos in the other.

"There you are, my precious little Nexus." Nathan said in an unnecessarily loud voice. Several people in class looked over at me, like I was an exhibit in a museum. "Why Chloe, it was very generous of you to keep my seat warm." Chloe huffed out a breath in annoyance but got up to take the desk on the other side of Jet.

"You don't have to change seats," I frowned, looking at Nathan in annoyance.

"We both know he won't stop until he gets what he wants, and I'll end up moving anyway. This is much easier, and on the bright side, I can block all the thirsty bitches from sitting by our hunky and mysterious Jet." She winked at him.

"Nothing mysterious about me," Jet stated, obviously annoyed at our antics.

"I agree with him. There is nothing the least bit interesting or mysterious about the guy." Nathan sat down. "He's my roommate, so I ought to know." Nathan then placed the large coffee and thermos down in front of me with a big smile. "This is much better than that stinky old coffee Zane brought you this morning. I was also thoughtful enough to bring you refills so you can stay caffeinated all day." I never ceased to be amazed at the lengths Nathan would go to win the imaginary competitions he had going on in his head.

"Thank you. I really appreciate the gesture, but the large coffee would have been sufficient."

"Nothing about me or anything I do is *just* sufficient." He twirled a piece of my hair around his finger that had come loose from my bun.

"Ain't that the truth?" I smiled in agreement.

Leaning over to kiss his cheek, I was startled when I never made contact. Nathan had disappeared.

"What the fuck?" I yelled, jumping to my feet.

"I think Emberhold decided it was time to initiate Nathan." Jet's eyes widened in shock.

"The lying one is not wrong," Pantar said, nuzzling the top of my head in comfort.

I closed my eyes and prayed that Nathan was as badass and clever as I thought he was. Not having him here was going to feel like losing a limb. I wouldn't feel complete until he was back where he belonged.

Right by my side.

CHAPTER 18
NATHAN

What the fuck is happening right now? I'd been sitting by my precious Nexi, and then I was standing at the edge of a massive forest. I could see a cute little village with stone cottages and thatched roofs, smell the smoke from the little chimneys.

Was this my initiation? If so, I was insulted. Someone as badass as me should be fighting four-arm beings with insectoid helmets or aliens with enormous dragon wings and a spider-face.

Wait, was I describing characters from *Destiny*? Shit, I was. That's how I had pictured my initiation since I learned about it. Not to toot my own horn, but I was a beast at that game.

Crouching down, I decided observing my surroundings for a while was best. I had no idea what was coming for me, but it better fucking not be killer gnomes or some such shit. I'd never live it down.

My new reality was insane. Finding out I wasn't human was a real trip. The best part of everything was knowing my bond with Reverie was unbreakable. As a human, I would've never let her go, but now, finding out I was Aurathion, she was genuinely tied to my side. I had been in love with Reverie for as long as I could remember. The fight I put up to have her was the most challenging thing I had ever gone through, including this jacked-up initiation. I should've been sickened at the lengths I had gone to have her, but I wasn't. I would fight anything to stay by her side, even Reverie herself. Getting through this would bring me one step closer to letting everyone know she was mine, so bring this challenge right, the fuck, on.

⮾

I pulled into the high school parking lot, ready to start my senior year. I saw that Reverie's baby blue jeep was in the parking lot. She liked to get to school early, so that meant I did too.

The fight to get Reverie to admit how she felt about me was mystifying. I was the total package. I'd had made sure of it.

In primary school, she was my best friend; we played together at recess and were inseparable. Then, at the beginning of our freshman year, Reverie wouldn't have anything to do with me. There was no explanation, just radio silence. I would have preferred a good kick to the nuts than the pain of seeing her laughing and talking with other people.

I did everything I could think of: I worked out; got good grades; I was good-looking; and extremely witty. What else could she possibly want in a man?

The most aggravating part of all was that I caught her watching me, the lust and love in her eyes more than evident to me. I didn't understand why she was doing this to us. I needed to be near her, and the rage I felt at being denied was all-consuming.

Over the last three years, I had done things I wasn't proud of, trying to get her attention. I was going to do one of those things this morning, in fact.

Entering the hallway, I spotted her looking at her phone, walking toward me, not paying attention. Glancing around to make sure there wasn't anyone else in the hall, I grabbed her and pulled her into the empty classroom nearby.

"What in the hell are you doing?" Reverie stumbled. I had to take her unaware, otherwise I wouldn't have been able to manhandle her. The girl was strong.

Lucky for me, it was a biology classroom with a doorway leading into a lab at the rear of the room. Putting my hand over her mouth, I dragged her into the lab.

Grabbing my hand, she jerked it off her mouth and punched me in the stomach. Damn, that hurt. Trying to breathe, I bent over and grabbed my knees.

"Let me out of here, Nathan!" Reverie screamed at me.

"No! I want to talk to you. I don't understand why you've cut me out of your life. We spent every moment together until freshman year. What changed?" Standing, I made sure I was blocking the door.

"I don't answer to you. I owe you nothing, and after the things you've done the last few years, I don't have any feelings left for you at all!"

I couldn't stand hearing those words coming out of her mouth. I felt my rage take over and grabbed her shoulders, yelling in her face, "I don't fucking believe you! I see how you look at me! Every single motherfucking thing I've done has been to make you see that we belong together. I love you, Reverie! What else can I do? Do I need to fuck someone right in front of you to get an honest reaction?"

"Screw whoever you want! Maybe that's what I need to do to

end this once and for all! Dane Taylor has been trying to get in my pants for years. This year just might be his year."

I completely lost it. I pushed her on the teacher's desk. Grabbing her shirt, I jerked it open, and buttons flew across the room. I held her hands over her head, both of her tiny wrists in one of my hands, restraining her. Pulling her bra down, her breasts were framed so beautifully by the pink lace. I leaned down and drew a plump pink nipple in my mouth and laved it with my tongue. The tip grew hard even as she fought me, kicking and yelling. She was stronger than an average girl, but the rage I was feeling gave me strength far beyond what I should have.

"What are you doing?" Reverie growled but ended the sentence in a moan.

Ignoring her, I took her lips, swallowing her words before she could say anything else. Sucking her tongue into my mouth. She tried to bite me, but I drew back before she could latch on. I kept my mouth against hers, trailing my free hand down her stomach, undoing the clasp of her jeans, then continuing until my hand was pushing at the waist band of her panties.

Reverie renewed her efforts to get away, bucking and kicking, trying to scream. I muffled the noise with my mouth and continued my descent. I could smell her arousal, the sweet honeysuckle scent permeating the room. Penetrating her tight opening with two fingers, I closed my eyes and took a deep breath. I was hard as a rock, but managed to get even harder when I felt how wet she was. Pulling my fingers from her, I started circling her clit. The fight suddenly left her. Reverie started kissing me and arched her body, trying to bring my fingers back inside her. With all signs of resistance gone, I placed a trail of kisses down her body. Dragging her jeans down her beautiful legs, I threw them on the floor, then spread her thighs. I almost came right then at the sight of her glistening pussy.

The moment was profound, hers was the first and only I would ever taste, or touch. Reverie's gaze was heated as she watched me lower myself to my knees. If she would only love me, I would stay on my knees for her the rest of my life.

I licked her slit, spreading her lips gently, then took her tiny nub into my mouth and sucked gently. Reverie went wild grabbing my hair and pushing my face against her. Feeling her tiny hands gripping my hair made my desire for her skyrocket, and I devoured her like a starving man. Pushing two fingers into her tight opening, I felt her body shake and knew her orgasm was close. With one last long suck of her clit, I felt her tighten around my fingers and her juices cover my face.

I released my cock from my jeans, squeezing the head tightly to stop me from coming before I found my way inside her. Bringing my mouth to hers, wet from her release, I kissed her with every bit of love and adoration in my body. Before she realized what had happened, I rubbed my cock in her wetness, then entered her abruptly. She screamed into my mouth from the pain.

Knowing I was the first to be inside her almost made me come right then and there. Tears ran down her face and I leaned over and licked the salty drops, wanting every part of her. I wish I could fit her inside my body and never be separated from her again.

I paused, letting her get used to my size and began rubbing her clit. When she began moaning and writhing on the desk, I started moving my hips. The pleasure was intense as her inner muscles clenched around my cock, I saw stars, losing my vision temporarily. Her hands were now clutching my arms, pulling me closer as I started slamming into her.

Reverie moaned as my cock hit the sensitive bundle of nerves deep inside. I released her mouth and stared into her passion-glazed eyes as her release grew closer. I felt my balls tighten and didn't know how much longer I would last, but I was determined to make her come first. Suddenly, Reverie threw her head back and began pulsing around me. My thrusts became erratic, and in the next moment, I found my pleasure, pulling out and spurting white ropes of cum all over her stomach.

I took my hand and rubbed it into her skin, wanting to know that she would smell like me all day. I leaned down and laid my head on her chest, hoping with everything in me, she would quit fighting and give in. I thought for a moment I felt her fingers tunneling through my hair. Feeling her tense up, I realized it was probably just wishful thinking.

Raising my head, I saw tears running down her face again. Standing up, I pulled her in my arms and held her as tightly as I could, knowing this may be the last time for a while. I didn't mean for this to happen, but I couldn't regret it. I wouldn't allow someone else to take what was mine, and I wouldn't give another what was hers.

I let go of her, squatted down, and pulled her pants back up her legs. I fastened her jeans and took my plaid shirt off, removing the henley I had underneath it. I gently lowered my shirt over her head, pulling it slowly down, hating to cover up her beautiful skin. She let me dress her like a doll.

"I can't believe that just happened," Reverie whispered.

I felt like she was talking to herself, so I didn't answer. I went to fasten my jeans and saw that my cock was covered in her blood. Knowing I should be horrified by my actions; bewildered that I wasn't. I now felt a sense of belonging and rightness. I knew I still had a fight on my hands, but there were simply no lengths I wouldn't go to make her mine.

～☙～

I crawled into a large bush, where I still had sight of the village. I had no idea what time it was here, but it felt like early morning. There was dew on the grass and a chill in the air.

I was thankful I had taken Reverie's advice and dressed in preparation for this eventuality. I wore cargo pants, hiking boots, and a long-sleeved, lightweight shirt. My body temperature ran hot like all Aurathions, so the cold wouldn't be a problem. I had a backpack I hadn't taken off since I was busy bringing my Nexi coffee. The backpack had water and a few granola bars. I also carried a knife Reverie had given me on my birthday. It was special to me, and I had it on me constantly.

Taking a sip of water, I sat and waited for the occupants to wake up and come out of their little cabins so I could see what I was dealing with. I hoped I could get this over with quickly and return to Reverie. I didn't like leaving her alone. She had no idea how much I stalked her. I very rarely left her alone. I gave Zeke and Zane shit, but when she was with one of them, I knew she was safe. That was the only time I could comfortably observe our enemies and ensure they stayed in their lane.

Oren was going to be a problem. I felt in my bones that he was hiding something. Kristine and her Bitch Brigade were filled with want-to-be mean girls who wouldn't be any real threat. My Nexi could whip their collective asses with her hands tied behind her back. The oldest Storm sibling watched Reverie constantly when she wasn't looking. Ever since she bonded with Pantar, he rarely took his eyes off her, and I didn't like it.

I watched Jet quite a bit, too. Something was off with the big guy. Jet was the perfect dorm mate. He kept to himself, cleaned up, and was quiet. But I had noticed him watching everyone around him as if he were memorizing their movements. The dean was on my list too, I'd gone to the office on a trumped-up errand to sneak into the dean's inner sanctum and go through his things. I found it suspicious he was only appointed to his position this year. I didn't trust him and wanted to find out what I could about the man, and why he was really at Ember-hold. I smelled a big steaming pile of bullshit.

Hearing a door shut, I noticed that the sun was beginning to rise. I heard talking, but in a language I didn't recognize. That was going to make things more challenging.

The voices were getting closer. I saw two women coming near my hiding spot. They were both tall and willowy. One had green hair cut in a short bob, and the other had lavender locks hanging in the middle of her back. The former had ebony skin that seemed to sparkle and the ladder had light pink. Their faces looked primarily humanoid, but the women's eyes were abnormally large, and their mouths were wider than the average human.

Even though I cared nothing for any other woman besides my Nexi, I could admit these two were exceptionally beautiful despite the strangeness of their faces. They were dressed in leather pants and a corset top laced up the front. Green hair was in a purple corset, and purple hair had on a green one. It was comical, especially if they didn't plan it that way. I could see other women in the clearing in front of the cabins. They were dressed similarly to the first two but with hair and skin in every color of the rainbow. Some were carrying spears made from a strange glass-like material.

Three women entered my line of sight, and I noticed the two in the back dragging someone between them. It looked like a large man, so large in fact, I was surprised they could move him at all. They went toward a giant fire pit in the center of the circle of cabins. There was a large cage near the fire I hadn't noticed earlier in the absence of light. The woman in the front opened the door to the cage, and the two women dragging the man threw him in. The first woman shut the door, then took a small rectangular object out of her pocket and trailed it along the outline of the door. Sealing the door in some way, I presumed.

Watching the man, I couldn't detect any movement. He was either dead or passed out. What kind of fuckery was this? Did the academy want me to rescue this guy? Was he a damsel in distress?

Biggest fucking damsel I'd ever seen. I shrugged, I guess that made me the prince. It made sense because I was rather princely.

I thought the best move was to find a safe spot to spend the day. Then come back tonight to check it out. I eased slowly out of the large bush I was crouched in and backed deeper into the woods.

I walked carefully, continuously scanning my surroundings. The trees were enormous. They looked like giant redwoods. The leaves were gold, red, and green. It reminded me of the forests in Oregon or northern Idaho during the fall. I approached a clearing and saw massive mountains in the distance with a blanket of mist covering the valley below. I could almost believe I was still in my dimension, except the colors were too vibrant. The mist had a purple hue, and the sky was a pale lavender. I saw a tree with a large limb at least a hundred feet in the air. I felt it was wide enough at the base to sit comfortably and still have a good view of my surroundings.

I reached for the well of power inside me and...nothing happened. Closing my eyes and concentrating harder, I was able to teleport, but it took everything I had. I was sweating bullets and felt like I had run twenty miles. This dimension seemed to be fucking with my ability, or the distance from Reverie was affecting it.

I could have climbed with no problem but why have an ability if I didn't use it.

I hated to give any credit to Storm, but his conditioning regimen was legit. I'd always been in shape. I'd played sports from a young age and liked knowing when I took my shirt off, I had Reverie's complete attention. After becoming Faction, and the training Reverie's fathers put me through, I reached a fit reserved for MMA fighters and Navy Seals. Storm had ensured that the students who were already fit maintained it, and the ones who weren't become that way. I thought it was more for his amusement than a concern about the Passives surviving initiation.

Once I reached my destination, I got comfortable and pulled out a granola bar and bottle of water. Munching on my food, I tried to put a plan together. Teleporting into the camp and grabbing the giant man wouldn't work. I was lucky to teleport myself to this limb, much less me and a massive man out of here. I would figure something out. I always did.

Getting back to Reverie and completing our Faction was my most important goal. I had a feeling her life may depend on it.

CHAPTER 19

NATHAN

I felt like my plan was a good one. I thought wandering into the village and pretending to be lost would be my best bet. Thinking they might offer some hospitality or let me camp close by. Thus, giving me more access to the captive and the strange key the woman had used to seal the cage.

Looking out through the bars with one eye, since the other was swollen shut, I was way closer to the captive than I intended. Those bitches were, well, bitches. And so fucking strong.

The guy was much larger up close than he had appeared from a distance, close to Jet's size, in fact. I just prayed he was friendly and would help me figure out how to escape. Hopefully, getting help from the man I was supposed to save didn't count against me. Now the big guy just needed to wake the fuck up.

Night fell, and Gigantor was still sleeping like a baby. The purple-haired chick had thrown a couple of what looked like turkey legs, into our cage. Since the guy I was here to rescue couldn't be bothered to wake the fuck up, I ate his. Gigantor owed it to me for the inconvenience he was causing by not WAKING THE FUCK UP. I was going a little crazy being away from my Nexi this long. Those two soulless gingers better not let anything happen to her, or I would skin them alive.

⤚☘⤙

I woke up when I felt a small prick in my arm. One of the warrior chicks pulled a long stick with a syringe-looking apparatus on the end back through the bars. I felt myself getting drowsy and, right before passing out, heard the cage door open. My last thought was that now I knew why Gigantor never woke the fuck up.

When I opened my eyes, I was looking directly at a set of the most enormous feet I had ever seen. Raising my head slightly I saw large calves that led to massive thighs and up to a huge chest.

Jumping to my feet, I stepped back, making room in case I needed to defend myself. The massive guy crossed his arms and stared at me like I was an idiot. I've seen the look many times, so it was easy to recognize.

I decided to go on the offensive. "Who the hell are you?" The big guy just continued to stare. "Can you hear me? I asked you a question."

"Who the fuck are you, boy?" Gigantor growled out in a crazy, deep voice.

"I'm here to rescue you," I smirked, winking at him.

The guy just stared at me like I had a screw loose. I

guessed I could see his point. I felt movement, and looking out of the cage, I noticed we were in some kind of wagon. Two large horse-like creatures were pulling them. I could only see the top of the driver's head, but there was no doubt it wasn't one of the warrior women. His head was bald and shiny, with no colorful hair in sight.

"Where are we going? Where are the warrior women?" I asked in quick succession, confused by my surroundings. Unlike the beauty of the forest, the road they were on was muddy and rutted from frequent travel. The scenery outside the cage was barren land that looked like several bombs had exploded—no sign of trees or grass. Everything was in shades of grey, brown, and black.

"Damn boy, do you ever shut up?" the giant inquired, running his hand down his face.

"Not very often, if I'm being honest. Possibly, if we did an exchange of information, I'd be less likely to keep asking questions." I huffed out, crossing my arms over my chest. The asshole reminded me of Reverie's Grumpy.

"We are on the way to the coliseum. The Pulchra, or warrior women as you call them, accepted payment, or in my case, a reward from the Brummond." Gigantor reluctantly spit out.

"Dare I ask who the hell the Brummond is? And why a coliseum?" I mean damn, was this guy charged by the word or something.

The giant's pale skin turned a mottled shade of red, apparently aggravated with even more questions from me. "The Brummond is the Faction that owns the Coliseum. I know you've heard of the Coliseum, boy, no need to pretend ignorance."

Faction? What dimension was I in? Could this be

Aurathia? I replied dazedly, still trying to figure out what was going on, "I don't know anything about the Coliseum, Gigantor, and I don't appreciate being called a boy when I'm clearly a man." This dude must be blind.

"Who the fuck are you calling Gigantor?" Gigantor growled out.

"I didn't mean any disrespect, but you haven't offered your name, and let's face it, you're freaking massive," I murmured, trying to calm the large man. The only way I could win a fight with this guy was by using my abilities, and they weren't dependable right now.

"You can call me Hayes, boy. I've seen no evidence of man-like behavior from you, so boy is what I'm calling you. What Faction do you belong to?" Hayes asked, narrowing his eyes.

I decided I should only give out information sparingly until I understood more of what was happening. "No Faction. I was just caught in the wrong place at the wrong time."

Looking at me doubtfully, Hayes replied, "I hope that's not true, because if it is, you're in deep shit. Fighting in the Coliseum is hard enough with a Faction, but without one, it's impossible."

"What Faction do you belong to?" I was starting to get worried. I needed to complete whatever task I was here for and get back to my Nexi.

Hayes looked utterly devastated for a split second, then his face cleared. "I've been assigned to the Tempest Faction."

I noticed the phrasing. Nothing about it sounded joyful or voluntary. "If you have a Faction, why were you trying to escape?"

"You act like you're new to this world, boy. I've been fighting in the Coliseum for years. My days will be numbered if I lose the ability to bring gold and prestige to the Tempest Faction." Hayes sighed. He then sat in the corner of the cage, leaned his head back, and closed his eyes. I thought I heard him mumble, "Why I continue to try to survive is a mystery to me."

I knew that the big man was done answering questions for now. Leaning my head back, I tried to get some rest. I would need to be at the top of my game when we arrived at the Coliseum.

～▲～

Waking at the absence of motion, I sat up. We had stopped at a set of massive doors. They had to be at least a hundred feet tall. The walls looked to be made from the same stone as Emberhold. I heard a whirring noise, and the doors started to open. This world seemed to be a strange combination of medieval and modern technology. I saw that Hayes was awake.

"Where are we?"

"Bellona, so it's called now." He whispered the last part. "We'll arrive at the Coliseum shortly. You better prepare yourself, boy. Don't make waves; follow instructions. I won't be in the practice yard tomorrow, but I should be the day after. I'll find you and help if I can." He seemed surprised that he made the offer.

I nodded and turned to observe my surroundings. We passed a market with many stalls and people everywhere. Some looked human, while others were utterly alien. I couldn't shake the feeling that this was Aurathia. But if so, why was there so much life and people around? The land we had traveled through was horrible and looked like a war had been fought, but the forest was beautiful and untouched. I had always assumed that Aurathia had been made primarily uninhabitable, but other than the dreary landscape, it seemed to be thriving.

After leaving the market area, in the distance, I saw a massive coliseum gleaming in the sun. It contrasted starkly with the walls surrounding the city because it was pure white.

Surprising me, Hayes spoke, "This was built about ten years after the war. Heads of the Factions come here to choose future members. Existing members like me fight to earn the right to remain in a Faction."

"Why would you fight to stay somewhere you clearly don't want to be?" I questioned in confusion.

"Where are you from?" Hayes asked, looking at me with suspicion.

"What does that matter?" I responded by dodging the question.

"It matters because you seem to have no knowledge of how this world works. I have no choice but to fight. If your current Faction rejects you, you must fight without proper food, shelter, and weapons until another Faction chooses you." Hayes told me, still looking at me in suspicion.

"What about the Passives with no Faction? How do they fight without abilities?" I asked.

"After the injection, everyone has abilities. You run the risk of going insane without a Faction and Nexus to stabilize you, but you're given no choice except to take the serum. Why do you not know this?" Hayes narrowed his eyes at me. I was saved from answering when we stopped at a gate guarded by two large, beefy guys.

"What do you have for us today, Eugene?"

The bald guy answered, "One newbie and Hayes."

"Hayes, you said?" the guy on the right asked. He had an eyepatch and greasy long hair.

"Yep. See for yourself." Eugene smirked. The two guys walked around to look in the cage.

"Well, what do you know? The great undefeated Hayes of the Tempest Faction returns in disgrace. I can't wait to see what Selene does to your ass. You'll be lucky if she doesn't skin you alive."

"He'll be lucky if that's all she does." The guy on the left smirked, around a mouth full of tobacco, spitting on the ground and wiping his mouth with the back of his hand. He leaned more toward fat than muscle, and his belly bounced disgustingly when he laughed.

"Go on and get them unloaded. Seamus is near the barracks and will take them off your hands." The tobacco dude motioned them forward.

Throughout the entire interaction, Hayes and I remained quiet. Hayes had a stoic expression, and from the conversation I had just heard, I felt like he was gearing himself up to face the consequences of his escape.

We rolled through the wooden gates. I thought this was the training area that Hayes had talked about. All kinds of training apparatus and weights were scattered throughout the yard. Stopping at an arched opening in the side of the Coliseum, a small man stood tapping his foot impatiently.

"What took you so long, Eugene? I have things to do, and I can't wait around on you all day." Not waiting for an answer, he walked over to the cage and asked Hayes, "Are we doing this the easy way?" Hayes walked to the side closest to the little man and leaned his head down where his neck was accessible. "Maybe you've smartened up." Pulling a small pen-shaped object out, he pushed a button, and it lengthened until he could reach Hayes's neck through the bars; there was a popping noise. Hayes flinched slightly but didn't make a sound.

"Now that's done. You know what happens if you try to leave the perimeter. You have fifteen seconds to return, or the device in your neck will explode. I have no idea what you were thinking running away like that. You've always been Selene's favorite and been given so much privilege. You disgraced her and your Faction. You'll be lucky to keep your head." Seamus sneered.

Looking over at me, he squinted his eyes and asked, "Am I going to have a problem with you?"

"I'm keeping my options open." I winked at the little man.

"A comedian. Fantastic. There isn't enough time in the day for me to deal with this shit. Lean your head down." He motioned to me.

I looked at Hayes, and he gave a slight nod of his head. I leaned down and extended my neck. I flinched because that shit hurt, but I didn't utter a sound. The big guy looked at me with the tiniest bit of respect.

Seamus motioned Eugene to open the cage. Hayes and I stepped out, and Seamus turned and led us into the tunnel. We walked a little way and then came to a large room. Seamus stopped and turned to us, "Selene will be sending for you as soon as I inform her of your return. You'll be put on the roster immediately if you survive her punishment. Turning, he looked at me, "We will have Joseph rate your skill and put you on the roster as soon as he thinks you'll be a challenge." Turning abruptly, he left back the way we had come.

At least three dozen men and women of all shapes and sizes were eating and gathered in groups. Two guys were levitating and trying to knock each other out of the air with a crowd cheering them on and a guy standing near them, taking bets. To my amazement, I saw a woman throwing fireballs in the air and a guy beside her freezing them and throwing them at a target.

A skinny guy with long white hair and midnight skin came running up. "Hayes, my man, I'm glad to see you. I hoped I wouldn't, but this place hasn't been the same without you." I was shocked when the guy pulled Hayes into a bro hug. I was even more amazed when Hayes hugged him back.

"Good to see you too, Damien. How have things been since I've been gone?" Hayes looked at Damien in concern.

I noticed the room had become completely silent, and everyone was giving Hayes their full attention.

"Selene has been in a temper since she lost her favorite gladiator. We've lost two fighters in the last battle and one in the solo events. Two of them weren't ready and didn't have the backing of a Faction." Damien ran his hand through his hair. "I tried, Hayes, I really did, but Selene knew how you felt about keeping unclaimed out of the fights, so she came down hard on them."

"Who was the solo fighter?" Damien bowed his head, not meeting Hayes's eyes.

"Mickey."

Hayes turned, picked up a chair, and threw it across the room. He then levitated a table and two chairs, smashing them against the wall. Turning, he stormed out of the room.

Damien held out his hand to me, "I'm Damien, a member of the Finnick Faction. Welcome to our Hell."

I was starting to suspect that this wasn't a normal initiation. I closed my eyes and tried to communicate with Reverie. No matter how hard I tried I couldn't reach her. I felt such emptiness and despair, for a moment I couldn't breathe. What was I going to do? How was I going to get back to my Nexi?

I finally managed to take a deep breath, letting it out

slowly, I raised my head. No, this wasn't who I was, I narrowed my eyes in determination. No motherfucker alive had the power to keep me from her. These people had never met someone like me. I smiled slowly, it looked like Hell was about to freeze, right the fuck, over.

CHAPTER 20

REVERIE

I didn't know how much longer I could take this. Nathan had been gone for a week, and I was losing my mind. The only reason I was still reasonably sane was thanks to the Moons. The three of them had proved I was correct in trusting them and our friendship.

Getting ready for class, I wore the usual T-shirt, cargo pants, and hot pink combat boots Zeke had bought me. I put my dark hair up in space buns, grabbed my go bag, and left the room. Waking up early wasn't a problem because I barely slept at all. I knew I needed to rest, I could be initiated anytime, but my worry for Nathan wouldn't let me.

Walking into the living room, I saw Zeke sitting on the couch, drinking one coffee and a large to-go cup on the table. It felt like déjà vu. It would be perfect, if only my psycho would only pop in.

Standing, Zeke walked over and pulled me into his arms.

"I guess I look exactly how I feel." I sighed, feeling like I'd aged ten years.

"You're always beautiful, but I know stressing about Nathan is weighing on you." He whispered in my hair.

I took a deep inhale of his shirt, fresh laundry, and a faint scent of pine. He was everything safe, and I didn't want the hug to end. "If it weren't for your family, I would be insane by now. I don't understand why he's not back yet. Most Passives that make it through are only gone a matter of days. I know he's alright because I would feel it through our bond if he wasn't." I took another deep breath, hoping the comfort he gave me would last through the day.

Pantar appeared in the room suddenly, making us jump. *"Nexi, you shouldn't worry so. I have complete faith in the crazy one. He fits perfectly in your Faction because nothing would keep him from you for long. You need to bond with more. I sense that a full Faction will be needed for what's to come."*

Seeing the frown on my face, Zeke asked, "What's wrong?"

"I'm not sure—just something Pantar said to me." I really didn't want to tell him.

"Said to you?" Zeke raised one eyebrow in question.

Wow, I was off my game. I hadn't told anyone I could communicate with Pantar except my parents. It's not that I didn't trust the guys. Worry for Nathan had put everything else on the back burner, and I still hadn't discussed it with Pantar.

"It's acceptable that they know. I have followed and observed the two brothers, and they will make fine members of your Faction. As you complete your bond with each of your men, they will gain the ability to communicate with me." Pantar yawned.

"So, you could have been talking to Nathan this whole time?" I asked, stunned.

"If I so chose. I didn't because I was waiting for you to tell him." He laid down and put his head on his giant paws.

Leading Zeke over to the couch, I started to explain about Pantar when Chloe entered the room.

"Good morning, bestie. How did you sleep last night?" she asked, sitting beside me and patting my leg.

"I tried, if that counts. Whenever I closed my eyes, I saw Nathan in every horrible scenario my mind could conjure up. I have complete confidence in his skills, but I just wish I knew what he was dealing with." Picking up my coffee, I took a long drink.

Chloe looked at Zeke with narrowed eyes. "Where is my coffee, dear brother?"

"Your juice is in the refrigerator. You know how you get with too much caffeine." Zeke smirked.

"I will cut off your balls. Nobody keeps me from my coffee." Chloe reached in her boot for the knife I had given her.

Zeke started laughing and motioned to the counter where another to-go cup sat. "I just wanted to get your heart pumping this morning."

Chloe punched him in the arm on her way to retrieve her coffee. "Did I say that my brothers were perfect for your Faction? If so, I take it back. They suck balls, and I think you should ditch them both."

"Hey Booger, I would never withhold coffee from Reverie. I can think of much better ways to get her heart pumping." He laughed, winking at me.

The twins had ramped up the flirting in the last week, and I had enjoyed every moment. If Nathan had been here, I would have sat down with them and seriously discussed their joining my Faction. They needed to know everything that was going on before they committed.

"I will fuck you up! I've already warned you once about calling me that. Coffee or no, one more time, and I'm telling

Mom." Glancing in my direction, she said, "You better think hard before accepting my brothers. I'm not sure the aggravation outweighs the benefits."

Turning to me, Zeke grinned and winked. "The benefits outweigh the aggravation. Of that, you can be certain."

Chloe started gagging, but I couldn't look away. He wasn't holding back anymore, and looking into those beautiful blue eyes, I felt myself begin to fall.

Seeing the look in my eyes, Zeke lost his smile, pulled me into his lap, and kissed me like he was dying of thirst, and I was a glass of water. I thought I heard Chloe say something about going to class and getting the hell out of there, but I couldn't be sure. The kiss was all-consuming, and I felt my nipples harden as Zeke's mouth wandered down my throat. I tunneled both hands in his silky hair and tilted my head to give him better access. I vaguely heard the door open, but jerked away from Zeke when someone cleared their throat loudly.

"I hate to interrupt, but you're going to be late to class," Zane said with a heated look in his eyes. "I also want to point out how rude it is to leave me out. I'm a much better kisser than him."

Zeke pulled me in, hugged me tightly and kissed my head. "He's delusional. My kissing skills are unparalleled."

"You'll certainly get no argument from me." I kissed his chin, hating to give up the safety and comfort surrounding me. "He's right about one thing, I'll be late for class if I don't get going." I started to stand, but Zeke wouldn't let go and pulled me down to give me another scorching hot kiss.

Zane walked over, jerked me away from Zeke, grabbed the back of my neck, and kissed me like it was his job. Pulling back, he gave me a hard look.

"No leaving me behind. Understand?"

I nodded my head because I'd lost my ability to speak. These men left me breathless, and I was lucky to have found them. I decided then and there to have the conversation with them later tonight. I would have liked Nathan to be a part of it, but it wasn't fair to these two to keep essential things from them.

Feeling that Nathan would approve, I hesitantly asked, "Can we talk later? There are things I think we need to discuss before you make the final decision to join my Faction."

Zeke came up and put his arms around me. Zane had never let me go, so I was cradled between the two brothers. Other than when Nathan held me, I'd never felt so safe and loved.

"I speak for both of us when I say it's too late. It doesn't matter what you tell us, we'll be a part of this Faction. The ritual is just a formality because, in our hearts, we're already yours."

That was just it.

We didn't need the ritual.

A fter morning classes, Pantar told me he was going to hunt for lunch in the forest behind the academy. I decided to go for an easier meal and headed into the cafeteria. I made a colossal salad with a little of everything and heaps of ranch dressing. Then, I went to the table Chloe was sitting at with two other first-year students. Paige and Joan were sisters. I thought Paige was a few years older. They were both found Passives, so they started Emberhold together. Neither had been called to initiation.

"Are y'all ready for ShitStorm's torture session?" I set my tray on the table beside Paige. Joan winced and peeked around the room.

"Be careful. Who knows the torture he'd put us through if he heard you call him that?"

"No shit. That man is a sadist." Paige whispered, eyeing Kristine, who was watching them from one table over with the Bitch Brigade seated around her.

"I hate to give him any credit, but he's the reason why we haven't lost more Passives to initiation this year. There is no doubt that the conditioning has helped." I popped a tomato in my mouth and winked at Kristine. At this point, I fucked with her every chance I got.

Kristine started whispering to her friends, and I saw Sophie stand. It continued to amaze me at the immaturity and entitlement they had. We were in this shit together. Why were there always a few assholes that had to make everything more difficult?

"Could you possibly get one more thing on that salad?" Chloe smirked while digging into her pizza.

I laughed, flicking a crouton at her. "I'll try next time." Chloe had made it her mission to keep my mind off Nathan. There was no way it would work, but I appreciated the effort.

I heard a throat clearing behind me and turned to see a handsome guy with dark blonde hair and blue eyes smiling widely. "Hey, Reverie. We haven't met, and I wanted to introduce myself. I'm Dean Mathews' nephew, Kyle."

"Hi, Kyle. It's nice to meet you." I smiled, hoping it looked sincere. With Nathan gone, this was the last thing I wanted to deal with. He was probably taking his chance now because Pantar and the twins weren't around.

Kyle sat down, putting his arm along the back of my chair. This was the first time I was thankful Nathan was being initiated. "How are you enjoying classes?" Before I could answer, he started talking again. "Most Passives have trouble when they first start the academy, but I had no issues." He puffed out his chest and crossed his ankle over his knee. I guess he was going to make himself at home.

"Classes are fine." I responded, hoping if I kept it short, he would get the hint and leave. I could already tell he was an entitled little shit.

"If you need any help, let me know. I'm available for tutoring." He winked at me flirtatiously, completely ignoring everyone else at the table, moving his hand from my chair to my back.

"I appreciate that, Kyle, but I'm doing okay." I leaned forward, dislodging his hand and took a bite of my salad. I wanted to punch him, but, for now, being in the dean's good graces was too important to indulge my temper. Kyle turned to face me, laying his other arm on the table and caging me in.

"Would you like to grab lunch tomorrow? I know a great place, and the lunch is free." He winked at me again.

Was this fool implying that I come to his dorm room? This was escalating fast.

"Hello Kyle, I'm Chloe. It's nice to meet you." She glanced in my direction and crossed her eyes.

I snorted out a laugh before I could stop myself. Kyle glanced at me and frowned before turning and smiling at Chloe. "Nice to meet you, too."

Feeling a warm hand on my other shoulder, I looked up and saw Zane standing beside me, frowning at Kyle.

"Reverie, could I speak to you for a moment?"

"Sure, Zane." I moved to scoot my chair back, but Kyle's arm blocked my progress.

"We were talking Moon. You can speak to her later." Kyle scowled at Zane.

I was shocked, what the actual fuck? Before I could part his ball sack from his body, Zane had me up and out of my chair, standing behind him.

"I will rip your fucking head from your body and shit down your neck. You don't keep her from me."

"You can't talk to me like that." Kyle stood and puffed out his chest, but I noticed he'd moved out of Zane's reach.

Since I was behind Zane, I couldn't see his face, but I felt the muscles in his back tense. "You're right, talking is over-rated. Why don't I just beat the fuck out of you instead, for touching what's not yours?"

Instructor Storm appeared beside our table. "Is there a problem here?"

Where in the hell did he come from? These days, it seemed he was everywhere I went.

I was at Java and Jam getting coffee. He was there.

I went for a run, and he just happened to be running too.

I walked out of my dorm, and he was outside my building.

It was a little disturbing, especially since Storm never said a word. He just nodded in greeting like it was all a big coin-cidence.

"No problem, just Moon being his usual dickish self." Kyle scowled at Zane.

"We can settle this in the arena if I've offended you." Zane stared at Kyle with a creepy as fuck smile.

"No need for the arena. I was just having a conversation

with the Nexus." Kyle glanced at me. "I'll find you later." He took off like his ass was on fire.

Did he refer to me as "the Nexus"? He probably already forgot my name. "What's the Arena?" I asked, stepping around Zane.

"I know this one." Chloe raised her hand enthusiastically. "It's behind the gym, close to the edge of the woods. Passives fight there to settle disputes. If they're lucky, they can prove themselves valuable enough to have a Nexus consider them for their Faction. Last year, two Passives died, so it's no joke."

"My parents never told me about that." I frowned. What the hell was wrong with these people? We were already losing Passives to initiation. Now we were killing each other.

"Probably because it only started three years ago," Storm smiled.

Damn, that smile was devastating. I looked away before he could see the admiration on my face. Why couldn't I shake these feelings for the tremendous asshole?

Strangely enough, Storm had been decent the previous week. He was still hard on me, but no more than he was to every other student. It was starting to freak me out just a little. No way could he possibly believe I would consider him for my Faction. My Nexus senses had to be wrong about this one, and even if they weren't, no way the other guys would accept him.

Storm left as quickly as he appeared, and Zane went to get food.

I was finishing my salad when I felt something cold spill down my back. Turning, I saw Sophie standing behind me, holding a cup. Paige jumped to her feet and shoved Sophie back.

"What the hell, Sophie? You did that shit on purpose!"

"I did no such thing." She smirked, not putting much

effort into denying it. "Her chair was in the middle of the aisle as if she owned the whole cafeteria. Just because she's Nexus doesn't mean she has more rights than the rest of us," Sophia hissed at Paige, pointing in my direction.

"You're just jealous that she's Nexus." Paige frowned at her.

"Please, I'm not jealous in the least of her fat ass. I'm not sure she's Nexus, anyway. Her mother probably helped her get that Fellat." She taunted.

I had been wiping the sticky liquid off my neck, listening to their interaction this whole time. Standing, I grabbed the back of Sophie's neck and slammed her face into Paige's mashed potatoes. When Sophie raised her head, mashed potatoes covered her face, and gravy dripped from her nose. She started frantically wiping at her eyes and nose, crying like the little bitch she was.

"You better watch yourself! Kristine is going to get your ass whipped. One more transgression against me or my friends, and we'll settle this in the arena." Now I felt like a hypocrite from my earlier thoughts, but these bitches were on my last nerve.

Zane walked up. "What the fuck is going on here?" He asked, then saw the food dripping down Sophie's face. He didn't try to hide his amusement.

"Nexus, are you responsible for this?"

Hearing Zane call me Nexus was the last straw for Sophia. She let out an enraged scream and ran out of the cafeteria. Looking less than pleased, Kristine followed behind her with the rest of their posse.

Chloe raised her glass to me. "'Maybe someday we could become friends—friends who ride majestic, translucent steeds, shooting flaming arrows across the bridge of Herndale.'"

I replied, "'I would follow you into the mists of Avalon.'" We both started laughing hysterically.

Zeke walked up. "What the hell are they laughing at?"

Zane looked at him and said, "Chloe finally found someone who loves *Stepbrothers* as much as she does."

They both groaned in unison. Chloe grinned at me, and I burst out laughing.

CHAPTER 21

REVERIE

After I changed clothes, Zane walked me to conditioning, holding my hand the whole way, mean mugging the fuck out of any guy that even looked in my direction. I was thankful, with worry for Nathan weighing me down, I appreciated his running interference. I think that Kyle approaching me in the cafeteria broke the seal.

Before we entered the gym, I pulled Zane to the side. "You know I have no interest in Kyle, right?"

Leaning down, he kissed me. "Yes, and I thank all our ancestors that's the case. I can't see him putting anyone above himself, even his Nexus."

"I'm not actively looking for Passives. I was raised to trust in my ability, understanding it would let me know when I've found the people that belong in my Faction. When I met you and your brother, I felt an instant connection. I don't understand how anyone would settle for anything less." I leaned in and squeezed him tight.

"That's why I love you, and I thank all the powers that be, every day that the ritual with Kristine didn't work." He squeezed me back.

I jerked back and looked at him. "Did you just tell me you love me outside a stinky gym on a Monday?"

"Looks like it." He grinned that cocky smile that I loved. I smiled so big I'm sure he could see my molars.

"I love you too. It'll be a crazy ride, but I wouldn't want it any other way. Now, let's get inside. I'm suddenly ready to kick some ass."

Holding hands and smiling with pure joy, we entered the gym.

If only my psycho were here, my happiness would be complete.

Zeke was standing inside the entrance, waiting for us. "Somebody looks happy." He smiled at his brother.

Zane clapped him on the back. "What's not to be happy about? It's a beautiful day, I'm holding hands with the most beautiful woman in the world, and I'm one handsome motherfucker."

"I can agree with the handsome motherfucker remark, and there is no more beautiful woman in all the dimensions than our Reverie, but it's cloudy outside and looks like rain." Zeke laughed.

"I didn't notice." He looked at me with complete adoration.

Chloe walked in and grabbed my hand. "We're going to change for conditioning, and I need to talk to my friend. You two need to quit hogging her."

I blew them both a kiss, reluctantly following Chloe into the locker room. I would have been content to blow off the rest of my classes and just hang with Zeke and Zane. I didn't suggest it because there would've been hell to pay from Instructor Storm.

On the first day, Storm made us do the course in the clothes we had worn to class. It felt cruel then, but it taught us a valuable lesson. We dressed now, keeping in mind that Emberhold could take us without warning. The last few weeks, we'd been allowed to change into something light-weight for conditioning. I made sure to pick clothes that would still work if I was taken to initiation.

"What made you smile so big out there? My brother looked happy enough to fart sprinkles." Chloe opened her locker, getting her clothes out.

I wrinkled my nose. "That's a disturbing visual. Never mention your brother farting again, sprinkles or not."

Chloe laughed. "You better get used to it. I have first-hand experience living with those two, and I can assure you they're toxic."

"You're an evil bitch, and they'd kill you if they knew you were telling me this." I pulled on black leggings and a short-sleeved pink moisture-wicking shirt.

"That's what they get for calling me Booger. How someone as fantastic as I am could get stuck with that nick-name is ridiculous." She tossed her hair and put her hand on her hip, striking a pose.

"I don't know, I think it suits you," I tried to look serious.

"Take that back, bitch!" Chloe laughed and punched me in the arm.

Joan and Paige came in and headed to their lockers.

"What are you two laughing so hard over?" Joan smirked.

"Nothing, really. Chloe is just being a booger today." I side-eyed her.

Chloe screeched, "Take that back, bestie, or I'll tell my

brothers what happened when we watched movies the other night."

I gasped, "You know I'm lactose intolerant. It's a medical condition and nothing to joke about."

Joan and Paige started laughing so hard they were leaning on each other.

"Bestie reset?" Chloe asked, arching her eyebrow.

"Absolutely." I agreed.

Joan and Paige looked on in astonishment as they watched us perform a fantastic series of hand motions and hip bumps, ending with us slapping each other's ass and blowing a raspberry. The sisters were in tears, but Chloe and I finished getting dressed like nothing had happened.

⌒⚜⌒

A fter our workout, I joined the twins, who were putting a group of Passives through an obstacle course.

"So, do y'all want to come over around six and talk?"

"That sounds good. We'll pick up some food." Zeke said, always eager to make sure I'd eaten.

Chloe and Joan walked over. "Paige is meeting a second year in the library to study, and we're going to get something to eat. Do you want to go?"

"Yeah, I'll hang out until the guys get finished here." I bent over and picked up my bag. "See y'all tonight."

I yelped when I was picked up suddenly.

"Were you actually leaving without kissing me goodbye?" Zane asked, cocking his eyebrow.

"No?" I squeaked out.

"You don't sound sure," Zeke frowned playfully.

Putting me back on my feet, Zane said, "Maybe a punishment is needed for this slight? Would you agree, brother?"

Zeke's eyes heated with desire. "I couldn't agree more."

A little confused about what they meant by that, I stood on my tiptoes to kiss Zane.

"It's too late for that, my Nexi." He gave me a peck on my puckered lips,

"You can settle up tonight for not saying goodbye to your men correctly."

Hearing the words "my Nexi," I felt my eyes tear up.

"What's wrong, baby?" Zeke pulled me into his arms.

"Hearing 'my Nexi' made me think about Nathan and how much I miss him. I can't stand not knowing what's happening to him." I cried into Zeke's shirt. Zane rubbed my back.

"I'm sorry, sweet girl. I won't call you that again."

"You can call me whatever you want. I'm being ridiculous. I have every confidence my sweet psycho will be fine. I just miss him and want us all to be together." I sniffed, tears running down my face.

Zeke leaned back and used his thumb to catch a tear before it fell. He brought his thumb up to his mouth and sucked off the moisture. A bolt of heat shot through me at his action, and I stopped crying.

"That crazy bastard will be fine. Nothing in this world or any other would keep us from you. On that you can count." He smiled and leaned down to give me a soft kiss. "Have fun with the girls, and we'll see you tonight." Turning to leave, I felt a sharp sting on my ass. I jerked around, and Zeke winked at me. "That's one. You'll get the rest tonight."

Feeling my cheeks turning red, both sets, I took off like I was being chased. I could hear the two assholes laughing, so I flipped them off over my shoulder but never stopped walking.

Catching up to the girls, we walked to Java and Jam. Finding a table in the back after getting some Snickerdoodles and hot chocolate, Joan grabbed a cookie and took a large bite.

"Girl, I think I got pregnant just watching you with those hot as fuck guys."

Chloe started gagging, "I don't know if I'm more grossed out by you talking about my brothers like that or seeing your mouth full of masticated cookies."

"I'd like a mouth full of your brother's cookies, if you know what I mean." Joan waggled her eyebrows.

We all laughed. "On a different note, are you doing all right in your classes? Finding out about this world and that you were Aurathion probably came as a shock to you." Chloe blew on her hot chocolate.

"It was a huge shock. We lost our parents in a car accident last year. Keeping a roof over our heads and food on the table has been tough. Paige and I have been holding two jobs, but we barely scraped by. Even as dangerous as this is, we welcome the challenge. At least we go to sleep with a full belly." She took another bite of her cookie.

I was shocked by her revelation. "I'm so sorry to hear about your parents. Losing two of my fathers before I was born sucked, but I have three other parents. I can't imagine what you and your sister have gone through."

"How did that work? That's something we've had a hard time grasping. Was there no jealousy? Did humans just accept the dynamic of your family?" Joan asked in rapid succession.

"Damn, girl, take a breath." Chloe laughed.

I smiled, "I don't know about Chloe's family, but I think

people assumed Mom was only married to one of my fathers and the other lived with us. My mom liked fucking with everybody by never confirming which one she was with. She's a unique individual," I smiled fondly. "Most Factions don't have that issue because they live in Aurathion towns. Those towns take measures to keep humans out."

"My dad is Nexus, and we grew up in an Aurathion community in Ohio. There was never any jealousy between my parents. It's hard to explain, but once your Faction is formed, those feelings don't exist." Chloe said.

"It's hard to wrap my head around. I see so much jealousy and cutthroat behavior here. I can't imagine how that's all put aside once your Faction is formed." Joan frowned in confusion.

"The important thing is that when forming your Faction, you trust your gut. You get a special feeling when you know someone is right for you. Choose a Nexus or Faction based on that instead of who they are and what advantages they bring." I took a sip from my mug. "The forming of a Faction can be a messy business. Just wait until more Nexus are revealed. Then things get ugly. Even with a class our size, there probably won't be more than ten." Chloe popped another cookie in her mouth. "Some Factions only consist of two people. That leaves lots of Passives out and unable to access their abilities. Nexus vary in strength, so the number of Faction members they can support depends on that."

"Wow, no wonder people are so desperate. That makes me feel bad for the Passives who have been here for years." Joan shook her head.

"Just imagine being unable to access your abilities and living a mundane life, knowing what could have been. There's nothing wrong with that if it's all you know, but it's like being at a massive buffet and starving to death when you've grown up in this world." I took another cookie.

"Good analogy, Miss Hawthorne." Instructor Storm said, startling us. This guy must secretly be a ninja.

"Instructor, we didn't see you walking up." Chloe put her hand on her chest.

"I would suggest keeping a better eye out for your surroundings. If you're this lax, you may not make it through initiation. Miss Hawthorne, could I have a word with you?" He gestured toward the door. I nodded my head and followed him out of the café. He walked to a small bench partially secluded by a large bush. Sitting, he turned to me. "Where is your Fellat?"

"Pantar went hunting. I think he needed a break from being around so many people. What did you want to talk to me about?" I was curious about what he could possibly want with me.

Storm looked hesitant but took a deep breath. "I wanted to know if you could meet me in my office tomorrow after lunch. I know I've been a bit of an ass to you, and I'm sorry for that. I could use your help teaching the students your techniques for dealing with the obstacle courses."

"I'm flattered, but you're amazing at it yourself. I saw you run through a course for the new Passives last week. I'm not sure how I can help." It was awkward speaking to him, or being this close, it made it harder to ignore the way he made me feel. We'd only interacted a handful of times, and those were hostile.

"You've had advanced training, and it shows. I thought coming from a fellow student it might make more sense. We could review some of your tapes this week and devise a plan. Then, you could demonstrate it to the students." Seeing my hesitation, he said, "I wouldn't ask if I didn't think it would help some of them survive initiation."

There was no way I could refuse, even if I only saved one Passive. Sometimes I truly hated being a nice person.

"Okay, I'll help."

Storm stood abruptly and began to walk away.

"I'll get back to you with an exact time. Thank you."

I couldn't see the sinister smile on his face. If I had, I would never have agreed to meet him alone.

CHAPTER 22
REVERIE

I went back inside the café and sat down.

"What did ShitStorm want?" Chloe asked wide-eyed.

"Can you believe he asked for my help with the new Passives? He even complimented me on my technique in getting through the courses." I grabbed another Snickerdoodle.

"You did kick ass on those courses, so I think it makes sense." Joan groaned, patting her belly. "There is no way I can eat anymore. I'm going to head back to my dorm. I've got a paper due in Professor Austin's class. Aurathion history is no joke."

"I finished that paper yesterday if you need any help." I offered.

"Thanks, but I've got this, plus the tutor I was assigned is hot. If I need any help, I'll ask him. I might ask even if I don't." She winked at us and then left the cafe.

We both laughed as she left. I truly liked the two sisters. I was glad my friend group was expanding, "Well, what do you think about me helping Storm?"

"I guess if it makes it possible for Passives to survive initiation, then it's worth dealing with the asshole. I'd be cautious. He started acting civil a few days after discovering your Nexus. Maybe he's hoping for a spot in the Hawthorne Faction." She grinned mischievously.

"Bite your tongue. No way would I want him or his fucked-up family a part of my Faction. I could never trust him, and the most crucial part of a successful Faction is having complete faith in each other." I wrinkled my nose at the lunatic, ignoring the way I felt sitting so close to him only a few minutes ago.

"That and a great sex life." Chloe waggled her eyebrows. "He walks like he's packing, so you might want to rethink that." I laughed despite myself and then downed the rest of my hot chocolate.

"I don't care what he's packing, bitch. I'm not interested." I flicked her forehead. "I'm going to head out to meet your brothers." She flicked me back, and we both giggled.

"Okay, I'll see you back at the dorm." Following me out of the café, Chloe blew me a kiss and headed toward our dorm.

That girl was something else. I was so happy Chloe had been assigned as my roommate. It felt like we'd known each other forever.

I waited outside the gym for Zeke and Zane, with my stomach doing flips. I was about ninety-nine percent sure they were going to be alright with everything, but that one percent chance was freaking me out. I looked forward to sharing everything, telling Chloe how vital honesty was in a Faction reinforced my decision to get this done. I hated that Nathan wouldn't be there, but it was the right thing to do. I wanted a Faction that was as strong as my parents, and this was the first step.

"Boo!!!"

I jumped. "What the hell?" I yelled, I was a little on edge.

"I couldn't resist. I called your name twice, but you were a million miles away." Zane laughed, poking my side.

Zeke pulled me into his arms. "Is everything all right?"

"Yes, I'm just looking forward to our talk tonight. I think it's past due." I squeezed him tight.

"Do you have any objections to having this conversation in our dorm instead of yours and Chloe's?" Zeke kissed the top of my head.

I looked up at him, "I was going to suggest that. Chloe is your family, and I trust her, but this is a Faction thing. Y'all can decide later if you want to tell her about our discussion."

Zane jerked me away from Zeke threw me over his shoulder and slapped my ass. "Let's get this party started then! Zeke, order some food, and let's put our future Nexus mind to rest."

"Put me down, Zane!" I yelled and grabbed two handfuls of his ass, prepared to squeeze the shit out of it.

Pantar appeared abruptly.

"Does the flame-haired replica need to be reprimanded?"

"Where in the hell did he come from?" Zane shrieked in surprise at seeing a giant Fellat appear right before him.

"I don't think he likes you carrying me like this." He must have agreed because he slowly lowered me to my feet. I walked over to Pantar and hugged him. "We were just playing, no need to reprimand him." I laughed, sticking my tongue out at Zane.

"The Nexus should be treated with dignity, not like a wayward youngling." Pantar huffed out a breath.

"They were trying to distract me from worrying about Nathan." I ran my hand down the soft fur on his back.

"The crazy one will be just fine. You should be worrying more about completing your Faction. I feel there is trouble coming, and it's important that you are at your strongest." He nuzzled my head.

"What's coming?" I stepped back with a frown.

"I am not sure, but I feel a sense of foreboding. Now, if everything is well, I will continue my hunt. I also need to be at my strongest." He disappeared as quickly as he had appeared.

"I assume he's gotten your power of teleportation, or is that something a Fellat is born with?" Before I could answer, Zeke continued, "I haven't forgotten how you implied you were speaking to Pantar." He walked over to me. "I hope that's one of the things we'll discuss tonight."

I took his hand, and with Zane following close behind, I led them away from the path and stopped at the forest's edge. Looking around to ensure no one was near, I turned and frowned at the brothers. "There's a lot I need to tell you both. I would've spoken to y'all sooner because my gut told me I could trust you from the moment we met, but it wasn't just my safety on the line if I was wrong." More serious than he was moments ago, Zane stepped up and grabbed my hand, weaving our fingers together, he tugged me back towards the path.

"Let's head to our dorm. We'll all feel better when we get things out in the open."

Zeke nodded and took my other hand. Hopefully, they both felt the same after I explained everything.

Entering the building that housed Zeke and Zane, I immediately noticed the differences between this structure and mine. Theirs was coed, housing both male and female, third and fourth years who had chosen to stay at Emberhold hoping to join a Faction. The building was also significantly larger, having six floors instead of four. Upon entering, Passives began whispering in the hallways, noticing that I was holding both Moons' hands.

Since bonding with Pantar had revealed my Nexus status, I'd noticed many of the advanced years hanging around the cafeteria and other public venues, staring at me and even trying to strike up a conversation. It was getting hard to go anywhere without someone approaching me. I was honestly surprised I'd been able to enjoy my time with Chloe and Joan without interruption.

Well, other than Storm popping in.

I understood why they were desperate for a Nexus and sympathized with their plight. Hopefully, as soon as initiation was over, another Nexus would be revealed, and I would fade into the background.

We stepped onto the elevator, and Zane punched the button for the sixth floor.

"There is nothing to be nervous about." Zeke reached over and grabbed my hands with his. I hadn't even realized I was fiddling with the hem of my shirt, twisting it repeatedly. "We're already yours. Nothing you can say will change that." He kissed the top of my head gently just as the elevator doors opened.

Exiting, we headed to the end of the massive hall and stopped at the last door. Holding his thumb to the scanner, the door clicked open. Zeke stepped back and gestured for me to enter first.

The first thing I noticed was the size of the room. It was more like an apartment than a dorm room. They had a full kitchen with an island separating it from the living room. A colossal television hung over the massive fireplace with an enormous sectional that looked like the perfect place to curl up with a blanket and nap. I could see a long hallway to my left that must have led to the bedrooms.

"Wow, this place is huge compared to our dorm."

Zane scoffed as he walked into the kitchen to grab some beer from the fridge, "When you move into this building, you know you may be here for the long haul. I guess the luxury is supposed to distract us from the reality that our days are numbered, and it's a good possibility we'll leave here without a Faction."

Handing us both a beer, Zane picked up his phone. "I know Zeke said nothing could cause us to change our mind about becoming your Faction, but depending on the answer to my question, we just might have to bail."

"What question is that?" I could feel the nerves returning and started twisting the hem of my shirt again.

"Do you like pineapple on your pizza?" Zeke walked over and hit Zane on the back of his head. Zane scowled at Zeke rubbing his head, "What the fuck, dude?"

"Really, jackass, can't you see how nervous she is?" Zeke growled at his brother.

Zane winced and huffed out, "I was just trying to lighten the mood. I'm sorry, Reverie." He frowned, seeing I had turned my back to them, and my shoulders shook. Rushing to me, Zane put both arms around me. "Please forgive me! Please don't cry! I'm so sorry!"

I pushed at his arms, and he reluctantly released me. I slowly turned and raised my face to his. Expecting tears, he was shocked when I laughed.

"Got you!" I stuck my tongue out at him.

Zane looked at me, stunned, then growled, "Brat! You scared me to death." He turned to Zeke and winked. "Your punishments are adding up."

"She needs her ass reddened for that." Zeke walked over,

pulling me into his arms. "We'll get to that later. For now, answer his question." He grinned.

I was stuck on the spanking comment. I couldn't believe this was coming from Zeke. Pushing the thought to the back of my mind, I answered, "No pineapple, of course. I'm not completely insane." Laughing, I looked at Zane solemnly. "Unfortunately, the same can't be said for Nathan. He loves pineapple on his pizza."

"That proves it. He is a psycho." Zeke frowned. Then, all three of us burst out laughing.

We got comfortable on the couch after handing out the beer and ordering our pizza. Taking a long drink, I rose and turned to sit on the coffee table facing the brothers.

"You were right, Zeke. I can communicate with Pantar. I gained the ability after we bonded in the cave. Nathan isn't aware either. I was still in shock, and I wasn't sure if Pantar wanted it known." I took another long sip of my beer. "Pantar explained that he could communicate with Nathan too, since we were Faction."

They looked thoughtful, "Do you know how it's possible?" Zeke took a pull from his beer.

"My dad can communicate with animals. Apparently, I inherited his ability." I shrugged my shoulders.

"I was amazed that you gained one ability without an entire Faction. Now, knowing you've gotten two, I'm completely stunned." Zeke stared at me in awe.

"Answering the question you asked earlier, I have no idea when Pantar gained the ability to teleport. He just started doing it, and I haven't questioned him. I'm assuming, as you did, he can do it through our bond." I tilted my head in thought. "Maybe it's an ability all Fellats have, I guess I need to ask him."

"I can't imagine why you thought any of this would be a

big deal. It just shows how exceptional you are." Zeke smiled proudly.

I winced. "Um, well, that's not everything."

Both twins leaned toward me. "Out with it then. I'm ready to get to the part where we kiss and make up." Zane grinned.

"Kiss and makeup? We're not fighting." I scrunched up my face in confusion.

"No, we're not, but the same theory still applies." Zane nodded his head like this was common knowledge.

Zeke frowned at him. "Really?" Looking back at me, he gave a soft smile. "Please continue, just ignore this moron." He gestured in his brother's direction.

I blurted quickly, "Ididn'tperformtheritualwithNathan." I took a deep breath and then slowly exhaled. "Damn, I do feel better getting that off my chest." Zeke and Zane just stared at me. I jumped to my feet. "I knew you'd be weirded out! I'll just leave, and you don't have to speak to me anymore, no hard feelings." I felt my eyes welling up with tears and headed for the door.

Zeke rushed to me and pulled me down on the couch between him and Zane. "No, baby, we just couldn't understand what you said! Calm down and say it slower this time." Zane lifted me into his lap, and Zeke grabbed my hands and held them between his.

"I didn't perform the ritual with Nathan." I turned my head and stared at the fireplace.

"What do you mean you didn't perform the ritual? Nathan is clearly your Faction." Zane was confused.

"I didn't say he wasn't my Faction. I said we didn't perform the ritual. There's a difference." I turned my head to look at Zane.

"If you didn't do the ritual, how did he become Faction?" Zeke grabbed my chin so he could look into my eyes.

Seeing nothing but love and care on his face, I explained, "We had several difficult years. I was trying to ignore how I felt about Nathan because I thought he was 100% human. Knowing I would leave for the academy and form a Faction made a relationship with him impossible."

"I've only known Nathan briefly, but I'm sure he didn't take that well." Zane smirked.

"That's putting it mildly. He was furious because he knew how I felt about him. I'm sure when he looked at me, it was clear on my face. Hiding it was difficult, and now I know why." I sighed in remembered pain.

"So, what happened?" Zeke urged me to continue.

"There was a scene at prom, and Nathan pulled me outside. He then proceeded to kiss the hell out of me. In the clash of teeth, we must have exchanged blood and before we could take another breath, we teleported into my living room in front of my parents. You can imagine the scene from there." I smiled wryly.

The guys were stunned into silence. When I tried to get up, they held me still. "Just give us a minute, sweetheart," Zane mumbled, looking at me in amazement.

Zeke was staring into space. Suddenly he pulled me away from Zane and into his lap, wrapping his arms around me. "Do you know how fortunate we are to have met you? There is no other Nexus in this world or any other that is as extraordinary as you, and we get to call you ours."

Zane started laughing. "Can you go into more detail about your parents' reaction to you and Nathan appearing out of nowhere?"

Zeke tried to keep a straight face but failed and began laughing too. I joined in, remembering Grumpy's face. Both

Moons leaned in to hug me, and our laughter subsided slowly. "No one can know out about this. The Council would use you as a lab rat if they found out." Zeke warned. "Not needing the ritual to bond is unbelievable."

"I just don't understand how it's possible." Zane frowned. "We need to tell Chloe, she's excellent with research, and maybe she can find something in the ancient scrolls kept in the archives."

I raised my head from Zeke's chest. "I'm glad you said that. I know Chloe can be trusted, and since she'll be family, she should know."

Zane's grin was huge. "I love hearing that. We'll be a family, and that's way more important than becoming a Faction or gaining abilities. This calls for another group hug. Bring it in, people."

Zeke and I started laughing again. Zeke with humor and me with relief. They had become vital to me, and I didn't know what I would've done if they'd wanted out.

CHAPTER 23
REVERIE

Wrapped up in their warmth, I only regretted that Nathan wasn't there with us. His presence would make this night perfect. I heard the floor creak as if someone were taking a step.

"Did you hear that?" I asked the guys.

"Hear what?" Zane asked.

"I thought I heard something over by the door." I untangled myself from their arms and got up to look around, Zeke right behind me.

"I didn't hear anything." Zane rose from the couch. Zeke opened the door and walked out into the hallway. I followed behind him, but neither of us saw anything. We entered the apartment as Zane was walking out of the kitchen. "I checked the entire apartment. Nobody's here but us. Did you two see anyone?"

"No, I'm probably just being paranoid." I was a little jumpy after our talk. Shaking off those feelings, I smiled. "Now that everything is out in the open, I've got my appetite back! Let's finish the pizza and decide when we'll tell Chloe." I grabbed another slice and sat down.

"I'm on board with finishing the pizza, but I'd like to make plans to complete our bond," Zane said, basically bouncing in his seat.

"I agree. I want to complete our bond before you're taken to initiation. Even though you can't communicate with Nathan now, if you gain more Faction and we develop our abilities, maybe your capacity to communicate will strengthen. You can check in on him, and we can keep track of you," Zeke said seriously.

"Wow. I can't believe I was worried about y'all's reaction." I smiled, thankful these two had come into my life. "I hope you're right, because I don't think I've slept more than a few hours since Nathan was taken."

"Maybe you need to be the meat in a twin sandwich." Zane winked. "I think I heard somewhere it was the cure for insomnia."

I really hoped he and Nathan never decided to join forces. Those two were hard enough to handle individually.

Together, it would be a losing battle.

Zeke frowned at his brother. "Let's not freak her out before she bonds us."

I smiled mischievously and said, "I love sandwiches." These two needed to know they couldn't fluster me that easily.

Both guys turned simultaneously to look at me. It was a little freaky when they did that. I started to squirm a little bit at the intensity in their eyes.

Maybe they could fluster me that easily.

Zane smiled slowly. "Could she be any more perfect for us, brother?"

"I don't think so," Zeke said, without taking his eyes off me.

Deciding a change of subject was in order, I said, "I'm a little nervous about purposely trying to bond without the ritual. Although I agree we need to do it sooner rather than later. I would like y'all to meet my parents first. I want to do it right this time, and if we appear in their living room, at least you've already met." I grinned at them.

"That can be arranged. I have a friend who found his Faction here at the academy. They stayed for advanced training, and he can create portals. I'll talk to him in the morning and see when we can go." Zane pulled me in for a kiss.

"Let him know it's urgent, and we'll owe him a favor. We need to complete our bond ASAP. I want her as strong as possible before Emberhold takes her." Zeke finished his beer, then stood and began cleaning up.

Zane walked into the kitchen to grab another beer for us, and I followed, sitting at the island. "I hope everything goes well, and I'll be strong enough to communicate with Nathan. It's painful being away from him."

Sliding me another beer and handing one to Zeke as he sat beside me, Zane said, "I can't believe I'm saying this, but I miss the ornery guy." He leaned down and rested his elbows on the island across from them.

I smile at him in affection. "I bet he misses y'all, too."

Zeke started laughing. "I'll take that bet. That's probably the one thing he's enjoying about initiation, not seeing us drool over you." His laughter died, and he looked at me with so much heat that I felt my face warm. Zeke leaned over and slowly pressed his lips to mine as if he was savoring his ability to do so. Ending the kiss, he said, "As much as I want you to stay, if you want us to meet your parents before we bond, you better let me walk you back to your dorm."

"I hate to agree with him, but I'm not sure I'd be able to resist forcing the issue if I got my hands on that luscious ass." Zane smoldered my way.

I turned up my beer, needing to cool down. "Yeah, you're probably right."

These two were gorgeous. I couldn't blame Kristine for trying to bond them. I could blame her for being a raging bitch, but not her desire for these guys.

We finished cleaning up and left the guy's apartment, heading to my dorm. I inhaled the crisp air into my lungs as we meandered down the path. None of us wanted to end our time together.

Zane walked slightly behind me, and glancing back, I saw his eyes glued to my ass. I stopped abruptly, and Zane ran into me. He smirked and wiped imaginary drool from his mouth. "No one could resist staring at an ass this fine, so I make no apologies." I laughed and grabbed his hand, pulling him beside me.

"Come on, perv. It's getting late, and you'll need your rest if you're going to meet my parents tomorrow."

Zane turned serious. "I've heard a lot about them. Our parents always talked about the bravery and loyalty of the Hawthorne Faction. I always thought of them as superheroes."

Zeke grabbed my other hand. "Our parents gave all the credit to your parents for holding back the Dark Factions, so the Aurathions that wanted to escape had the chance." He raised my hand and kissed it gently. "Mom cried when she told us about Adelaide losing two of her men. Those stories are why Chloe sees your mom as a hero."

"I think she should come with us tomorrow. I want to introduce them to her, anyway. We can let her in on everything then and get her help finding answers." I was excited to come clean with her. That girl was special, and her friendship was important to me.

Zane grinned in Zeke's direction. "She's going to lose it. This might be the only time she's ever been speechless." They both started laughing.

"I wouldn't count on it. Chloe never runs out of things to say."

As we rounded the corner of my building, still laughing, Oren stepped in front of us.

"You shouldn't be out so late, Miss Hawthorne. You need your rest if you're going to help with my class tomorrow."

The man was everywhere I turned. It was starting to worry me a little, especially since I felt the tingling start up with his abrupt appearance.

There was *no way* this guy would be a part of my Faction, tingles or not.

"As you can see, we're heading that way, Storm. Maybe you should take your own advice and get some rest. You're not getting any younger." Zeke narrowed his eyes.

"That last part was just mean. In all fairness, you're not much younger than me." He gave the twins a menacing smile. "You should be careful walking back to your apartment. I've heard that it can be dangerous around here for Passives with no abilities this late at night." Whistling, he turned and walked away.

"How in the fuck were we ever friends with that dick," Zane growled out through clenched teeth.

"He wasn't always such an asshole." Turning to me, Zeke said, "I don't like how he looks at you. Let me know if he steps out of line even the slightest bit. I've about reached the end of my tolerance with him, and Passive or not, I will fuck him up."

I reached up and cupped Zeke's face with my hand. "I appreciate the sentiment, but you know I can handle him."

He turned and kissed the palm of my hand. "I know you can, but defending our Nexus is my privilege. You wouldn't deny me that, would you?"

I swayed toward him, entranced by his words. "Do you know how sexy I find that?"

"I called him a dick. That's sexy, right?" Zane pouted.

I turned to him and, standing on my tiptoes, kissed his plump lips. "It was, you are the King of Sexy, Zane Moon."

Zeke grabbed my hand, laughing at his brother, "Come on, your highness, and let's get our Nexus to bed. She needs her rest because we have a busy day tomorrow."

We finally made it to my dorm. Before I could enter, Zeke grabbed the back of my neck with his large, calloused hand and pulled me toward him. He leaned down, and I parted my lips in anticipation of his kiss. He softly rubbed his mouth against mine, gently biting my bottom lip, and breathed me in. Zane stepped up behind me, and I felt the heat from his muscled chest seep into my back. He leaned down, lightly nipping my neck, then tenderly kissing it better. Zeke slowly deepened the kiss as Zane began sucking and licking my neck with more intensity.

I moaned, and Zeke swallowed the sound, licking into my mouth. I felt my nipples harden and clit pulse in time with Zane's attention to my neck. Zeke placed his large, warm hand over my pussy and gently squeezed me through my pants as Zane brought his hands around and cupped my breasts, rolling my nipples between his fingers. My head fell back against Zane as Zeke rubbed two of his large fingers directly over my clit.

I felt Zane push his large erection into the crease of my ass, rubbing back and forth slightly. I was overcome with sensation, and even though I didn't want the pleasure to end, I felt my orgasm wash over me.

I was relaxed and drowsy and didn't protest when Zeke picked me up and carried me into my room. He pulled back the covers while Zane undressed me, pulling his shirt off and slipping it over my head. After they both tucked me in, I was already falling asleep, but felt each of them place a kiss on the top of my head.

⌒☖⌒

I awoke abruptly to find Pantar spread out beside me, partially hanging off the bed, snoring slightly. I'd been dreaming that Nathan was fighting beside some huge guy in what looked like a Roman coliseum. As I felt my breath even out, I prayed that my psycho was well and that bonding with the guys would strengthen me enough to communicate with him. I snuggled back into Pantar's warmth and pulled Zane's shirt over my nose. Breathing in his scent, I closed my eyes and drifted back asleep.

CHAPTER 24

JET

I was up and out of my dorm by zero six hundred and headed to do some conditioning before class. I did my best thinking during my workout. I needed this time to wrap my mind around the insanity of this place. I had been at the academy for several months, and every day, I found something new that amazed me. An Aurathion's power after joining a Faction was tremendous, and, in my opinion, a danger to my country and the world. They had abilities that the military could only dream of, and instead of manufacturing them, they accessed them with the flick of a hand.

The problem was, I didn't know if there was anything the United States or any other country could do to defend itself against the Dark Factions. If they found a way to come here, I hoped the Factions that fought against them the first time would defend this world again. There was nowhere for us to go if they failed. Using weapons of mass destruction would be the only option, and no one would win in that scenario. Luckily, it wasn't my job to find solutions; I was only to report what I saw without blowing my cover.

I hadn't heard anything nefarious from any Aurathions at Emberhold. Mostly, they seemed to concentrate on teaching students Aurathion history and biology and training them in case the Dark Factions tried to infiltrate the world they now inhabited. Initiation was a mindfuck, and realizing the academy was sentient freaked me right the fuck out. Did Emberhold know I was here as a spy? And if so, why would I be allowed to stay? If I was being honest, this whole experience had been fucked up.

Joining the military was a tradition in my family, starting with my paternal great-great-grandfather dating back to the First World War. My father had met my mother while serving in Afghanistan. She was a military doctor, and they fell for each other immediately. As a child, I loved hearing them talk about their first meeting. Of course, my father incorporated explosions and gunfire, and he even claimed to rescue my mother a couple of times. Clinton Lockley was quite the character. I took after my mother, Viola Lockley. She was quiet and liked to weigh her words before speaking. Her account of their first meeting was quite different from my father's. I tended to believe my mother's version rather than his.

Both of my parents had chosen to serve in the Army. I decided to follow my grandfather's path and joined the Marines. My dad loved to give me shit about it, but I knew I had their full support no matter what branch of the military I chose to serve in.

I excelled in my training and, after serving three years, was approached by a senior officer to apply to MARSOC (Marine Forces Special Operations Command). The organization is comprised of the Marine Raider Regiment, Marine Raider Support Group, and Marine Raider Training Center. Marine Raiders specialize in direct action, special reconnaissance, foreign internal defense, unconventional warfare, and counterterrorism. I was proud to be a part of this organization and loved the challenge it provided.

During my service in the military, I had many medical evaluations. My blood had been drawn more times than I could count, so the Council getting access to my test results wasn't surprising. What was still a mystery to me was how they narrowed their search. Millions of people were in this country alone, not to mention other countries. There is no way they went through everyone's blood samples. I suspected they only researched people they thought would somehow enhance a Faction. I was approached while having a few drinks with some of my buddies in Oceanside, CA. I had been stationed at Camp Pendleton for two months at that time.

～⚜～

"*H*ey, shithead, you owe me a beer for saving your ass in Yemen." *Josh, a good friend and fellow Raider, said clapping me on the back and laughing.*

I held the door to the hole-in-the-wall bar that all my fellow Raiders preferred. "Sure you did. I remember that incident a little differently."

"So do I!" The third member of our trio, Deshawn, laughed. "I saved both of your candy asses." We all laughed as we took a seat at the bar.

"Sure you did, fucker! You couldn't save your ass with both hands." Josh responded.

"No, but I could save yours with one!" Deshawn cackled.

Josh flipped him off just as the bartender showed up with three beers. We had been here so often in the last two months she didn't have to ask us what we wanted.

After she left, Josh turned to Deshawn. "Did you tap that ass? She was throwing it at you enough last weekend."

Deshawn turned up his beer and took a large swallow. "I don't fuck and tell," He smirked, "but if I did, I would say she was well worth the money I spent taking her out."

"That's not saying much. Isn't McDonald's your go-to date night restaurant?" Josh asked, trying his best to look serious.

"Absolutely, have you seen the price of a Big Mac meal lately? It's practically fine dining." He winked at the bartender serving a lady at the other end of the bar. She blushed and turned back to her customer.

I felt a presence at my back and turned. I saw a man who was way too overdressed for this establishment.

"Can I help you with something?"

"I'd like to speak with you, if I may?" He said haughtily.

"Do I know you?" I frowned.

"No, Jet Lockley. You don't, but I know you. It won't take but a moment." He gestured toward a table in the back.

"Who the fuck is this guy?" Josh turned, giving the stranger the stink eye.

"I have no idea, but I guess I'll find out." I finished my beer and then stood to follow the man.

"If you're getting an inheritance from a rich relative, remember the guy that saved your ass!" Deshawn yelled out.

"I saved both of your prissy asses. I'm the one he needs to remember!" Josh whined. I smirked as I walked off, the debate of who saved whose ass still going strong.

After I sat down, the guy at the table began speaking immediately: "My name is Reginald Wayne, and I'm here to share some astonishing news concerning your ancestry." He reached into a briefcase and pulled out a file that he slid to me. I eyed the file and then looked at Reginald.

"Who are you with, and what is this concerning?"

"I would rather you examine the file first, then I'll give you the information you're asking for," he said in a no-nonsense way.

I was annoyed at his response but too curious not to open the file. It was most definitely a character flaw. The first page was a copy of a blood test, followed by a DNA analysis. I picked up the paper with my DNA results and read through it several times. Looking up at Reginald and then back at the paper, I asked, "What does this mean?"

"It means, Mr. Lockley, that you're not entirely human."

Standing, I frowned down at the man. "Fuck off, I don't have the time or patience for this shit. I have no idea how you got that blood test, but I know it wasn't legal. I'll be keeping my paperwork, and if I see you again, I'll beat your ass first and ask questions later."

The man grabbed my arm. I tried to jerk it out of Reginald's hold, but I couldn't do it, no matter how hard I pulled. What the fuck was going on? The guy wasn't even half my size, and I couldn't break his grip. I looked at him in astonishment as Reginald glanced around the room, making sure no one was looking. He brought his other hand to my face, and a flame shot up from his index finger.

"If you are even remotely curious to find out how I'm doing this and about your ancestry, I'll leave my card with a time and place to meet. The decision is yours, but if you don't show, you'll never hear from me again, and the opportunity to be so much more than you are now will have passed." Reginald threw the card on the table, picked up his briefcase, and left the bar.

The next day, I was called to the Sergeant Major's office, where a man in civilian clothes was waiting. The Major left the office, giving us privacy, and the man explained that they had been watching Mr. Wayne for quite a while and thought I was the perfect candidate to gather more information. The rest was history.

~⚜~

The letter departments in the government, CIA, FBI, etcetera, knew nothing about the Aurathions.

The organization I had become a part of was hidden so deep that once you became a member, only death saw you leave. Their knowledge of the Aurathion people and what amounted to an invasion was gained late in the game after the Aurathions were already well-established in this world. Several military personnel had Aurathion ancestry, but none had my special training, so I was recruited to gather information about their culture and technology. Sometimes, I felt that my superiors had difficulty swallowing the information I passed on about Aurathions' abilities.

My reports read like comic books, and I sometimes had trouble processing them, even though I had witnessed it all firsthand. I felt like everything had been going well until I met Reverie. Not growing up as Aurathion, I was stunned at how powerful the pull was to her. I had researched Factions and how they connected, but my research had made it seem more clinical and not so emotional or instinctual.

I hadn't put Reverie in any of my reports so far. My loyalty to this country had never been questioned, but I found that my feelings for Reverie superseded everything. My first instinct was to protect her at all costs, and so far, I hadn't been able to overcome it.

Nathan had been gone for a couple of weeks, and I could tell it was taking a toll on her. The guy was a lunatic, but I admired his loyalty to Reverie. Nathan was also new to this world, but took everything in stride, focusing entirely on his Nexus. I envied him because he could explore his new circumstances and owed nothing to anybody.

I was curious about my initiation and excited to discover what challenges would be thrown at me. I wouldn't be in this position if I didn't thrive on the impossible. The level of physical fitness was crazy, and I was here for it. In fact, I loved everything about my new culture and the possibilities it offered. Only the love I felt for my parents and my country kept me on track and the knowledge that I had no choice but to continue my mission unless I wanted to disappear.

I had kept my distance from Reverie for the last few weeks, only observing her from a distance. I had seen her relationship with the twins developing and knew they would be made a part of her Faction. I'd also seen Storm following her everywhere. I knew she wasn't fully aware of how extensive Storm's obsession was, but calling it stalking was not enough. What I couldn't understand was why her scary Fellat allowed it. (I'd have loved to see the looks on my superiors' faces at finding out about the Fellat species and their level of intelligence.) Of course, I had left out Reverie's involvement with the beast.

I quietly entered the workout room and jumped on the treadmill to warm up. I was almost finished with my five miles when I saw Kristine slip down the hallway toward Storm's office. She didn't see me, so I quietly stepped off the treadmill and followed her. Staying in the shadows, I stepped close to Storm's door to see if I could find out why she was there so early. I didn't trust either of them, and lying to myself, I pretended it was for the organization and not Reverie.

"What the fuck do you want now?" Storm growled out.

"I want to know when you're going to get rid of that

bitch! She in no way, deserves a Fellat. There must be some-thing wrong with the animal to bind itself to someone so inferior. I'm sick of everyone acting like she's something special." I heard the crazy bitch stomp her foot like a three-year-old.

There was a brief silence. "I'm amazed that you believe I give a shit about your petty issues. Your mother didn't do you any favors, spoiling you like she did. It gave you a false sense of self-importance." I heard him push his chair back, then footsteps stopping near where I thought Kristine was standing. "The best advice I can give you is to stay the fuck out of my office. I'm meeting with Reverie after lunch today, and I don't need you fucking up my plans."

I heard a squeal and took a chance, gazing through the tiny crack in the door. I saw Storm had grabbed Kristine's chin and leaned in close. "If you do anything to jeopardize what I've put in place, don't think your being my stepsister will save you. I'm going to warn you one last time, don't seek me out and stay the fuck away from Reverie." He shook her face and then released her.

I could see the marks on her chin from Storm's fingers. Wow, there's not much sibling love between these two. I slipped back into the shadows just in time to see Kristine storm out of the office with tears running down her face. As I returned to the workout room, I knew I would be following Reverie to her meeting with Storm. I had no idea what the asshole was planning, but Reverie wouldn't be facing it alone.

CHAPTER 25

REVERIE

I opened my eyes to hazy sunlight shining in through my window. I couldn't believe that I had slept all night. Since Nathan had been gone, I usually only got three or four hours of sleep.

Sitting up, I yawned and rubbed my eyes. Pantar was already gone. He probably went hunting again this morning. Taking Zane's shirt off, I brought it up to my nose and inhaled deeply. His smell comforted me. I knew it was the reason I was able to go back to sleep after the strange dream I'd had about Nathan. I folded his shirt and placed it under my pillow.

Grabbing my robe, I headed to the bathroom to shower. Chloe must still be sleeping because I didn't smell coffee or hear her moving around. I turned the water on as close to scalding as possible and let the water cascade over me. Thinking back on my night with the twins, I couldn't help but smile. Their acceptance just cemented my feelings, and I knew they were meant to be mine. Knowing about my ability to bond without the ritual should've made them want to take things slower. Not informing the Council of the incident was risky and could put them and their families in danger. But if anything, it seemed to excite them more.

Now, if only my psycho would return. The ache I felt at his absence was intense. I knew I loved him, but didn't realize how much his presence comforted me. Knowing he always had my back gave me an undeniable sense of security. Hopefully, bonding with the twins would strengthen me enough to communicate with him and find out what the hell was going on. He should have been back by now. The only thing keeping me from losing it completely was Zeke and Zane, and knowing that if he had been killed, I would feel it.

Getting out of the shower, I threw my long, dark hair up in a towel, slipped on my robe, and went to my room to get dressed. These days, my clothing choices were repetitious. My hair was the only thing I changed. Today, I wore Viking braids. My mother had taught me to do them a few years ago. Mom said that she wore them during battle, and since I was meeting with ShitStorm later today, I felt like the hairstyle was appropriate.

Looking in the mirror, I was satisfied with the result. I grabbed my bag and left the room, almost running into Chloe.

"Hey girl, you look ready to kick some serious ass! You've got to teach me how to braid like that." Chloe smiled, heading into the kitchen to make coffee.

"How about I do your hair tonight before meeting my parents?" I smirked, waiting for the explosion.

"Yeah, that sounds……. WHAT??!!!! I'm meeting your parents? Bitch, you better explain!" Chloe ran over to me and grabbed my shoulders, shaking the shit out of me.

"Calm down and quit shaking me before you give me

whiplash!" I was laughing so hard I could barely speak. "I wanted to introduce your brothers to them, and we thought you might want to tag along."

"Hell yes, I do! Oh shit, I should probably skip class so I can decide what to wear. Should I bring a gift? What does your mom like? I bet she would love some donuts from Java and Jam! I should head there now. See you later, my most favorite person in the world, except for your mother," she slammed the door behind her. I stood there with my mouth hanging open, left silent in the wake of Hurricane Chloe. It was amazing that she had that much energy before coffee.

I waited for the coffee, grabbed a to-go cup, and left for class. I wanted to get there early and maybe grab a seat by Jet. He'd kept his distance lately, and I wanted to check in with him. The fact that he was a found Passive concerned me and was part of why I had agreed to help Instructor Storm. Not that Jet needed any help in that area. He zipped through the courses almost as fast as I did. As good as he was, it seemed like he might have had some kind of training.

Unfortunately, initiation wasn't just about physical skills. Knowledge of other dimensions was also necessary, as well as past initiations. I wanted to help him with these things if he'd let me. I was just going to ignore the reason I was so concerned.

Leaving my building, I saw Zeke waiting, holding a small white bag.

"Hey, handsome, how long have you been out here?"

He smiled and pulled me in for a hug. "Not long." After squeezing me hard, he handed me the bag. Opening it, I could immediately smell the delicious aroma of glazed donut holes.

"I wanted to make sure you had breakfast before class. I

know you haven't been eating right since Nathan was taken." Zeke gave me a concerned look.

I went up on my tiptoes and kissed him. "Thank you. It's very thoughtful."

He immediately pulled me back in for a longer kiss. "It's not hard to be thoughtful when you're always on my mind. Are you headed to history?"

"Yes, I thought I'd get there early and see if Jet needs help with anything." I dug into the bag and ate one of the delicious little dough balls.

"I'll walk you." He took the bag from me and popped a donut hole in his mouth.

"Hey, I thought you bought those for me?" I grabbed the bag back.

"I did, but I made sure there was enough to share." He winked. "I may have had an ulterior motive."

"And just what would that be?" I smiled at him.

"Other than seeing your beautiful face, I wondered how Chloe took the news of meeting your parents." He grinned.

I laughed, "I didn't get another word in after giving her the news. She started talking a mile a minute and headed out the door."

"I can't wait to see her reaction when she meets them. Zane and I made a bet. He's taking the speechless option, and I'm going with verbal diarrhea." He waggled his eyebrows.

I punched him in the arm. "Hey, watch it. That's my friend you're talking about."

Zeke rubbed his arm and grinned. "Holy hell, that's quite a punch you have. My girl is strong!" He looked proud, like he was personally responsible for that.

"You got that right, so you better be sweet to Chloe, or else." I held up my fist and growled. I tried to keep a serious face, but when he suddenly crossed his eyes at me, it was so out of character that I started laughing.

"We're her big brothers, and she expects us to be assholes. If we weren't, she'd be disappointed." He said innocently.

"Sure, she would." I smirked.

By the time we reached my class, we had finished the donut holes. Zeke took the bag and threw it away.

"I'll see you at lunch. Zane will be here to walk you to Biology."

"Y'all know I can get to class fine on my own." I reached up to cup his cheek.

Turning his head to kiss my palm, he said, "We know you can, but it makes us feel better to do it. You wouldn't deny us that, would you?" Zeke pouted. He could pass for Zane with that pout and flirty eyes.

"I don't think I'm going to be able to deny y'all anything." I sighed.

"Good." He leaned down to kiss the tip of my nose, then turned and walked away. I continued to stand there, staring at his ass, completely mesmerized. I tilted my head to the right, then the left. Yep, it looked damn good from any angle.

"Hey Bitch! Quit staring at my brother's ass." Chloe jerked me into the classroom.

"Where the hell did you come from? I thought you were skipping class?" I held my hand to my chest and tried to keep my heart from jumping ship.

"Nope, I decided not to deprive you of my company." She rolled her eyes. "I called your name, but you couldn't tear your eyes away from Thing One's booty." She pulled on my braid. "All of us Moons are blessed with exceptional glutes." She slapped her ass and a guy walking in behind us tripped over his feet. She waggled her eyebrows. "Now come on, Jet's saving us a seat. Let's hurry before the thirsty bitches steal it."

I followed behind her, laughing. I didn't even try to deny the accusation. Thing One's booty was worth staring at. Although to be fair, Thing Two's booty was just as nice.

Jet watched us walk his way and stood, motioning for me to take the seat next to him, putting Chloe on his other side next to the aisle. This was a surprising turn of events, since he had been avoiding me for weeks.

"It's about time you got to class. I've been saving these seats for a while," Jet said, his eyes darting around the room like he was looking for something.

"Are you alright?" I observed him in concern, he looked a little stressed.

"Yes, I'm fine. Why wouldn't I be?" He glanced in my direction but continued to watch our surroundings with narrowed eyes.

"I don't know. But you're looking around the room like you expect us to be attacked at any time." Chloe was watching him in concern.

He turned to Chloe and started to reply, but stiffened when Storm walked through the door, closing it behind him. I was surprised at Storm's appearance, too.

"Hello, class. I'm lecturing in Professor Austin's place today. We have a lot to cover, so please take your seats." Storm smirked, and I could swear I heard panties dropping. I would admit he was handsome, especially today. He wore jeans and a black Henley, his dark hair brushed back from his face, touching the top of his shoulders in tousled waves, like he frequently ran his fingers through it. His green eyes were piercing, his very presence demanding attention.

Stepping behind the podium, he began, "Today, I want to talk about the ritual we perform when Passives are trying to form or become part of a Faction. The ritual is performed here, at Emberhold, but in special cases, and with the Council's permission, the ritual can be performed in other settings. It's been vital to Aurathions for centuries to bond Passives together and reveal the center of a Faction, the Nexus. I'm sure most of our born Passive students have looked forward to performing it and having their abilities revealed. Found Passives have probably heard many accounts of what it is and how it's performed, but today, I'll give you the facts, so you know what to expect."

The class was focused entirely on him. Their attention was hanging on his every word. "Dionysus is commonly known as the Greek god of winemaking, fertility, ritual madness, and religious ecstasy. What is unknown to humans is that he was an Aurathion that had the ability of potion making and was Nexus to his Faction. He was only worshipped after Aurathions began visiting this world through portals. A few years after his Faction was formed, Dionysus mixed a powerful potion, golden in color, that Aurathions named the wine of Dionysus, which became an integral part of binding Passives together. A knife made of pure silver is used to cut each Passive's palm. They then join hands over the Kapala, a small skull cup also made of silver and covered in precious Aurathion stones. After, the Kapala is half full of their combined blood, a drop of the wine of Dionysus is added. If they're compatible and one Passive is Nexus, the liquid in the bowel will turn fully golden."

"What happens if they aren't compatible, and neither are Nexus?" A student in the front row asked.

Looking annoyed at the interruption, he continued, "If they aren't compatible, and neither is Nexus, then the blood will remain just that— blood." Storm strolled from behind the podium and leaned against Professor Austin's desk. "All that I've explained is true and part of why the war was fought. A significant number of the population in our world was growing restless. Fewer Nexus have been born as the years have passed, leaving many Passives no choice but to abandon hope of ever gaining their abilities. A serum was invented that allowed babies to access these abilities if administered during pregnancy- without the ritual or a Nexus." He paused as a few of the students gasped at this revelation. "The Aurathions, now called Dark Faction, didn't think it was fair that the serum was only available to embryos and wanted to see if it would work on Aurathions of different ages." You could've heard a pin drop, most Aurathions knew nothing about any of this. "Does anyone know why the serum wasn't entirely successful on adult Passives?"

I knew the answer but didn't raise my hand. I felt like this lesson had taken a weird tone and had no idea where he was going with this. He looked around the room in expectation. I was surprised when Chloe raised her hand.

Storm nodded for her to speak, "Their abilities became unstable without a Nexus to balance them. Many lost their minds, and some even committed suicide."

"You're partly correct, Miss Moon, but that's not the entire story. The General of the Tempest Faction didn't show any signs of insanity and did, in fact, plan and execute the removal of all Factions that didn't agree with his stance." He stared out at the class like he was waiting for something.

I couldn't contain myself. "I think his grasp on sanity is debatable. He did betray his people and start a war."

Storm looked pleased by my response. "I suppose that's true, but it depends on which side you were on, now, doesn't it? If you were part of a Faction and already had your abilities, could you really judge what they did?"

"Yes, I wouldn't ever cause chaos and grief for my people just to benefit myself. The loss of life and the destruction of our world weren't worth the price. The serum was already proven to work on babies, and our future was looking bright, but greedy, corrupt Aurathions ruined that." I spoke passionately, enraged by his words.

Storm smirked, but looked oddly proud. "Maybe, maybe not. You'll never know what you would do because you already know you're a Nexus and won't ever have to live without your abilities. It's impossible to judge them when you'll never walk in their shoes."

When I remained quiet, he continued, "Since it looks like Miss Hawthorne doesn't have a response to that, I'll continue my lecture." I heard some tittering from his fan club in the front row. They were all just being shitty because they didn't get to sit by Jet. I really hoped every single one of them developed hemorrhoids as big as their head.

"All of this could have been prevented if we still had access to scrolls before Dionysus's time. Most of them were destroyed in a fire that some believe was done purposely. Stories have been passed down that imply our Aurathion Ancestors didn't need a ritual. That we, in fact, just needed a simple blood exchange with a Nexus to bond into our Faction." I couldn't contain the gasp that escaped me at hearing this.

Storm stared directly at me and continued, "My family was lucky enough to obtain a few scrolls that were still partially intact. We were able to interpret a few of them and they allude to the loss of these abilities for reasons we're just not sure of. They also refer to a hundred years with no new Factions until Dionysus formed his. The stunning part is that Dionysus formed his Faction years before he conjured his potion. In fact, some scholars believe that the potion Dionysus conjured was successful because it contained his blood."

The class was completely silent, it felt like everyone was holding their breath. "It's true that the serum was invented to help Aurathions have access to their abilities without needing a Nexus to stabilize them. What isn't known is that we're running out of the wine of Dionysus and when we do, unless a Nexus is found with blood as powerful as his, able to create a Faction without the ritual, our race will die out."

CHAPTER 26

REVERIE

I felt like I was going to pass out. My breathing became erratic, and sweat broke out on my forehead. Just when I felt my vision narrowing, Jet leaned down and whispered in my ear, rubbing his massive hand up and down my back. "Breathe with me, big breath in, and exhale. That's it. Take another deep breath and now exhale."

The soothing timber of his voice combined with the heat from his hand on my back, and I found myself calming and able to breathe. When I finally tuned back into my surroundings, no one else had noticed my reaction because the class had exploded into chaos. Panicked questions were being slung at Storm, and some students were even crying.

"Are you back with me, precious girl?" Jet asked, still rubbing my back in a soothing manner.

"Yes, thank you. I've never heard that information before, and it shocked me." I gave him a small smile. Did he realize he had called me precious? Terms of endearment spoken in that growly voice should be outlawed.

"What the actual fuck is he talking about?" Chloe leaned

forward, eyes widened in panic. "I've never heard about a shortage of D's wine, and I grew up in a town of Aurathions. If it's true, this will cause a full-blown panic."

"My parents have never said anything about this. But I bet the Council is aware of it. If Storm's family is the only ones with access to the scrolls, then I bet there' are a lot of things they're keeping to themselves." I leaned my head closer to Chloe. "We'll talk to my parents about it tonight."

"You're going to your parents' house tonight?" Jet questioned.

Damn it. I was so focused on Chloe that I didn't pay attention to what I was saying. "Yes, but please don't say anything. We aren't exactly getting permission."

"I won't say a thing," Jet assured me. Before I could sigh in relief, Jet continued, "As long as you bring me with you."

"What?" I looked at him in disbelief.

"I said that I won't say a word to anybody as long as you take me with you." He repeated, not apologetic in the least.

Chloe appeared just as shocked as I was by his request.

"Why do you want to go?"

"I'm new to this world, and I want to be there when Reverie questions them about what Storm has revealed." He looked at Storm, still fielding questions, with a death glare. What was that about?

"I can just get with you tomorrow and tell you what was said." I tried to reason with him. There were many other things I needed to discuss with my parents that couldn't be said in front of Jet.

"No, I want to hear it for myself." Jet transferred his gaze to me. He could be extremely intimidating when he wanted to. Too bad for him Grumpy raised me.

"I thought you were my friend. I can't believe you're

blackmailing me to get what you want." This guy had some balls.

"Believe it. You wouldn't take me otherwise, and I want to go." Jet didn't seem to be the least bit intimidated by me, either.

"Fine. Meet us in our dorm at six o'clock. Don't be late, or I'll leave your ass." I huffed out.

"Don't worry, I won't be late." The bell rang, and Jet headed straight for the door without saying another word.

"What the fuck? He's always been cold, but I didn't think blackmail was in his wheelhouse—good looks and possibly a little villain sprinkled in. Girl, you better tie that up, literally. He seems like a freak." Chloe fanned her face.

I threw my head back and laughed despite still being pissed at Jet. I got a lot of heated looks from students who were still in panic mode. Even Storm looked at me in confusion. I guess it did look bad when I was already Nexus and didn't seem to care about what Storm had said.

"Chloe, you're going to get me drawn and quartered for laughing at a time like this."

"Nah, they'll all be too busy kissing your ass trying to get into your Faction. Knowing you're Nexus, if the shortage is real, then there won't be a problem letting you perform the ritual with other Passives. It won't feel like a possible waste of D's wine. I wonder if that's why we have to wait until after initiation to form Factions. No use wasting it if we may die."

"It probably is. I'm sure I won't be allowed any other members until I return, either." I sighed, exhausted by everything.

Chloe and I gathered our things, but before we could leave, I heard Storm call out, "Don't forget our meeting. I'll be waiting in my office before workouts start."

I nodded my head but just kept walking with Chloe at my side. Zane was waiting outside the classroom for us.

"What the hell happened in there? Everyone coming out was hysterical. Even stone-faced Jet looked upset." He leaned down to kiss me and then grabbed my hand heading in the direction of my biology class.

Chloe hooked her arm with mine. "First off, Professor Austin was replaced today by Storm, and boy, did his lecture give us a good kick in the nuts."

Zane smirked. "Do we need to have a talk with you about boys and girls and how they differ?"

"It's just a figure of speech, dick." Chloe glared at him.

God, I loved this family. No matter how upset I was, they could always make me laugh.

"Anyway, he just casually put out there that D's wine was running short because the main ingredient is Dionysus's blood, and since he's been dead for several hundred years, there won't be anymore." Chloe took a deep breath and then blew it out.

"What the fuck? How can that be the first any of us heard of this?" Zane looked stunned.

"He also told us that in the scrolls his family possesses, before D's wine, there hadn't been any Faction formed for several hundred years. Leading them to conclude that Dionysus formed his Faction with only a blood exchange. The only hope for Passives seems to be finding someone with that same ability." I gave Zane a wide-eyed stare.

"Well, good luck with that. I didn't even know that was possible until today. The chances of that are about as slim as me meeting Liam Hemsworth in a bar, falling on his dick, finding out he's Aurathion, and his ability is to give orgasms by pointing his finger at me." Chloe laughed, realizing no one was laughing with her, she made a face at me. "What, like you've never had that same exact fantasy?"

"I can't give you orgasms by just pointing my finger, but I can give them in sixty seconds or less, using my finger." Zane winked at me. Pulling me close, he whispered, "No need to fantasize about anybody not in your Faction. At least two stone-cold studs surround you."

Once again, I was laughing when I should have been panicking. How in the fuck was it possible to be turned on and amused all at the same time? Hearing Chloe gagging just made me laugh harder.

Zane walked us to our classroom door. "I'm going to talk to Zeke and let him know what's going on."

"There's one more tiny detail I forgot to tell you." I ducked my head and then looked up at Zane through my lashes.

"I'll see you inside, sister," Chloe smirked.

What an ass. She could have hung around until I broke the news that Jet was tagging along.

"What's up, and why am I getting flirty eyes?" Zane asked suspiciously.

"Well Jet's-"

"I'm going with you to Reverie's parents." Jet walked by and entered the classroom like he didn't just drop a bomb.

"Why in the fuck is he going with us, and how did he know we were going in the first place?" Zane asked between gritted teeth.

"I may have accidentally mentioned it in front of him. You can't blame me because I was a little distracted by the crap that ShitStorm had just told us!" I whisper yelled.

"Calm down, I'm not blaming you." He ran his fingers through his scarlet curls. "There are things we need to discuss that he doesn't need to hear." He paused and then pulled me into his arms. "Is there a possibility he does need to hear it?"

I pulled back to see his face. "Why would he need to hear it?"

"I know we haven't known each other long, but I pay much closer attention than you think I do. You look at Jet the same way you look at me, Zeke, and Nathan." He smiled and leaned down to steal a kiss, letting me know he was fine with it. I didn't know what to say. I guess when in doubt, the truth was best.

"I'm not sure. I get the same feeling when I'm with him as when I met all of you, but I've been trying to ignore it. He's so aloof most of the time I'm not sure he feels what I do."

"Believe me, he feels it. He's always watching you and even sitting in the middle of his fan club, his eyes follow you everywhere you go. You have to remember that he's new to all of this and may not realize what his feelings mean." Zane kissed the tip of my nose.

"Well, it'll have to go on the back burner. We need to figure out what the hell is going on and how we're going to deal with it all. Maybe I need to let the Council know what happened with Nathan because if my blood can help my people, then I have to do it." I looked up at Zane and tried to smile.

"Let's talk to your parents before we make any decisions. They know the Council a lot better than we do." He smiled at me reassuringly. "Now get to class, and don't worry about it. That's what we're for." Zane leaned down and gave me one more soft kiss.

I entered the classroom and took my seat beside Chloe. I saw Jet was surrounded by the usual suspects, trying to get his attention. Right now, I was glad for it because I didn't have anything to say to the giant asshole.

I missed Nathan so much it was painful. I needed my psycho to come home to me. People who didn't know him thought he never took things seriously, but his advice was invaluable to me. He never failed to make me feel better, and I trusted he always wanted the best for me. I just prayed he was okay. I didn't want to do this life without him.

"It's going to be OK, bestie. We'll figure everything out, and that crazy man of yours will be back before you know it." Chloe put her hand on my arm.

I laid my hand on Chloe's. "What would I do without you, Moon?"

"Since I'm going to be your sister-in-law soon, you'll never have to find out." Chloe smiled reassuringly. "I have one question since we're going to your childhood home tonight."

"What's that?" I asked.

"Does your bedroom have enough room for activities?" Chloe smirked.

This girl and her obsession with the movie *Stepbrothers* never failed to make me smile. Once again, this incredible redhead brought me laughter when I was close to tears. What more could you want in a friend?

CHAPTER 27
OREN

I whistled as I walked toward my office. What an excellent time to be alive. I honestly didn't know how my day could get any better. The look on Reverie's face after my big revelation was fantastic. I knew my father would be pissed I shared that information, but I could give a fuck less about that old bastard's opinion. The agenda that was in the works was my own and didn't include the fucked-up Faction that raised me. After the things that had been done to me as a child, any feelings I had for my parents were long dead.

Entering my office, I was surprised to see Pantar stretched out on my floor. Shutting the door behind me, I leaned back in my chair and waited to see what he had to say.

Rising slowly to his feet and showing all his sharp teeth in a jaw-cracking yawn, Pantar turned his gaze to me.

"Is the complicated web you are weaving coming together as you expected?"

"I'm not sure I want to tell you. You haven't been subtle in your favoritism to your newly bonded." I crossed my arms behind my head.

"It is not just favoritism. She is unequivocally my favorite." Pantar smiled, displaying those deadly teeth.

"Ouch! That stings, my old friend." I grinned, contradicting the hurt in my voice.

"I think you lie, Storm. You care not that my loyalty is to your Nexus."

"So, all the secrets are coming out?" My grin grew even more prominent.

"There have never been secrets between us. Luckily, I know your intentions and approve of most of them. I would prefer you go about them differently, but our goals are the same." Pantar leveled a look at me.

"I'm sure you would, but just because she's going to be my Nexus doesn't mean I won't put her through shit to make sure she's strong enough to deal with what's coming. Her other bonded are too blinded by their feelings for her. I want her survival more than her approval." I smiled wryly.

"My pack has passed down stories from days long past, and I am glad you understand more about the Factions of old. When I was observing your lecture, I noticed you left out some information."

Once again, a grin graced my face. "I can't tell her all of my secrets if I want her as my Nexus sooner rather than later."

"Tread carefully, my friend. Her other Faction members aren't going to forgive easily, and neither is she." He brushed by me, stopping to lick the side of my face with his rough tongue.

I narrowed my eyes at him and wiped my face. "The information I found leads me to believe she will forgive way quicker than her Faction might, but I can deal with them.

With her as our focus, we will come together to protect our center."

"I hope all goes as you plan, Storm. I must check on Reverie and continue hunting to strengthen my skills." Pantar was gone in the blink of an eye.

Well, that went much better than expected. I knew Pantar disagreed with my methods, but acknowledged they had a purpose. Things were on the horizon that would require every bit of my ruthlessness and cunning to keep my Faction intact.

Until now, everything had been to test Reverie's ability to deal with adversity. If I am correct about things to come, she would need every bit of the stubbornness and strength her sexy body contained...... and what a body it was. Those eyes were liquid gold, and when she trained them on me, even in anger, I felt chills up and down my spine. Not to mention I could drive nails into concrete with my dick when I watched her complete the courses like they were nothing. Reverie was my perfect match and here, just in time to save me. Some would say it was luck, but luck had fuck all to do with it. I made shit happen. I didn't wait around like a bitch.

Whether I deserved it or not, I was eager to complete my Faction. Reverie had begun to call the strongest to her soon after she arrived. I knew she wasn't aware of this, but it didn't change the truth. I approved of all her choices. Fortunately, otherwise I would have been forced to make some hard decisions. No weakness could be allowed in a Faction I would be a part of.

Jet was interesting. I had observed him extensively, and I knew Jet's secret. His allegiance was divided, but I knew that his loyalty would lie solely with his Faction as soon as the bond was complete. More importantly, his Nexus. Jet's contacts may come in handy if shit goes down as I expect it to. His ability to integrate into the Aurathion culture so quickly impressed me, along with his athleticism in the obstacle courses. He was going to be an impressive Faction brother.

Reverie's first Faction member initially concerned me. However, on closer observation, his loyalty and strength became obvious. Nathan could be vicious and, he had little doubt, a killer when defending his 'Nexi'. I looked forward to teaching him more discretion at the first opportunity. The nickname didn't matter now, but other things would. Plus, I owed the little shit for the punch in the face. Nathan and I would probably have to take a turn in the Arena, and I was looking forward to it. I knew I was going to end up being Reverie's bitch, but I'd be damned if I was going to wear a t-shirt announcing it to the world. Some things needed to be kept on the down-low for the sake of my reputation.

The twins were a bonus. We had been good friends before I was forced to put distance between us. I expected their abilities to be tremendous and help us through the days ahead. They were both loyal to the extreme and almost as ruthless as me. I knew they would be invaluable in helping our Faction work together as a unit. It was vital that we accomplished that, the future of Aurathion and humankind might depend on it.

I felt like everything was coming together on schedule. I just hoped things would hold off until we were ready. My sources thought it would only be a matter of weeks, possibly even days.

Reverie was due in my office soon, and I needed to decide what to do with the information I'd found out last night. The ability to become invisible had come in handy before, but nothing like it did yesterday. I couldn't stop smiling when I thought about her reaction to my lecture, I was sure she had no idea it was a warning. I wanted her to begin to wrap her mind around how important she was and, if I was honest, see how she handled the information. I couldn't believe she was the one my father had been searching for.

This changed things and made it even more critical for us to complete the bond. Now that I knew she didn't need the ritual, I had to devise a way to initiate our joining, with or without her consent. The completion of our Faction needed to happen sooner rather than later, and I was sure that as soon as I bonded with Reverie, the rest of her guys would insist on following me. I was counting on it.

My mouth curled up in a sinister smile. I had just decided on a plan of action. My meeting with Reverie was going to be fun. If everything went as I wanted, I would meet Reverie's family as a member of her Faction. The next few hours were going to be life changing. However, I doubted my future Faction would enjoy it as much as I would.

I hurried out of my office. I had a few tweaks to make before Reverie arrived. They better buckle the fuck up. Daddy was coming home. My laugh echoed down the hallway at the thought.

CHAPTER 28
REVERIE

I headed to the cafeteria with Chloe. I needed to find some calm before the ShitStorm. The corners of my mouth turned up in a tiny smile. That was funny, no matter who you are. I took my laughs where I could these days. Since Nathan had been taken, it was hard to smile, and the longer he was absent, the harder it became.

Emberhold had taken two students from biology for initiation. Even though it was becoming more common now, it still upset everyone. Passives had been together long enough now that they had developed friendships, so tensions were high, waiting to see who was next.

I was startled out of my thoughts when Chloe suddenly stopped in front of me and turned and flicked my forehead.

"What the actual hell, Chloe?" I rubbed the spot on my head and looked at her in confusion.

"You need to get out of your head. You're welcome! That's what besties are for." Chloe smirked as she started walking again. I rolled my eyes and took off after my bestie. Hearing me speed up, Chloe looked behind her. Her eyes widened, and she started laughing as she broke into a run. "What are you doing, Bestie?!!"

"Getting out of my head!" I laughed as I reached for Chloe's shirt. Right before I grabbed it, I was pulled off my feet. Apparently, my men thought since I was fun sized, it was okay to pick me up whenever they wanted.

"What's going on with my two favorite girls?" Zane grinned, kissing me on the head before setting me back on my feet.

"Did he just call us girls?" Chloe winked at me when he turned his head.

"You know, I think he did. The question is, what should we do about it?" I walked over to Chloe, and we both turned to face Zane.

"I clearly misspoke. You're both women, and your behavior reinforces that." Zane tried to appear sincere, while obviously laughing at us.

"I feel like he's trying to placate us," I gave Zane the stink eye.

"I agree, and as strong, independent women, we need to show him the error of his ways." Chloe whispered in my ear, "I'm going to do absolutely nothing."

My eyes widened, and I started laughing. "You're completely diabolical, and I love it."

"Hey now, you two need to take a breath and remember who you're talking to. Chloe, you know I'm the prank king in our family. You and Reverie don't want to start something you can't finish." Zane was starting to sound a little nervous.

"You're completely right, and we're just going to drop the whole thing." Chloe nudged me with her elbow.

"I saw that, and I'll be on high alert. Just be sure you're ready for retaliation." Zane walked up and turned me in the direction of the cafeteria, slapping me on the ass.

I frowned at him, rubbing my butt to get the sting out. "You Moons are a violent family."

Zeke met our group at the entrance to the cafeteria and took over the rubbing of my ass. "Those Moons are, but I'm not. I'll be glad to massage the ache out later tonight. Now, come take the seat I saved you, and I'll get you something to eat."

I turned to follow Zeke, sticking my tongue out at Zane. Chloe laughed and put her arm through Zane's.

"Come on, brother. You clearly need to watch and learn from your eldest sibling."

"Just by a few minutes, and I can promise you I don't need any tips on how to treat my woman." Zane glowered at his sister.

Chloe just laughed and pulled him toward our table. After I had taken my seat, Zane leaned over to kiss me on the head, and left to get his food.

"So, the plan is to do nothing?" I smirked at my friend, who could give Dr. Evil a run for his money.

Chloe giggled, "He'll be way more tortured anticipating what we might do than by anything we actually did."

"You are an evil genius." I died laughing. "I do feel a little bad for him because he didn't do anything wrong."

"He loves things like this. Plus, I know you could do with a distraction, and this is the best I can do." Chloe laid her head on my shoulder.

I smiled as I leaned my head on Chloe's. I couldn't wait for Chloe to find her Faction. She was going to run them in circles.

Zane looked our way, when he saw our heads close together and both of us looking in his direction, he started frowning in suspicion.

"See, he's sweating right now, wondering what I just told

you. He won't eat or drink anything he hasn't fixed himself for weeks." Chloe booped me on the nose with a smug smile on her face. "That's how it's done."

I stared at her in amazement. "Thank the good Lord you're on my side. Your mind must be a fascinating place to be."

"You have no idea." Chloe said in complete seriousness.

Zeke returned to our table, setting a plate in front of me and Chloe. He took a seat across from his sister and leveled her with a look. "What are you planning to do to my twin?"

Chloe took a large bite of her sub sandwich and grinned at Zeke. "Not a single thing."

Zeke started laughing. "You make your big brother proud."

Returning to our table, Zane handed his twin a plate piled high with pizza, staring at us in suspicion. He sat across from me and started eating, still watching us with narrowed eyes.

Chloe leaned close and whispered, "I told you so."

I couldn't hold in my laughter when Zane threw down his food and stomped out of the cafeteria.

"Aww, come back, we didn't mean it," I yelled.

Zane flipped us off and kept walking. I was concerned that we had really upset him until Zeke started laughing.

"He's going to meet with the guy about setting up a portal for our visit with your parents tonight."

"He wants to look as pitiful as possible, hoping you'll make it up to him later." Chloe said in disgust.

I wasn't completely convinced, but took the word of the people who knew him best. After eating all my delicious spaghetti, I looked at Zeke. "I'm nervous about my meeting with Storm. Hopefully, he's not a complete dick and truly wants my help with the Passives. There were no better trainers than my fathers, and I'd love to pass on some of their advice."

Zeke inhaled a piece of pizza, I wasn't even sure he chewed it. "You can almost guarantee he's going to be a dick but, if he fucks with you too much, I'll fuck with him."

Damn, he gave good threat! I felt my blood heat at his words. Was there anything sexier than a man defending his woman? I was fully capable of protecting myself, but it was nice not to get my hands dirty.

"Quit lusting after my brother where I can see." Chloe leveled me with a look. "We're going to have to make some rules going forward. I can't digest my food if I'm gagging." She paused, then glanced at Zeke, giving me a mischievous wink. "I'd much prefer to gag in more pleasurable scenarios." She licked her spoon suggestively.

"What the fuck, Chloe! Now you've ruined my lunch." Zeke tossed his pizza on his plate in disgust. He rounded the table and kissed me. "I'll be waiting for you in the gym to find out how your meeting went." He threw his food in the trash and gave Chloe the evil eye as he left.

"Now we can enjoy our lunch in peace." Chloe dug into her pudding, grinning at me.

"You're something else. You could get rich teaching torture techniques." I stared at her in amazement.

"I've thought about it, but I prefer to share my talent with only a chosen few. Aren't you the lucky one?" She winked at me.

We both laughed, but it was cut short when we heard Kristine's whiny voice talking to her gang of ball sniffers.

"Did you see Zeke and Zane run from her? They couldn't get away fast enough. I told all of you it wouldn't be long before they realized their mistake."

Sophie started giggling. "I know. Did you see her head

straight for Jet in history this morning? It was funny when he avoided her in biology as if she had the plague or some nasty venereal disease. Somebody needs to let her know that stalking is illegal."

As they passed our table, Chloe took a big spoonful of her chocolate pudding and launched it at them. She hit Sophie right between the eyes. Sophie froze in shock as the pudding slid down her face to land on her white shirt. Everyone in the cafeteria started laughing and pointing. If it was anyone else, I would have felt sympathy for them and probably kicked the person's ass that threw it, but in Sophie's case, she just wouldn't leave well enough alone.

I stood and handed her a napkin. "Bless your heart! I hope that doesn't stain your nice shirt," I cooed in mock sympathy.

"You'd think the bitch would be getting tired of leaving the cafeteria with our food on her face." Chloe grinned.

Kristine got up in my face and said through gritted teeth, "You better be grateful there are people around. When I catch you alone, you'll regret getting on my bad side."

"There's nothing between us but air and opportunity, bitch." I smiled, spreading my arms wide.

"Come on, girls. Let's leave these two thirsty sluts alone so they can continue feeding their fat asses." Kristine growled out, shoulder-bumping me as she passed. Before leaving the cafeteria, Sophie turned and flipped us off.

"It just doesn't come off that threatening with chocolate running down her face." I smirked, sitting back down.

"True story, now let's continue to feed our fat asses so you can get to your meeting, you thirsty bitch." We both laughed, but managed to finish our meal in complete peace.

◦⚜◦

I arrived at Oren's office a little early, but he told me to come in when I knocked, sounding out of breath.

Entering his office, I saw he was performing a series of chin-ups using a bar installed in the ceiling. It was in an area that also contained a bench press and weights. Storm wore a tank showing his defined pecks and eight-pack, with his massive dick on full display in a pair of grey sweats.

I knew I was eye fucking him, but how could I be blamed when he was dressed so alluringly. He was practically begging to be objectified with that get-up. Grey sweatpants! Really, universe?

Trying to get my head on straight, I took a seat in front of his desk. Taking a deep breath, I tried to think unsexy thoughts: dog crap, vomit, old man balls.

"I'll be with you in just a minute, I'm almost done." Storm grunted out, drawing my attention back to him.

I barely heard him since I was hypnotized by the anaconda in his pants bouncing around every time he did a chin-up. It was very distracting. There was no way he had on underwear. I felt my skin heat up and knew I was probably drooling.

I closed my eyes against the tempting sight. I refused to believe he was part of my Faction. I planned on fighting this as long as possible because I couldn't imagine living with the giant asshole. I jumped when I felt him touch my arm.

"What's wrong, Hawthorne? You seem to be sweating, and your face is flushed." He asked in concern. When he touched me, goosebumps broke out, and my voice sounded breathless, much to my annoyance.

"Nothing's wrong. I'm just ready to get this meeting started."

"Well, let's not delay any longer." Instead of sitting in his chair, he sat on the desk in front of me. "First, I'd like to see if you have any suggestions regarding conditioning. Then we'll move on to training." He shifted, causing his massive dick to change position, drawing my attention since I was basically at eye level with it. As I stared, I noticed it getting hard and growing even larger. How in the actual fuck could that thing possibly get bigger? Hearing a throat clear, I looked back at Storm, "Anything bothering you? You're looking flushed again."

"Nothing at all." I rubbed the back of my neck and coughed. "So, good talk. Anything else we need to discuss?"

"We haven't discussed anything yet. Are you sure you're alright?" He stood up and put his hand on my forehead, his massive dick brushing against my shoulder. "You do feel a little hot."

I jumped up and backed toward the door. "I do feel a little funny. Maybe we should…" I ran into the door, "I mean…." I tripped over my foot. What was wrong with me? I finally got the door open. "…continue this at another time."

I was so busy fumbling with the door trying get the hell out of there that I missed the satisfied smile on Oren's face.

CHAPTER 29

REVERIE

I entered the gymnasium like my ass was on fire. I sat off to the side and started stretching. These feelings were getting extremely uncomfortable. The longer I was around men I knew were meant to be in my Faction, my resistance to them became non-existent.

It was like an illness, and it pissed me off. The drive I felt to bond with them was nothing like I had ever heard of. My mother had told me about the goosebumps and shivers but not the burning need to touch and be touched by them. The mark that appeared between my breasts was unique, too. I needed to find out what it all meant.

There were so many differences between us and what I knew of other Factions that it worried me. I tried not to dwell on it. Nathan being gone this long was my biggest concern. However, my feelings for Jet (and he-who-shall-not-be-named) were getting hard to ignore.

I had no relationship with Jet, other than friendship but, could feel my Nexus instincts pushing me toward him in a much different capacity. I wouldn't force anyone to bond with me, but maybe Jet and I needed to have a conversation. Zeke and Zane kept telling me that Jet had feelings for me and watched me when I wasn't looking. I guess it was time to woman up and find out if all that was true.

Storm was an entirely different matter. I had no idea what I was going to do about him. His behavior had changed, and I had grown to respect his brilliance in training Passives. That didn't mean I agreed with his technique, but I thought he cared more about their survival than he admitted. Still, no matter how good-looking he was, and yes, I wouldn't continue lying to myself, I didn't know what my Faction would look like with him in it. It made me a complete idiot, but I would try to delay the inevitable for as long as possible.

"Reverie. Earth to Reverie." Zane sat beside me and had apparently been trying to get my attention for a while.

"Sorry, my mind was a million miles away. You're not mad from earlier, are you?" I gave him my best attempt at puppy dog eyes, hoping it didn't make me look constipated.

"No, baby. I wasn't ever mad." He laughed. "We Moons love our prank wars. I'm just laying the groundwork for catching Chloe unaware." He picked me up and moved me between his legs, all without showing the least bit of strain. I felt my blood heat seeing that kind of forearm porn. After watching Storm work out and Zane's display of strength, I was turning into a thirsty bitch just like Kristine and Sophie had said. Zane buried his nose in my hair and inhaled deeply. "You smell so good. I'm one of the luckiest men alive, and I can't wait to complete our bond. Being inside your head and always knowing where you are will relieve most of my stress."

I turned slightly so that I could reach his mouth. He leaned down and kissed me like he hadn't seen me in years. I lost myself entirely and just enjoyed the moment, wrapped securely in Zane's strong arms.

"That's enough PDA for the moment, Miss Hawthorne. I hope you put that much enthusiasm into your performance today." Storm's voice startled me. My eyes flew open, and I saw him wink at me and then return his attention to direct Passives to the first obstacle course.

My jaw dropped, and I pushed to my feet. What was that? Had he dropped a weight on his head? Zane used his finger to close my mouth, and then narrowed his eyes on Storm.

"Did Oren just wink at you?"

"Thank God you saw that, too. I thought I'd lost my mind," I whispered, still in shock.

"Why are you whispering?" Zane whispered, grinning.

"I don't want to draw Storm's attention. If he winks at me again, I might pass out," I said, still whispering.

Zane laughed, "I think it's too late for that. Seems you already have his attention." He shook his head. "Our Faction is going to be unique." He kissed me then walked to his station, yelling at his group to line up.

～☖～

After gym, I was even more confused by Storm's actions. He didn't flirt or give me special treatment in any way. He was as much of a hard ass as he always was. I didn't want to be treated any differently, but his actions were confusing, to say the least. Maybe luck would be with me, and I could delay the inevitable a little longer.

Zane walked me back to my dorm and said he still hadn't located his portal making friend. He was worried because the guy's Faction hadn't seen him since yesterday. Zane was going to help them search for him, and much to my surprise, Jet volunteered to help as well. I wanted to believe it was out of the goodness of his heart, but I suspected it was to ensure we made it to my parents' house. I'd wanted to help, but Chloe had shown up and recruited me to decipher some ancient books she had found in the library. Thinking they could answer some questions and possibly help my Faction, I agreed.

"This is hopeless. The writing is so old that I can't make out half the words, and translating this ancient Aurathion script takes forever." Chloe whined.

We were sitting on the floor with several old books spread out on the table. Zeke brought snacks and then left to help Zane look for their friend. That guy always ensured I was fed, and I loved him for it. He was a caretaker at heart, and what a lucky woman I was that he was mine.

"We'll get it. It's just going to take time. I bet my parents can help us, and maybe they know some of the old stories of Dionysus's time." I leaned my head back on the couch. It was getting late, and we still hadn't heard from the twins.

Just then, we heard a knock. Heaving myself up, I opened the door, but nobody was there. I saw a picnic basket with a bow tied to the handle. Picking it up, I closed the door and sat the basket on the coffee table.

"Who sent that?" Chloe yawned, flicking the bow with her finger.

"I have no idea." I opened the basket and saw two eclairs, one chocolate, and the other raspberry. There were also two mason jars with what looked to be hot chocolate. Each jar had directions on a cute little tag that gave the amount of warm water or milk to pour in to get the perfect cup of chocolaty goodness.

"Wow, that's thoughtful. I bet Zeke sent it to impress you.

He's the chef in our family." Chloe pulled out the raspberry éclair, as I knew she would.

"I guess I'll take the chocolate." I sighed heavily in mock disappointment.

"Don't act like you wouldn't eat that one, anyway. We both know you have a serious weakness for anything chocolate," she narrowed her eyes at me.

Chloe opened her mouth to take a bite of her éclair, then paused. "You don't think Zane is fucking with me, do you?"

"Normally I would, but he's obviously worried about his friend, so I don't think he would take time out of his search to fuck with you." I bit into my éclair and moaned. "Damn, that's delicious."

"Screw it." Chloe joined me in the enjoyment of our unexpected treat. As I took the last bite, I licked the delicious cream filling from my fingers and then let out a massive belch.

"My compliments to the chef."

"What the hell? That was terrible." Before I could call her out on her bullshit, Chloe let out a burp that shook the walls and lasted at least thirty seconds. "Now that's how it's done." She smiled at me smugly.

"Ya basic!" I said with a straight face, trying to hide my amazement at that manly burp. Chloe flipped me off, and we both laughed until tears poured down our faces. Chloe made our hot chocolate, and we sipped it while continuing to decipher the ancient books.

About thirty minutes later, I let out a jaw-cracking yawn, followed by Chloe's. "I'm exhausted. I say we go to bed and attempt this again tomorrow."

"I agree. I can barely keep my eyes open." Chloe yawned again.

"See you in the morning," I staggered to my room, shut the door, shed my minion pajama pants, and fell into bed.

⸙

L ater that night, I woke slightly when I felt a sting on the palm of my hand. I smelled cinnamon and embers, and those two scents triggered my internal alarm. My eyes were too heavy to open. Feeling a gentle kiss on my lips, I heard a soft whisper, "Go back to sleep, Nexus of mine."

The voice comforted me, and I fell back into a deep, dreamless sleep.

⸙

W hen I woke up the following day, I felt groggy. I had trouble getting myself out of bed, but finally made it to the shower. Turning the cold water on, I let it do its job. Thank God it was Saturday, and I didn't need to be anywhere. What in the hell is wrong with me? The water had perked me up a little, but my vision was still blurry.

I threw on some sweats, having to sit on my bed to pull my pants up. I didn't even put on a bra, pulling a t-shirt over my head, I sat back on the bed to put on my shoes. I strapped my ankle sheath on and slipped my knife in, I was groggy but not out of it enough to forget that. Heading into the kitchen to make coffee, I absently scratched my Nexus mark as I pulled two cups from the cabinet.

Chloe entered a few minutes later and didn't say a word until she took her first sip of the hot brew.

"I didn't think I was going to be able to get out of bed

until I smelled coffee. Bless you, bestie, for making it. I feel like I downed a fifth of tequila."

I opened the refrigerator to get the creamer and started scratching at my mark again. Was I getting a rash? I discreetly pulled the neck of my shirt out to see what was going on. Was that another mark? A fucking lightning bolt was in one of the spots that was previously blank. I dropped the creamer, and it spilt all over the floor.

My body felt like it was on fire, getting hotter each second as I went into a full-blown panic.

Suddenly, my fingers began to tingle, and fire shot out from them, headed directly for Chloe. We both screamed, and Chloe dropped to the floor and rolled out of the way just in time to avoid being burned alive.

Pantar suddenly appeared out of nowhere and stepped in front of the stream of fire shooting from my hands. The fire hit his side, but he didn't flinch as the flames engulfed him. I screamed again, pleading with everything in me for the fire to stop. Much to my surprise, the fire immediately disappeared.

I ran to Pantar, scared to death that I had hurt him, but when I got to him and ran my hands down his side, there were no burns or marks of any kind on him.

"Calm, Nexus, your power cannot hurt me."

I fell to my knees in relief, hugging Pantar tightly.

"What the hell is going on?"

"I'll give you one guess, my sweet Nexus." A different voice said in my head.

I felt my eyes roll back in my head, and for the first time in my life, I passed out.

CHAPTER 30
REVERIE

I woke and found myself lying on my bed with Pantar sitting beside me on alert. Seeing my eyes open he nuzzled my face encouraging me to sit up.

"What happened?" Immediately after asking the question, the memories started to flood back in. I quickly got to my knees and ran my hands down his side, making sure there weren't burn marks I missed the first time.

"Oren went through with a plan that I was not aware of. He meant well, but I don't appreciate the trauma he put my Nexus through, and he will be punished." He growled, as if to punctuate his statement.

"He's pissed with me, as I'm sure you are. Do you think you could come to my apartment so we could discuss this? Your feral roommate won't let me come into your dorm and threatened to feed me my dick if I attempted it one more time." Storm's voice had taken on a pleading tone.

"What the hell have you DONE?!!" I mentally screamed at him.

"I did what was necessary, sweet Nexus. Now come to me,"

Storm urged in a seductive voice. I felt him close the communication between us to give me privacy.

I felt lost. There was only one person who could comfort me when I was feeling this way. Maybe the one advantage of this bond would be to strengthen me enough to communicate with Nathan. Closing my eyes, I concentrated, *"Nathan... NATHAN!"* I screamed, *"Please answer me."* I begged and then started sobbing when all I got for my effort was complete silence.

I bowed my head and prayed that my sweet psycho was well and would come back to me soon. I didn't know how much longer I could stand the pain of his absence. Digging deep to find the strength I would need to deal with this situation, I turned to Pantar. "I think you have some explaining to do."

He bowed his head. *"Yes, Nexus. I do."*

I sat back on my bed and waited. I didn't like the feeling of betrayal that I felt toward Pantar now. My bond with him felt damaged, and I hated it. I could feel his regret and wanted to give him a chance to explain before I lost my shit.

"I have been a companion to Storm for several years now. He is not the villain he portrays to the world, but a product of his environment." Pantar shook his massive head, letting out a growl. *"I felt called to him and couldn't understand why, since I knew he was not Nexus. Deciding to stay by his side until I could figure it out, I followed him to Emberhold."*

I couldn't stand how dejected he looked, so I laid my hand on his neck and gave him a small smile in encouragement. *"After coming to the academy, my instincts told me this is where I needed to be. Several years later you showed up and I knew that I was destined to be your Fellat and help guide your Faction."*

"Did you know what he had planned?" I felt hurt at the thought.

Pantar shook his head. *"I knew he had something planned and warned him against doing anything that would cause you pain. This may not comfort you, but he means you no harm. In fact, his intentions are to protect you. His life has not been an easy one, so he did not go about it as he should have. I will not tell you what he has been through because that is his story to tell. Just know that my loyalty is to you first and then to those that you choose to join with."*

I thought about everything he said. I didn't think Pantar would or even could betray me purposely. "I believe you, but I'm still angry that you didn't mention having a connection with Storm."

"I regret not telling you, but I preferred not to get involved with your joining. He needed to find his own way and not use our connection. I never expected he would take the route he did." Pantar bared his teeth in anger.

Satisfied with his explanation, I attempted a smile. "I love you, but from now on, I would appreciate it if you kept me in the loop."

"I will try to be more forthcoming with information as it pertains to you." He then leaned down to nuzzle his nose in my hair. I put my arms around his neck and hugged him tightly.

"Well, I guess I better go see what Storm has to say for himself. The bond is already dragging me in his direction." I frowned, beyond pissed. Our bonding was probably inevitable, but the choice being taken away from me for a second time, was fucked. A strong Faction usually consisted of extremely headstrong people, but we needed to come to an understanding. I wouldn't tolerate my choices being taken away.

Leaving my room, I saw Chloe sitting on our couch, holding a baseball bat, frowning. Her head jerked up when I entered the room and she rushed to me, hugging me so tightly I couldn't draw a breath.

"Reverie, what in the hell happened? How in the fuck did you gain the ability of fire? Why did you pass out? I've been so worried, and Storm has been banging on the door like a fucking maniac trying to get to you. I wanted to go get my brothers, but I didn't want to leave you alone."

I extracted myself from the stranglehold Chloe had on me. "I promise we'll talk about all of that when I get back, but I need to talk to Storm first."

Proving once again that she was a great friend, she just nodded her head. "Okay, as long as you're alright. I'll talk to you when you get back."

Now it was me squeezing Chloe. "I love you and I promise to let you in on everything ASAP." Giving Chloe one last squeeze, I left to find Storm.

◦⚬◦

I entered the building that housed the teaching staff and went to the fourth floor, where Storm's apartment was located. Pantar had given me directions before he disappeared. I knocked on his door and it immediately opened. Storm pulled me inside shutting and locking the door behind me.

"I'm so glad you came, my sweet, Nex-." I balled up my fist and hit him directly in the mouth. I followed that up with a kick in the dick that sent him to his knees.

"You no good, piece of shit! Did you ever think about courting me instead of forcing the bond on me?! You don't even like me! Why would you do this?"

Trying to breathe, cupping his dick, with blood running

down his face he looked up at me. "You never would've accepted me when you found out about my family. I was dying, Reverie." He wheezed out. "I needed my Nexus sooner rather than later. Please hear me out before you hurt yourself."

"Hurt myself? You're the one lying on the floor, I think I'll be okay. Now, what is this bullshit about you dying? You look healthy to me, omitting the broke dick, I hope you're rocking now." I kicked out at him again and he grabbed my leg making me lose my balance. I tried to catch myself, but Storm wouldn't let go and caused me to fall in his lap. He wrapped both arms around me, holding me so tight I couldn't struggle.

"Stop Nexus." He whispered in my ear. "Let me show you what I can bring to this Faction." I started to struggle as he picked me up and took me to his bedroom. He laid me on the bed and when I tried to get up, I found that I couldn't move.

"What the hell? How are you doing this?"

"I'll tell you everything as soon as I show you how it can be between us." He pulled his shirt over his head, exposing a body that could only be described as divine. The eight pack he was rocking was unreal. But it was the tattoo covering his entire left arm that shocked me into silence. The entirety of his arm from shoulder to wrist was black with white cracks throughout, giving the illusion of lightning. How appropriate, considering the bolt of lightning that appeared this morning in my Nexus mark.

"Like what you see, sweet Nexus?" Storm ran his hand down his muscled chest, drawing my attention once again to his amazing body. He grinned, the blood coating his teeth from my punch to his face making him look like a savage. With his hair disheveled and piercing green eyes, he looked completely deranged. Did this crazy bastard think we were going to have sex? He might be more deranged than Nathan. I closed my eyes and turned my head to the side.

"Look at me, Nexus." I refused to give in, it was hard enough to continue fighting the newly formed bond without seeing that amazing chest and the massive tent he was rocking in those slutpants, damn it, sweatpants.

I felt fingers on my chin turning me forcefully back to him. Storm wasn't touching me physically; his power was unbelievable. I felt invisible hands pulling my shirt up and over my head, so my breasts were exposed.

My nipples immediately puckered from the cold air. Feeling the lightest of touches trail down my throat and over my breasts, goosebumps popped up all over my body.

I was beyond furious with him. He was an absolute dick and had caused a lot of misery for me and other Passives. Not to mention his crazy sister and the scary thought that his family was involved in starting the war. But the hard truth was I had been fighting how I felt about him and now with the Bond in place it was a losing battle. I could feel my desire and his inside my mind and body. I knew when I looked at him, he could see and feel all the fury and need I had bottled up inside me.

"Let me go, asshole!"

The crazy bastard smiled with pride. "My Nexus is strong, denying our bond even with every instinct you have fighting against you. I bet you could break free from my hold if you truly wanted to." Storm grinned, looking at me with such hunger I felt my blood heat in response.

He was right. I had gained the ability of fire that could only be his, so surely, I had gained this ability, too. Closing my eyes against the desire in his, I reached into that well of power, deep inside, startling when I saw the beautiful red strand encircling Nathan's green, both nestling the ball of amber power swirling in the center. It was beautiful and in the right circumstances, I would be excited to have another full Faction member. These were not the right circumstances. Focusing on the red strand I was amazed at the power that flooded my body. It was like he was Nexus too. I had lots of questions for him, but now wasn't the time.

Concentrating hard, feeling sweat pop out on my brow, I broke the hold he had on me and sprung to my feet. Knocking him on his ass, I sat on him to hold him in place as I pulled the knife from my ankle sheath and put it to his throat.

Expecting to see rage on his face, I was surprised to find him with a satisfied grin "You're perfect. Together we're going to make this Faction untouchable."

Pressing the knife to his throat, I watched a drop of blood seep out and run down his neck. Fighting the urge to lick it off, I snarled, "I'm in control now, NOT you, and I'm leaving!" I felt calloused hands slide up my naked sides, ending with them cupping my breasts and thumbs rubbing across my pointed nipples. "Stop doing that!" I growled, trying and failing to keep the desire out of my voice.

Oren leaned up, causing another drop of blood to follow the first, "Do you have control?" he asked as he narrowed his eyes. "Prove it, show me how strong my Nexus is." Caught up in the intense desire I felt, I decided to stop denying myself and take what I needed from him. After I left, he could lie here in misery and contemplate everything he'd done. It was the very least he deserved for his actions, and if I got a little pleasure out of the deal, that was even better.

I slammed my mouth to his. I could feel our bond thrumming through me, making our kiss an explosion of desire. I started grinding on his dick, putting pressure on my clit, and moaned in his mouth. Our tongues were thrusting in time to the movement of my hips. I raised my head slightly. "Touch my breasts, let me feel the ability that you seem so proud of." I threw my head back when I felt a warm tongue lap at my nipples and not the touch of hands like I was expecting. Storm's power was next level.

"That's it, Nexus. Take what you need from your Faction. Use me for your pleasure," he urged, this time speaking directly in my head. Through the bond, I could feel the pleasure he felt, and it brought my orgasm even closer.

"I'm in control of this Faction and I'll make the decisions of who I bring into it and when!" I rolled my hips and ended my statement in a long moan as my climax hit. Forcing my will on him and taking my power back felt amazing!

Feeling the heat from his gaze I was surprised to find him grinning widely. "The funny thing about control is, taking it is easy, but keeping it is another matter entirely. It's all about perception."

The knife I was holding flew from my hand and stuck in the wall behind him. I felt myself being lifted and thrown on the bed as he followed, quickly lowering his weight on me. My hands were thrown forcefully above my head and restrained by his power. He lowered his head and began licking and biting my nipples in a frenzy.

I tried to use his power against him like I did previously, but the pleasure was too much. Our connection demanded we complete our bond, and I was caught up in the intensity of the moment.

Oren licked and bit his way down my body, as I felt the rest of my clothes being removed. Hands pulled my thighs apart and I lifted my head, watching his progress. He licked into my navel and then raised his head to meet my eyes, seeing the raw need on his face, I had to look away.

"Give me those beautiful amber eyes, Nexus. I want you

watching everything I do to you." Unable to fight his command, I brought my eyes back to him. He smiled slowly in satisfaction and lowered his head to continue his journey down my body. I arched my back as I felt him lick up my slit, reveling in the moisture left by my previous orgasm.

Oren inhaled deeply. "You taste and smell divine. This is now my favorite place to be." I felt his power release my hands when he began sucking on my clit. Instead of pushing him away, I clutched his hair, pushing his head closer to me. I felt him all around me, hands in my hair, lips on my breasts, hands cupping my ass and running down my legs. I had no idea which ones were his and which were his ability. He continued his ministrations, and I moaned as I felt another orgasm cresting, right before it broke, he stopped.

"What the fu...." before I could complete the sentence, I felt him slide back up my body and plunge his massive dick into me with no warning. Giving me a minute to adjust to his size, he took my mouth in another searing kiss. As he started to move, we both moaned in unison, I felt an intense heat coming from his dick, making me clench around him in pleasure. Opening my eyes in shock, I found him grinning down at me.

"My Faction brothers are going to need to step up their game." He smiled smugly.

Just as I started to reply I felt a finger touch my clit with a shock of heat and I lost it. My orgasm was so intense I saw stars. Oren let out a shout and I felt his warm cum paint my walls, triggering yet another orgasm.

I must have passed out for a moment because when I came to, Oren had a warm rag cleaning me, then he left the room returning with a bottle of water. He helped me prop a couple of pillows behind my head. Handing me the bottle of water, Oren cleared his throat and lowered his eyes.

"You're so much more than I hoped for or deserve." He raised his head, and I could see the shine of tears in his eyes. "I'll do whatever it takes to gain your forgiveness for the things I've done, but I will never be sorry for making you mine."

I could feel his sincerity through our newly formed bond. I truly hoped I could find a way to forgive him, because he was a part of my Faction now, for better or worse.

I thought it would have been awkward between us. But as he climbed back into bed and pulled me into his arms, my last thought before drifting off to sleep, was how natural it felt. Almost like it was meant to be.

CHAPTER 31
OREN

I left Reverie sleeping in my bed and headed to the cafeteria to grab us something to eat. The need to take care of her was riding me hard. I couldn't believe that I was now part of a Faction and had a Nexus to take care of. I regretted how it came about but I didn't have time to court Reverie properly. My very life was on the line.

Reverie didn't know it, but I had put plans into place to become part of her Faction before she stepped foot on campus. Those plans changed when I slipped into the twins' apartment using one of my most useful abilities. There was a learning curve to mastering invisibility, but my father had made sure I became proficient. Remus Storm had a lot of enemies and liked to stay two steps ahead. Learning Reverie didn't need the ritual to bond made things a great deal easier.

I was at a gathering of Aurathions to celebrate the New Year when I first saw Reverie. She was only fifteen or so, and I was on a winter break from Emberhold. My father had pointed out the Hawthorne Faction. Then, of course, went into a long monologue about their disloyalty to the Aurathion people. At that time, I was just starting to realize my father was not the man I thought he was. It was my second year at the academy. I hadn't found my Nexus and was starting to get discouraged. Thanks to my father, it was critical that I find one sooner rather than later.

I heard laughter and tuned out my father's words to see a small teenager with midnight hair. She punched one of her fathers in the arm, and he picked her up and tossed her to what was obviously his twin brother. Adelaide walked up and pulled her out of his arms and stood in front of Reverie protectively. (I knew who Adelaide was, all Aurathions did.)

Suddenly, a massive tiger came out of nowhere and pounced on the two tiny females. I started forward when the tiger transformed into one of her fathers. They were all laughing, even as her other father pulled him off and thumped him on the forehead.

I felt the need to get closer to the girl, and as soon as my father turned his back, I slipped away. Staying to the shadows, I drew near enough to see her stunning amber eyes. Those eyes, combined with her midnight hair, and pale skin made her stunningly beautiful. I felt drawn to her, and when she turned my way like she could sense me there, I knew she was destined to be my Nexus.

~☙~

I had kept close track of her over the next few years until she made her way to Emberhold Academy. I knew Nathan had become part of her Faction but had assumed her mother had performed the ceremony or found someone else to do it. Imagine my surprise when I found out the truth.

I wasn't a good guy, and I knew it. Honestly, none of the guys that were going to be my Faction brothers were. Except, possibly Jet. To defeat what was coming, it was going to take every bit of ruthlessness we possessed. I hoped it would be enough. I would give my life ten times over to protect my Nexus and I knew that was the hook that would bring my Faction brothers together.

Entering the cafeteria, I threw some sandwiches and chips together. There was a cold selection of food available to students or teachers twenty-four hours a day. I had drinks in my apartment but had spent so much time following Reverie there hadn't been time to stock up on food.

Turning to head for the door, I heard my name being called.

"Oren!"

Fucking Kristine! Just great. I stopped, knowing it was useless to try and ignore her. She would just follow me back to my apartment and I didn't want any of my family to know I had become part of Reverie's Faction...yet.

"What do you want?" I sighed in exasperation.

"Well I had news, but with that attitude I don't know if I'm going to tell you." She pouted. I turned back toward the door and started walking. "Hey, where are you going? Didn't you hear that I had news?" Kristine stomped her foot. I turned around once more.

"I don't have the patience for your shit, Kristine. Either tell me or don't."

"You're no fun. I'll tell you but only because I can't tell anyone else." She walked closer and leaned in. "Mommy told me that things are beginning to come together, and it won't be long now."

I felt chills all over my body.

"When?"

"I don't know. She did say that when students went home for winter break, they were going to have quite a surprise."

Sophie walked in, halting our conversation.

"Hi Oren." She batted her eyes, not even acknowledging Kristine.

"Hey Sophie, I was just headed to talk to you. Did you see Zane on your way over?" Kristine asked, obviously annoyed with her friend.

"No, but I think Lindsy said she'd seen him earlier near the library." Sophie licked her lips, eyeing me like I was the last tampon in an all-girl's school. I knew I shouldn't have worn these damn grey sweatpants in public.

"I'm out. I know if I can catch him alone, I'll be able to convince him to stay away from that stupid Hawthorne bitch." Kristine said over her shoulder as she hurried away.

Sophie sidled closer to me, lowering her lashes. "So, do you want to come over to our dorm? Kristine will be out for a while looking for Zane."

I felt the need to throw up just from the thought.

"Fuck no I don't. I've told you more than once that I'm not interested."

Sophie stuck her lip out. "But I've been practicing, and I can swallow a whole pickle without choking." She ran her hand down my chest.

I stepped back, not being able to stand her touch. "I'm sure your digestive system thanks you. Now fuck off." I hurried away before she touched me again.

Fuck, change of plans. I had to collect the guys from the wild goose chase I'd sent them on. Things were moving faster than I had anticipated.

᠁ ⚜ ᠁

I found them regrouping in the twins' apartment. I enjoyed immensely the look on their faces when I appeared out of nowhere.

"WHAT THE FUCK?" Zane screamed like a little girl while going for the knife he kept in his boot.

"How the hell did you get in here?" Zeke growled, heading my way.

I held my hands out. "Calm the fuck down. I'll explain everything, just hear me out."

"Talk fast." Zeke demanded in his no-nonsense way.

Jet remained quiet, just observing us. He had positioned his body so that he could see everyone and keep an eye on the door in case anyone entered. Yep, military, no doubt about that.

"I'm going to explain some things, and you're going to want to kick my ass. Don't do it. We don't have time to fight with each other." I crossed my arms over my chest and narrowed my eyes.

Zeke and Zane stood side by side. I took a moment to gather my thoughts, and Zane motioned me to get on with it, always the impatient one.

"Shit is about to go down and my family is responsible. I've been gathering information, but it's gotten harder over the years. I think my father has begun to suspect I'm not on board with his plans." I relaxed my stance, but still watched the guys cautiously.

"What shit, exactly?" Zeke questioned.

"The Dark Factions are planning on invading our new world." I said, then waited for the explosion.

"What the fuck!?" Zane yelled.

"The fuck you say?!" Zeke thundered.

"What kind of timeline are we talking?" Jet asked, much calmer than the other two.

"Unfortunately, sooner rather than later." I cleared my throat, "We need to wake up my Nexus and make plans." All three guys looked confused.

"You don't have a Nexus." Zane muttered, still distracted by the news I had just delivered.

"I didn't have a Nexus, but that changed tonight." I took a small step back when Zane's eyes widened, and he immediately gave me his complete attention.

Zeke narrowed his eyes. "How did you get a Nexus tonight? There haven't been any rituals performed in several weeks, much less tonight."

Zane and Zeke looked at each other, then turned and stared at me with rage.

"What the fuck have you done?" Zeke said in a voice that raised the hair on my arms.

"I did what needed to be d-" Zane lost his shit and punched me before I could finish my sentence. I let Zane have that hit before I used another of my abilities and froze him on the spot. I knew I deserved that and more, but it would have to wait until later, if we survived what was coming.

"What the hell have you done to my brother?" Zeke grabbed me and shook me hard.

I pushed him away from me. "I'll let him go, but you two have got to get ahold of yourselves."

"Where are you? I can feel how upset you are." Reverie sounded drowsy.

I closed my eyes so I could savor the feeling of my Nexus communicating like this for the first time. I had waited years to make Reverie mine and everything I'd gone through was worth it.

"Everything will be ok, but you may want to get dressed. I'll be there soon and I'm bringing company."

"Oh shit! Okay, *I'm getting up. What the hell have you done now, Storm?"* I could hear the exasperation in her voice.

"I like when you call me Oren much better, sweet Nexus." I smiled.

"Then I suggest you earn it." Damn, she was something else, and she was mine.

I smirked, loving that sass. Even with everything that was going on, I knew how lucky I was.

"I think I earned it several times over tonight." I was jerked out of our conversation by another punch to the face. This one knocked me on my ass.

"Now unfreeze my twin, motherfucker." Zeke stood over me with his fists clenched. When he came into his abilities this bastard would be invincible. Thank fuck he was in my Faction. I waved my hand, Zane blinked his eyes and slowly looked down at me.

"I know that look, Moon, and I promise we'll have our reckoning, but we don't have time for it now."

Zeke walked over to Zane. "Come on, brother. Let's get to Reverie and make sure she's okay."

"I'm holding you to that reckoning, Storm." Zane turned and followed his brother toward the door.

I stood and wiped the blood from my nose. "Are you coming?" I asked Jet, sure I knew the answer.

"Yes, I am." Jet turned and headed out behind the twins.

Man of few words, he may have just become my favorite brother. Time to fill my Nexus in on what was going on and decide what to do next.

CHAPTER 32

REVERIE

I jumped out of bed and headed for the bathroom. I took a quick shower, but before throwing my clothes on, I took a moment to admire my mark. It was beautiful. It glowed slightly, looking more balanced with the dagger and lightning bolt on either side of the ash tree. There were three spaces left, and I felt a strong need to fill them.

I didn't know how much time had passed with me staring at my beautiful mark, but I quickly finished putting my clothes on and pulling my hair into a messy bun. Just as I walked into the living room, the door opened and Storm entered, followed by all the guys that made my heart race faster. Minus my beloved Nathan.

Storm walked up and leaned down to kiss me. I turned my head. He kissed my cheek, like that was his target all along. Then he had the gall to put his arm around me and face the guys like we were a united front.

Shaking his arm off, I moved a few steps in front of him. Zane rushed up to me, pulling me into his arms. Zeke was only steps behind and jerked me away from him, then proceeded to look me over, for what I didn't know. He looked less than thrilled seeing the hickeys and bite marks on my neck.

"Are you alright?" Zeke murmured, looking for any signs of distress on my face.

I reached up and put my hand on his face. "I'm fine, Zeke."

He pulled me into his arms and hugged the shit out of me. These Moons gave the best hugs. I couldn't wait to meet their parents.

I felt Zane move up behind me, engulfing me in the warmth of their bodies, one of my new favorite places to be.

"You may not be our Nexus yet, but we couldn't adore you any more than we do now." He was such a charmer.

"You're speaking bullshit and don't even know it. The feelings you have now will strengthen tenfold." Storm grunted.

The guys just continued holding me and didn't acknowledge him. It was obvious they were upset, and I didn't blame them. Storm had jumped the line, and both men were pissed. They'd put in the effort to court me properly and now were left on the outside looking in. I planned to correct that as soon as possible.

I saw Jet looking me over but keeping his distance.

"Are you good?" He murmured like the words were pulled out of him against his will. I nodded my head and reluctantly pulled away from the twins.

"What's going on?"

"Please everybody, take a seat and I'll try to explain." Oren gestured toward the couch.

Everyone sat down except for Jet, he moved to stand directly behind me. I immediately felt protected when the massive man took the position.

Storm stood in front of us and cleared his throat. "I explained some of this in my lecture yesterday in class." I interrupted him before he could continue speaking.

"Zane, can you please go get Chloe? I think she needs to be part of this conversation." I looked at Storm, expecting him to protest, but he remained quiet.

"Yes, I'll be right back." He left, but not before kissing me gently on the mouth, giving Storm a smug look. Storm was smart enough to let him have it.

"I brought sandwiches back for you, Nexus. Can I make you a small plate?" Storm headed toward the kitchen before I could answer.

Zeke frowned. "What kind of sandwich did you get? She prefers turkey and tomatoes with lots of mayo."

I hid my grin because I knew Zeke enjoyed the role of providing me with food and didn't appreciate Storm horning in on what he considered his responsibility.

"I've been watching her for weeks. I know what kind of sandwich she likes." Storm said over his shoulder.

"Are you people really talking about sandwiches? There are way more important things to concentrate on." Jet frowned, impatient with all the delays.

Storm turned and looked at him in admonishment. "There is no more important thing in this world or any other than caring for our Nexus."

I was a little stunned when Zeke grunted in agreement. Jet just stared at them like they were both crazy. Maybe they were but, I had to admit, I dug it. The Nexus in me preened at their words and attention.

I was used to this attitude since I was raised in the Aurathion culture. From Jet's perspective I was sure it looked ridiculous, but to Faction the health and welfare of a Nexus was of utmost importance. I grew up seeing my fathers treat my mother like she was made of glass. I remember asking my mother why they did it when they both knew how strong she was.

"They don't do it because they think I'm weak. They do it to show me they are worthy to be Faction." Mom smiled at me.

"You don't think they're worthy already?" I was mad in my *fathers' defense.*

Mom pulled me close and kissed my forehead. *"Of course they're worthy. There are no better men in Aurathia or any other world, but if it makes them happy, who am I to deny them that?"*

I understood what my mother meant now. I could feel through my connection with Oren how important it was for him to show me he cared and that all my needs were met. I couldn't imagine how intense Zeke would feel after we bonded, he was a natural caretaker.

Oren returned with my food, and although he had a lot to make up for, it was hard not to forgive him when I could feel how much I meant to him.

"Thank you." I groaned as I bit into the sandwich. It was perfect, and I hadn't realized just how hungry I was.

Storm smiled in satisfaction and in a move that was completely out of character for him, he stuck his tongue out at Zeke.

I busted out laughing but quickly covered my grin when Zeke frowned in my direction. Storm winked at me before his face regained the arrogant expression he usually wore.

Zane and Chloe came through the door at that moment. Chloe walked directly up to Storm and punched him in the face.

She then jumped up and down, cradling her hand, "Fuck, shit, damn! Your head just broke my hand, you rat bastard." Chloe groaned, narrowing her eyes at Storm like he had walked up to her and hit her on the hand with his head.

I stood and went into the kitchen putting some ice in a towel, I led Chloe to the couch and put the ice on her hand. Chloe smiled and thanked me, then continued her death glare at Storm.

"No ice for me?" Storm pouted at me while wiping the blood from his already swollen nose. Lucky for him, Aurathions had advanced healing. His nose and Chloe's hand would be back to normal in no time.

"You deserved that, and you know it." I smirked at him.

"Maybe so, but the next Moon that hits me is going to get their ass lit on fire." He narrowed his eyes at everyone, his patience at an end with all the punches to the face. Maybe it did trend and I just wasn't aware, I gave a small smile at the thought.

"Okay, enough of this bullshit. What the fuck is going on?" Jet was clearly pissed at all the delays.

"I ran into Kristine when I went to grab food. She said some things that I found alarming. I've known for some time my father has been involved with what happened to our world. I can even understand it, to a point." He looked at Zeke when he made a sound of derision at his comment, but continued. "My father lost my loyalty when I found out the serum worked on embryos. Our culture would have been saved in just one generation, but that wasn't good enough for the high society Aurathions that didn't want the stigma of unbonded Passives in their families." It was my turn to narrow my eyes at him because I think I brought that point up in class.

Jet spoke, "I don't understand why there is a stigma on Passives just because they haven't found a Nexus. It's not like it's by choice."

"I might have misspoken. There is a stigma, at least in their eyes. I've heard my father speak about it a hundred times. He couldn't stand the thought of my Uncle Trent being weak and shaming the family. But that's not the only reason they wanted the serum for adult Aurathions. The family would be much stronger if every member had the use of their abilities. Therefore, keeping them in power and on the Council. Unfortunately, my father wasn't the only one that felt like that." He paused, seeming to be upset at old memories.

"Why would your Uncle Trent agree to take an experimental serum?" Jet interrupted again, asking way more questions than he usually did in class.

"Wouldn't you if you could extend your life by about a hundred and fifty years?" Storm questioned.

"Depends on the quality of that life, and what you have to do to get it," Jet said, using about ten more words than he usually did.

"That's exactly right. Unfortunately, not everyone has your ethics." Storm smirked. "I know I don't, as I'm sure you've all figured out. But it really wouldn't have mattered since I didn't get the choice."

"What do you mean, you didn't get the choice?" I asked, mad on his behalf even though I was still pissed at him.

"I mean, sweet Nexus, that my father started injecting me with the serum when I was just thirteen and starting puberty. I think he wanted to see if it worked better when it was injected in a younger subject." He smiled sadly at me.

I stood up and walked directly to him, wrapping my arms around him. He hugged me back and kissed the top of my head.

"You saved me, Reverie. I felt the insanity trying to take hold, then I saw you at a gathering of our people. I knew you were my Nexus, and it gave me the strength to hang on."

"He's still a rat bastard, and nowhere near good enough

for my bestie, but I understand a little better why you did what you did." Chloe murmured, still frowning at him.

"Can we get to the pending invasion of my world?" Jet growled, clearly at the end of his patience and looking strangely annoyed at my arm around Storm.

"I knew that my family, along with a few other Factions had been meeting frequently. Unfortunately, he had the place shielded, so I couldn't listen in. They're all power-hungry and resent having to hide what they are." He pulled out of my arms and started pacing. "Kristine said, and I quote, 'Students are going to have quite the surprise when they go home from winter break.'"

Jet started for the door but before he could open it, Pantar appeared.

"Nexus, you must get home. Your family is in distress and needs your help immediately."

I felt my heart drop, and Chloe jumped to her feet, running to me. She was pushed out of the way by both of her brothers.

"Do you have any details?" Oren asked, looking at Pantar.

"You can hear him?" Zane asked in surprise.

"Yes." Storm answered abruptly, then gave his attention back to Pantar.

"All I know is the shields I placed around my Nexus's family have disintegrated, and that shouldn't be possible." Pantar growled in obvious distress.

"Everyone, get to your rooms and pack a small bag. Only pack things that are necessary. We'll meet in Reverie's dorm and Pantar can create a portal. Hurry." Oren gave me a scorching kiss before walking into his room.

Chloe and I rushed back to our dorm, packing things we thought might be important. Meeting again in the living room in less than ten minutes. "Chloe, you don't have any abilities yet and this might be dangerous-" She cut me off before I could finish.

"Don't insult me by finishing that sentence. I'm coming with you. I'll contact my parents when we find out what's going on and they can help." She narrowed her eyes.

I held my hands up in surrender. "Okay, I just don't know what's going to be waiting for us."

"I'll stay close to her." Pantar told me, appearing next to me.

The door burst open, and the guys came in together. I was anxious to get to my parents, so as soon as the door shut, I turned to Pantar. "Can you create a portal?"

"Yes, Nexus." He turned and pointed his tentacles at the hallway. A swirling circle appeared just big enough for a large man to fit through. We were all amazed, but now wasn't the time to question him.

I wasted no time heading for it, but was pulled back suddenly. I was surprised to see Jet holding my arm. "Let us go through first. We have no idea what's on the other side."

"You do know I can take care of myself. I have access to abilities, and you don't." I now knew he was feeling the connection, too.

"I don't need abilities." He stepped into the portal without another word.

"Well, doesn't that make the rest of us feel a little inadequate." Zane grinned at Jet's arrogance despite their situation, before following behind him.

Zeke kissed my forehead, then took Chloe's hand. "Let Oren bring you through."

Chloe waved before stepping through with her brother.

"Looks like it's our turn, little Nexus." Storm put his arm around me.

I stopped him before we stepped through and turned to Pantar. "Are you coming?"

"Yes, Nexus I will be right behind you." He nodded his head regally.

I looked up at Storm and he smiled in reassurance. We both turned and walked through the portal.

The portal brought us out directly in front of my house. I felt my legs collapse and the only thing holding me up was Oren's arms around me. The house I grew up in was on fire. Smoke and flames were billowing out of the windows upstairs and I didn't see any sign of my parents.

Zeke and Zane were running around the house yelling my parents' names and trying to find a way to get in. Chloe ran to my side and took me so Storm could help the guys. Jet came from behind the house and shook his head at Storm, letting him know that he didn't find any evidence of my parents back there.

Pantar appeared and roared in outrage at the destruction of my home, joining the guys in searching for my parents. They all returned shortly, and I knew by the looks on their faces that they hadn't found any trace of them.

Suddenly, a small portal appeared. The guys all took up a defensive stance around me and Chloe with Pantar in the front, teeth bared ready to tear into any threat leveled at his Faction.

I heard the twins yell in shock and pushed my way to the front, so I could see what was going on. I couldn't believe my eyes when I saw Nathan and a massive man step through the portal.

"NEXI!!!!! WHERE IS MY NEXI?!!!"

I felt like my heart was going to beat right out of my chest. I was frozen in shock, but Nathan didn't have the same issue and appeared right in front of me faster than I could blink. He stopped before taking me in his arms and just stared at me.

"Oh, my precious Nexi. I've missed you." Nathan raised his hand to catch a tear running down my face. He brought it to his mouth and the spell was broken as we both reached for the other at the same time. Nathan kissed my face everywhere he could reach, and I held him with all the strength in my body. "My Nexi, I'm sorry that we're too late. We tried getting here in time to stop it." He frantically explained in between kisses.

"What is it?" Storm asked, interrupting our reunion.

Nathan stopped kissing me abruptly and narrowed his eyes at Storm.

"Why do I feel a connection to you?"

"I'm now your Faction brother." He reached for my arm, but before he could make contact, Nathan punched him directly in the nose. Storm fell to his ass for the second time today.

I put my hand out to intervene, when the large man that came through with Nathan appeared. "There's no time for this bullshit."

I couldn't believe my eyes! I'd seen pictures of him and been told stories for as long as I could remember.

"Dad?"

He startled, looking into my amber eyes that were so like my mother's, and fell to his knees. Putting his head in his hands for a moment, he looked up at me once more. With tears streaming down his face, he leaned his head back and screamed,

"ADELAIDE!"

AFTERWORD

Thank you for picking up a copy of my very first book.
(Squee) If you liked it please leave a review. Reviews are the
life blood of Indie authors. The next title is up for pre-order
the date is just a placeholder, and it will be released sooner.
Thanks for your support.

Inter
Emberhold Academy Series Book 2

ABOUT THE AUTHOR

Frankie James is a brand-new indie author. She's been an avid reader all her life and decided to try her hand at creating her own stories. She raised her babies in a small town in Texas. After they left the nest, her husband decided to take a job traveling. They bought a fifth wheel RV and haven't looked back. Seeing this beautiful country gave her all the inspiration she needed to put pen to paper.

When not reading or writing, her favorite things are loving on her grandbabies, cooking, and hanging out with her husband.

Come hang out with her at page or join her group.

Instagram: @frankiejamesauthor

Tiktok: @frankiejamesauthor

Scan the QR code for quick links to all Frankie James social media.

I found the resolve to write this book after the death of my beloved father. Even as I write that sentence, it still seems unbelievable. By the time this book is released, it'll be eleven months, and yet it seems that only hours have passed.

He was always larger than life and made every day in his presence one of laughter. Losing him was the loss of a best friend and not just a parent. He was one of my biggest fans, no matter what I did. He would cheer just as loudly over me cooking him a simple meal, as he would the writing of this book. (Not that this would've been his kind of book lol)

I'll miss him every single day of my life, and I hope he's looking down still cheering me on. I know he is because his family was the most important thing on this earth and not a day passed without him telling each of us how much he loved us. Frank James, this one is for you. I love you.

Mom, I haven't forgotten about you. Being married to him for fifty-four years and together since the age of sixteen, I know you'll never recover from his loss. But I thank God that we still have you and hope that's true for many more years to come. Y'all are the best parents anyone could ever have. You two made hard times fun and left us with stories that we've all told over and over but still find hilarious. I love you.

I don't want to leave my husband, children, and grandchildren out. You people are the best of me, and I love you, each and every one.

When I say children, this includes y'all, Adaira, Brian, and Nicole. My kids did good when they chose each of you.

Special thanks to Hayley and Adaira. I couldn't have done it without your help. Thank you for the time you put into making this book possible.

Thanks to my ARC team, Karah, the two Angies, Jamie, Charlotte and Lexie. All your input was important and made my book better.

Thank you, Laura Marrero, for your input! Check out her Facebook Pages: Bullymancers and My Dungeon of Books.

Melissa Adams, I appreciate all your advice. It was invaluable. If you haven't been lucky enough to read her books, be sure to check her out.

SCAN ME